Praise f
The Outrageous ⌐
Redefining L⌐

This book should be read to every young girl, maybe even as young as middle school. Kate shows you how and why you may be feeling what you are feeling—giving you the answers to look within rather than seeking outside validation. This book was also one to not put down. I read it in a day. When I met the author, Amy Cady, I told her she would be the miracle child. She truly is.

—Dr. Ming Chee, Author of *Money Blues to Blue Money-Alchemy for Creating Everlasting Wealth*

A hilarious, moving and touching journey of self-discovery that beautifully explores the struggles we all experience in relationships, men and women alike. Kate's journey helped me better understand my own past relationships and the challenges that women go through to find love. At the same time, I could also relate to the insecurities, the inner voice, and the highs and lows that accompany our quest to find deeper connection with others, and ourselves. Ultimately, this book offers a heartfelt and deeply profound message on what it takes to create the ideal relationship, teaching us that true love begins with self love.

—Akshay Navati, best-selling author of *Fearvana*

I believe this is a very important book for all women who have been struggling to find Prince Charming and experience happily ever after. It is a must to read and one to reflect upon, so women can realize the power they have to experience true love that lies within them. As I read through the stories, I was transported to many experiences I had myself in some of my own adventures of dating various Dicks. I warn you this is a different kind of fairytale that is raw, funny, real and sometimes a painful journey that Kate takes you on. But in the end, all of the adventures are worth the final surprising outcome.

—Dr. Mayra Llado, best-selling author of *Run Your Race*

Amy Cady
Upcoming TOADD Anthologies

The Outrageous Adventures of Dating Dick: Her Stories (2018)
The Outrageous Adventures of Dating Dick: His Stories (2019)

iamamycady.com
@iamamycady Facebook and Instagram

The Outrageous Adventures of

Dating Dick

Redefining Love One Dick at a Time

Amy Cady

Copyright © 2018 Amy Cady.

All rights reserved. No part of this book may be reproduced, stored, or transmitted by any means—whether auditory, graphic, mechanical, or electronic—without written permission of the author, except in the case of brief excerpts used in critical articles and reviews. Unauthorized reproduction of any part of this work is illegal and is punishable by law.

This is a work of fiction. All of the characters, names, incidents, organizations, and dialogue in this novel are either the products of the author's imagination or are used fictitiously.

ISBN: 978-1-4834-8165-4 (sc)
ISBN: 978-1-4834-8167-8 (hc)
ISBN: 978-1-4834-8166-1 (e)

Library of Congress Control Number: 2018902442

Because of the dynamic nature of the Internet, any web addresses or links contained in this book may have changed since publication and may no longer be valid. The views expressed in this work are solely those of the author and do not necessarily reflect the views of the publisher, and the publisher hereby disclaims any responsibility for them.

Any people depicted in stock imagery provided by Getty Images are models, and such images are being used for illustrative purposes only.
Certain stock imagery © Getty Images.

Lulu Publishing Services rev. date: 03/21/2018

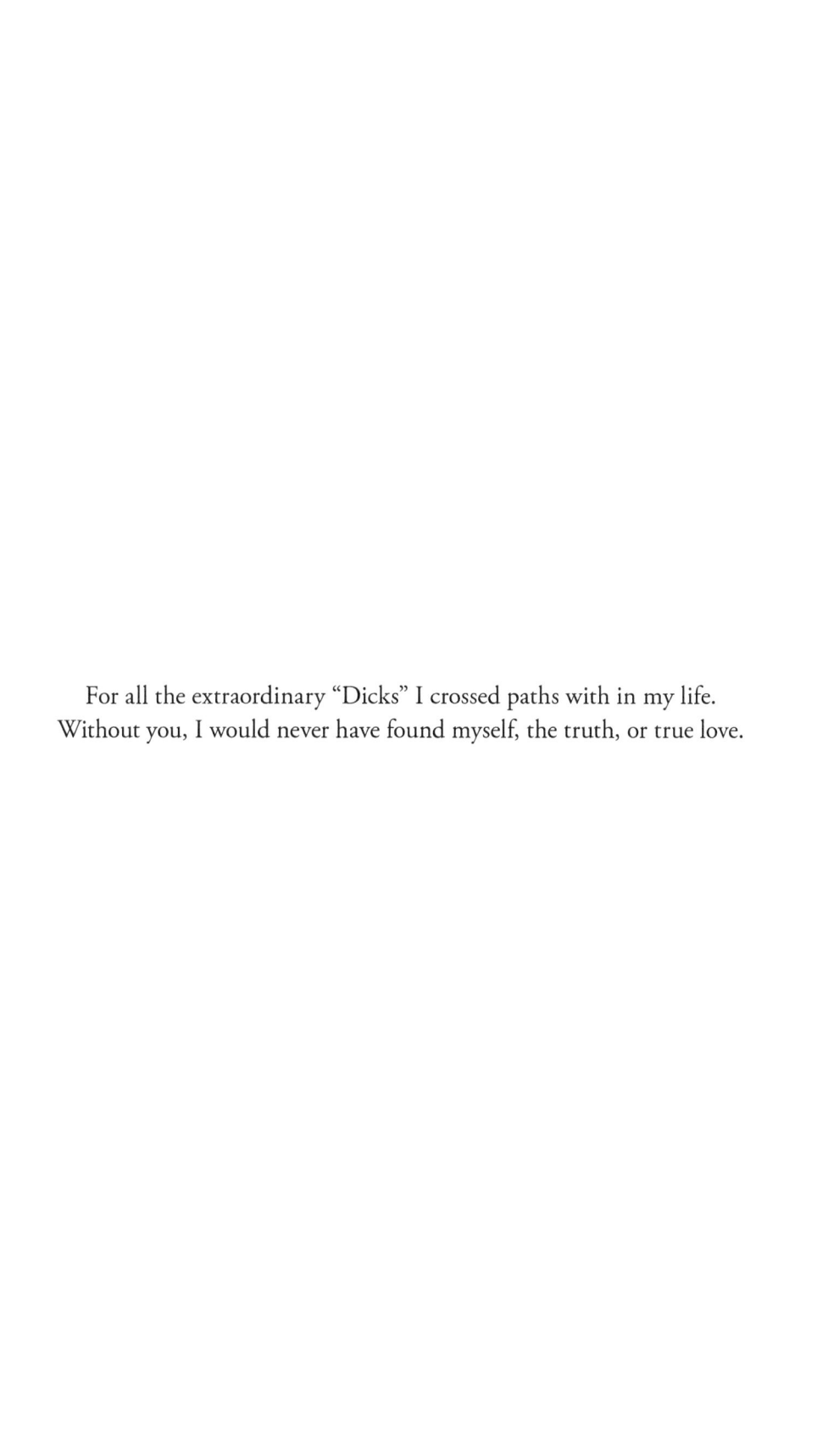

For all the extraordinary "Dicks" I crossed paths with in my life. Without you, I would never have found myself, the truth, or true love.

Preface

I am bending the rules of the acronym TOADD a bit to serve my purpose in this book. You will see the word toadd misspelled throughout this book as a play on the word. The acronym stands for the title of the book, *The Outrageous Adventures of Dating Dick.* And while Kate searches for the toadd of her fairy tale dreams, the reader will realize that it's not toadds that hang out on lily pads. It's really frogs that turns into Prince Charming in fairy tales. Hence, hers was a fairy tale doomed from the start.

The inspiration for the TOADD anthologies came about during an outing with a married girlfriend of mine. We were sipping champagne and talking about my experiences dating a multitude of Dicks, as we called them, before divorce, during marriage, and postdivorce. I, like so many hopeful romantics, had been searching for true love all my life, thinking it existed wrapped up in a fairy tale. The stories I recalled were comedic and sometimes ended in tragic events, but even so, they all ended with a poignant outcome. It turns out my fairy tales sounded more like tales of woe. We laughed and cried for hours. She begged me to write them down and come up with answers as to why I thought these relationships did not work out. It would become a sort of soul-searching exercise that served to open up space as a way to heal and forgive the past so that I could someday meet my true love.

As I relived each and every story and penned the painful experiences onto paper, I stumbled upon the root of the problem, and sure enough, the healing began. While unraveling my assorted past relationships, I realized that I could write about my experiences by telling a unique story of one woman's search for love. It's a story that could change the lives of others too.

This book, while fiction, will propel other hopeful romantics to take a good look at themselves and their own complicated relationships and hopefully get them moving toward the path of discovering true love. Because for me, no matter what happened to make love turn into heartache, I still never gave up on true love. I still believe in fairy tales. I still believe that love conquers all. And … I still love Dick.

One other thing: I use the term *Dick* to protect the names of the innocent and not because I believe men to be dicks—just fascinating creatures, like you and me, looking for love. My message is less about Dick than it is about the man behind Dick. Reason being, I believe men are amazing and very loving if you know *how* to love them. The question is whether you love yourself enough to take Dick on an adventure with you. But first, let's start with another question.

Will the real Dick please stand up?

Acknowledgments

I would like to thank the following people, who graciously contributed to the success of my book and continually supported my efforts:

Lori Aldana, senior editor extraordinaire, who is an angel on earth and a master at interpreting what is in my mind and helping me put it on paper in a way that is beyond this world. Because of her angelic touch, I am now able to share my message globally.

Dana Bouse, always willing to listen to my stories and no matter what I was going through remained positive and my biggest cheerleader.

Jack Canfield for writing *The Success Principles*, a book that paved the way to my love, joy, peace, and freedom. With his work, I saw the light, cleaned up my mess, and found success. His book and work heavily influenced Kate's discoveries and Little Katie's advice.

Dr. Ming Chee, another angel on earth who was, and still is, my accountability partner, pushing me beyond my limits and believing in me when no one else did.

Dr. Mayra Llado for being my champagne-sipping girlfriend and sharing in the hilarious birth of TOADD.

"Love had a message to be heard, and so she roared with the heart of a lion."
—Amy Cady, author

Prologue
The Fairy Tale Dream

Once upon a time, there lived a little princess who, like many little girls her age, had a fascination with the magical fairy tales she read of the beautiful princesses who would be found and rescued by Prince Charming, fall in love, and live happily ever after. So it was no surprise this little princess wished for and fantasized about her own happily ever after—living the magical fairy tale of falling in love with a prince who would find and rescue her. Which she did … well, sort of. Except her fairy tale takes place in a preposterous kingdom that attracts princesses looking for love in all the wrong places. The fantasyland she conjured up turned out to be a distorted picture of her happily ever after by some cocked-up series of events.

The princess landed in the fantasyland of Dickland, a quixotic place of love and desire where princesses venture in the hopes of finding prince toadds to rescue them. This place hardly resembled any of the fairy tales she had grown up idealizing. In Dickland, all the wannabe princes are named Dick—and not by coincidence. And they spend most of their time near the enchanted pond disguised as toadds. They sit on their lily pads waiting to prey on the unsuspecting, naive damsels in distress who are all searching for true love.

Alas, the little princess would grow up one day and realize that for the greater part of her life she would undertake the disheartening pursuit of kissing not just a couple of toadds but dozens of toadds while revisiting the enchanted pond more often than not.

But why, she wondered, were these toadds not giving her the life she was led to believe a princess ought to have? Perhaps there was a magic spell she needed to break? As she contemplated this, she fell into a deep, reflective daydream, reliving her past fairy tale romances from beginning to end, hoping to find an answer to her mystery.

❀

Growing up, the princess's mother taught the princess she should look for a rich, handsome Prince Charming to marry—one who would take care of her and provide her with a lifestyle that was not too different from the fairy tale she had dreamed for herself.

According to her mother, that fairy tale lifestyle was composed of one Prince Charming to provide her with a gigantic diamond ring; a gigantic house with a white picket fence; a gigantic closet with tons of designer clothes, shoes, purses, and jewelry; and a gigantic SUV to cart around the adoring children she would someday birth.

Although her mother was not able to live the fairy tale herself, she would tell the little princess it indeed existed and she should never settle for anything less. However, the princess always thought there seemed to be something missing. *Where is love in this fairy tale?* she wondered.

One day the princess wandered away from home to pursue a fairy tale, beguiled by her mother's portrayal of what that should look like and a desire to find love. She followed a mysterious path that led her to the kingdom of Dickland and coincidentally stumbled across an enchanted pond by following the odd noises coming from it. As she came closer, her view opened up to an endless sea of toadds croaking excitedly as they perched on lily pads.

She couldn't believe her eyes. She had discovered a pond filled with toadds in all different colors, shapes, and sizes. But these weren't just any old toadds. They had one thing in common: each of the toadds wore a crown bearing the name Dick.

These were prince toadds!

The princess was ecstatically delighted by her thrilling discovery, for she had read about these prince toadds in her fairy tales. She knew all she had to do was answer to the right one and kiss him, and he would turn into her handsome Prince Charming. She was so excited to see so many Dicks ready to pounce into her arms she could hardly contain herself.

Is this what love looked like? Could it be this easy to find Prince Dick Charming after all? She saw so many attractive toadds all in one pond, making it difficult for her to decide which one to fall in love with. The princess closed her eyes, listening for the loudest croaking toadd she could hear, for the loudest toadd meant he was the most attentive Dick. She decided the most attentive one would be the one to pounce into her arms and gain her affection.

However, as her luck would hold, she sadly learned with her first prince toadd that he was just another Dick. A Dick who, precisely like all the other prince toadds who came afterward, ended up jumping back onto his lily pad—back to his space, back to his rules, and, more to the point, back to his hunt for another unsuspecting princess who would come to the enchanted pond looking for love in all the wrong places.

Before long, the young princess became disillusioned with the fairy tale and finding her prince because her mother's idea of Prince Charming proved wrong over and over … and over again. Time after time, she went back to the pond to kiss Dick after Dick—different looks, different lines, different promises, different attitudes, but all with the same failed outcome. It soon became obvious to her that if she'd heard one Dick, she'd heard them all:

"C'mon, baby. Just one little kiss. I swear I'm a prince."

"Trust me. Look at this face … Would I lie?"

"Noooo, I don't have a girlfriend … Sure I love you."

"She will never know. Please, baby, please."

"Of course I'll respect you. I'm not like all the other guys—I swear."

"I'll call you. Really!"

One day as she sat near the pond brokenhearted again, the princess asked herself, *Why do all the toadds I pick leave me and return to their lily pads?* The only obvious answer was because they were the wrong Dicks for her. She figured maybe these toadds were not looking for love after all.

"At least not with you!" she heard a little voice chime in.

Who was that? The startled princess jumped up and looked quizzically into the pond, searching for an explanation of where the little voice had come from. She caught her own reflection looking back at her. This reflection, however, was of her childlike image, and the voice seemed to be coming from inside the child.

Astonished and confused, the princess looked into the pond and slowly asked the little voice, "But why not me?"

The little voice exclaimed, "Because it's a fairy tale!"

Then the little voice softened and spelled it out for the princess. "Okay, so truthfully, the outcome involves *you* and, well, how you're responding to these toadds. And to be frank, darling girl, in order to find your prince, you just need to kiss a few toadds, not fool around with the whole pond!"

Then the little voice enlightened the princess about how these toadds from Dickland had no intention of committing to any princess. The only intention they had was to remain perched safely upon a lily pad day in and day out. They were either on the hunt for unsuspecting princesses or in hiding from any would-be predators, a.k.a. princesses looking for love. They played it cool, spending all their lives by the pond in the hopes of briefly mating with the plenteous prey at their beck and call.

Consequently, upon the princess learning this, it was bestowed upon her that she must write her own fairy tale to find her perfect Prince Charming and stop chasing her mother's dream. In order to take on this new mission, she needed to have a clear vision of two things: what type of Prince Charming she was looking for and, more importantly, what type of love she was looking for.

"I've got an idea. Let's take an adventure together to get to the bottom of this so-called love thing once and for all so we can finally live happily ever after," the little voice compellingly suggested.

And in that moment, they embarked on a journey that would take the princess back to where it all first began with *The Outrageous Adventures of Dating Dick*.

1

The Disturbing Dick

INTRODUCING THE INNER CHILD (LITTLE KATIE)

Kate had believed in the same fairy tale dream of meeting Prince Charming ever since she was a little princess. Her parents called her a princess, but in the real world, she was simply Kate—although there was nothing simple about her. Kate was a beauty with very feminine traits, chestnut hair, and deep-set eyes the color of amber sea glass. She had no problem attracting the opposite sex. The problem Kate faced was that she did not know how to be discerning. Before discovering that the enchanted pond was only a loveless cess-"pond" of Dicks, she could not help being a serial Dick lover who kissed one toadd after another, searching for her one true love in every Dick adventure. Yes, that's right. She referred to them all as *Dick*. At some point, she had to wonder whether the connotation was just a generic tag name for all men, a label for their attitudes, or a term used to refer to their packages. You know—the package: Action Jackson, Captain Winky, Cock-a-saurus Rex, Cocktapus, Big Jake the One-Eyed Snake … you get the picture.

Be warned—these adventures may get a little raunchy, but the story is painfully real as Kate reiteratively dated and kissed different Dicks with hard consequences and lessons that followed. Every time she thought she had found Prince Dick Charming, she soon became disenchanted, heartbroken, and/or too weary to carry on. No matter how much Kate meant well with every Dick affair, she always ended up choosing the wrong Dick: the bad-boy Dick, the noncommittal Dick, the-one-who-thinks-I'm-batshit-crazy Dick, and so on.

Every adventure left Kate mystified with a bemused look of *Huh?* or *WTF!* etched on her face and a voice in her head asking, *Did this shit seriously just happen to me again?* And all because a Dick is a dick! All of Kate's past Dick adventures had only shown her that love was sometimes crooked, drunk, gay, tiny, black, bent, big, and everything else in between. For Kate, in her botched-up fairy tale dream, this was love.

※

Kate grew into her sexuality like a caterpillar emerging from her cocoon—a butterfly receiving extraordinary attention from male onlookers. When she became an adolescent, she adored the attention she received from the power of attraction she possessed. Kate fluttered her wings around every attractive Dick who gave her attention, giving in to their charm and affection. She was fooled repeatedly while mistakenly equating Dick with love, because, frankly, what more could a Dick want than sex? She did not know a single man who would say no to sex, and she became extremely good at giving it. Kate figured that sex was naturally the way to a man's heart.

Her very first Dick encounter was with an adolescent toadd named Disturbing Dick. Kate was at that age when she was old enough to recognize feelings of attraction, such as who gave her the stirring butterfly feeling in her stomach and who made her turn away and head in the opposite direction. That was the extent of her understanding of sex—primarily attraction.

Luckily, the Dick she had been crushing on for so long wanted to go out with her too. And now, here they were. It was a decisive moment. Kate had no idea what to do with Dick in her first encounter with him. She was too embarrassed not to go through with it, and the same was probably true for him. She stared at him, and he stared back, trying to be cool, while she tried not to show how nervous she was feeling.

She looked at it, a little frightened as she noticed the head was strangely a bit larger than its body. The thing was hairy too. What was a girl at that age supposed to do with it anyway? Caress it? Feed it? Stoke its ego? So she just went for it, foolishly touching it because she felt bad about the way it looked. As she started to touch it with awkward strokes, it sprung to attention and became aroused enough that it started crying all over her. Kate didn't understand what was happening.

"Why did you do that?" she had to ask.

Then Dick went dormant!

What the fuck? she thought. *What just happened? What am I supposed to do now?* This was all disturbingly new to her. So many questions were rambling through her head, and there was no one to answer them.

✧

Maybe Kate's thirst for love stemmed from when she was growing up, being called little princess and being told she was Daddy's little girl and a special little girl by her parents. Suddenly, this little *special* girl began receiving *special* attention from boys. She couldn't remember exactly how the attention was initiated, only that she was seven years old. Whenever she went over to her best friend's house to play, she got more attention from her best friend's brothers than she got from her best friend.

As Kate recalled the incident, a voice interrupted her thoughts. "Hold on, wait. Stop there. What's that you're talking about?"

It was the impatient little voice in Kate's head speaking to her again. Kate very well knew that if she didn't let that little voice have her say, she would not be able to get to the bottom of this adventure without her irritating interruptions.

The voice was seven-year-old Little Katie. She could be a bit menacing, somewhat outspoken, and at times a little too demanding. Little Katie was Kate's inner child or that annoying little voice inside her head responsible for ringing the alarm bells whenever Kate went off on another toadd adventure. She came to attention, speaking to Kate every time she met a Dick she was remotely interested in. When Kate first met Little Katie, she wasn't sure whether she was her voice of reason or an alter ego protecting her from reopening the wounds of her childhood.

"Remember—I was only seven when it happened," Little Katie spoke in her mature, yet childlike, defensive voice. "I didn't know what was happening, and I was afraid to stop it," she reminded Kate.

Little Katie blamed herself for what happened, although she didn't understand why no one had helped her and why her parents never did anything about it. She didn't know if they even knew what was being done to her, but the troubling thing was that she kept going back for more. However, more of *what* was the question.

The special attention came from her best friend's older brother, and to make it worse, the other members of the pack peered through the window and watched it happen. The brother would tell Kate's best friend, "Hey, go get your little friend and bring her over to the house to play."

Her best friend couldn't grasp what was happening, so she would go get Kate to come over and play. Kate would be led away by the brother, leaving her friend playing dolls or watching television. Kate would go off alone with him, and he would tell her they were playing a game. It seemed like a strange game, but she felt too scared to stop it. It was a game of show and tell. The other boys would peer through the window, watching young Kate with curiosity and intrigue.

Little Katie would ask that burning question of Kate all the time. "Why did I keep going back for more? Did I like it?"

Ugh. Kate didn't know how to answer that. To shield herself from blame, she came up with the most reasonable explanation she could think of: "Maybe I felt it was a form of attention that I wasn't getting during my childhood." Yes, that was it. Kate went back for more attention. As a result, it was that kind of attention from Dick that would constantly show up to thrill her and gradually lead her to become promiscuous.

As Kate navigated life, trying to make sense of it all, she placed a lot of blame on her father for the choices she made when it came to seeking love or, many times, just approval. Her dad traveled extensively, and when he was not traveling, he would work all day. Then he would come home, pour his scotch, grab the remote control, and watch television until dark, falling asleep in his rocking chair. He was pretty much absent from Kate's life for most of it.

Kate felt like she never received the confirmation, attention, or approval that a daughter needs from her father to feel worthy and supported—to feel secure as a woman. She felt alone and desperate for attention, longing for the fairy tale her mother had described to her as a little princess. She desperately wanted to feel loved and be adored. It's conceivable that Kate was looking for the approval she was not getting from her dad. And, oh boy, she certainly found a way to get the approval! Because Kate was a lost soul when it came to men, sex became a cry for attention.

She also grew up watching her parents barely communicate with one another, hopelessly lacking in the role-model department of what an intimate relationship was supposed to look like. She quickly discovered she did not want the same relationship as her parents, which was another reason she turned to what she knew would attract men—the power of her sexuality.

The trouble with all this was that she didn't understand how to use that power. Right or wrong, Kate returned to the enchanted pond many times over, always picking the wrong toadd, who would string her along, jump back onto his lily pad, and leave her standing there feeling wet, cold, used, and duped. She came to deduce that perhaps the problem with all these different Dicks had something to do with not learning from her parents how to treat a Dick, much less knowing how a Dick should treat her.

That's when Kate began to hear the voice of Little Katie in her head chiming in. She was the voice that would show up and try to rationalize with Kate, sometimes scold her, sometimes feel sorry for her, and many times just put up a protective shield. Nestled away in Kate's head, she sat in fear from that traumatizing experience as a little girl and was terrified of repeat abandonment and humiliation that took place with Disturbing Dick.

As for Kate, she would just dive into the pond headfirst, preferring not to think about it. She did the best she could with the lack of role models and information necessary to make better choices. Kate suppressed Little Katie a lot in the early years because she thought of her as the scared little child. After all, what did she know?

Kate felt that attracting a Dick with her sexual energy would definitely keep him *forever*. She felt that as soon as she had sexual intimacy with a Dick of her choosing, he would instantly fall in love with her. In reality, this unconsciously turned out to be a destructive way to her longing heart and an emotional mistake she would keep making for years to come.

She couldn't help but ponder self-demoralizing and desperate thoughts, like *Will I ever find true love's Dick? Will the real Dick please stand up and be the man I am looking for? Is he out there? Is he looking for me too?*

The real question Little Katie wanted her to think about was this: *What am I truly looking for?*

This question burned in Kate so much, in part because she needed to fill the emptiness inside of her with true love, but also because Little Katie insisted she narrow her sights with some sort of idea of the love she was looking for. Little Katie did not want to go through what happened in the first encounter with Disturbing Dick ever again!

So, Kate came up with a brilliant idea—she created a Fairy Tale List of the Prince Dick Charming she wanted. It looked pretty good to her.

My Prince Dick Charming Fairy Tale List:

- ☐ Has money
- ☐ A good-sized, tall Dick … but not too tall—ouch
- ☐ A confident Dick
- ☐ Straight, not crooked
- ☐ A Dick that is dark, white, Latino—not too concerned with ethnicity
- ☐ Handsome—I have got to be able to look it in the eye and still want it
- ☐ No hairy Dicks
- ☐ In shape, no fat Dick's allowed
- ☐ Smart, but not a smart-ass
- ☐ Sense of humor
- ☐ Loves to travel
- ☐ Loves to dance
- ☐ Drinks and eats good food
- ☐ And, of course, loves to fuck (Because if Dick can't keep up with my libido, my insatiable appetite, my love of the dick, then he is not the Dick for me.)

"It's pretty shallow, but I guess it's a starting point," observed Little Katie.

"It's all the qualities of a Prince Dick Charming," replied Kate.

Little Katie told Kate she could count on her to help her find him.

In a voice imparted with so much wisdom, she began, "I will have a powerful effect on us, Kate. During our adventures together, I will be your inner chatter or, for better understanding, what I like to call your inner guide for right or wrong. I want you to listen to me when I try to steer you in the right direction. You will need to take into consideration that I am helping you get closer to what you really want—which is love."

Then she told Kate how she was going to help her.

"I will be motivating you to change some of your behaviors. You will hear my voice in your thoughts. I will help you create greater success and happiness with every fleeting toadd until you finally find your final Prince Dick Charming."

Little Katie knew Kate even better than Kate knew herself.

"I see you blocking me with fear and self-doubt during these adventures when you ignore me, but consider the awareness I bring to you. Try to be present, listen, and do not wander aimlessly throughout these adventures. Each encounter will bring up a new set of emotions, and if you listen to me, you can avoid pain and suffering and move toward falling madly in love with the final Prince Dick Charming."

It sounded daunting to Kate, and she had doubts as to whether she was going to be able to do this alone. *Do I really have a choice*, she wondered. So Kate agreed.

"Okay. Next step. Where do I meet these Dicks?"

"There's only one place to start," said Little Katie. "At the enchanted pond in Dickland where the land of many toadds awaits your arrival."

2

The First-Time Dick

BE CLEAR ABOUT WHAT YOU WANT IN A RELATIONSHIP

After Disturbing Dick, it would be a few years before Kate considered returning to Dickland—the land of love. A little more mature and just two years shy of surpassing her adolescent years, Kate had bottled up the troubled memories of her childhood so she could forget about Disturbing Dick, get past the trauma, and fall in love. As Kate prepared to take a leap of faith in love's direction, Little Katie's ethereal presence was cautiously optimistic at best. She trailed behind Kate, trying to keep up with her pace as she made swift strides toward the enchanted pond.

Kate caught a whiff of a distinctive aroma in the air as she neared the pond. Oddly enough, it smelled of fried chicken. Hanging out, perched on a greasy green lily pad was a toadd dressed in white cook's attire. It wasn't hard to identify him as the one serving up fried chicken. He reeked of burnt cooking oil. His odorous stale scent slightly grossed her out, but Kate couldn't help noticing something so adorable about this toadd. As their hungry eyes met, he jumped off his lily pad and into her open arms.

Little Katie registered that the smelly one had won this round and prepared with trepidation to engage in this new adventure with Kate. "Oh boy, I can already sniff out what this adventure will be like, and I don't think it's going to leave a good taste," she remarked.

※

Kate waited to have sex until she was a senior in high school when she became attracted to First-Time Dick. The entire experience with her first toadd (who had cried on her, for God's sake) left her scarred—a scenario she never, ever wanted to repeat. After that, she fooled around with a Dick every now and again, but never got past third base. Kate wanted her actual first time to be special. Unlike the attributes of Disturbing Dick, First-Time Dick was long, dark, and less hairy.

"Okay," Little Katie observed. "At least those qualities are on your Fairy Tale List if you are actually considering going through with this. I have to warn you, though. He's not going to fully satisfy you, because he's missing quite a few ingredients from your list."

She didn't need Little Katie to point it out. Kate also had an inkling he was not the right Dick. Being a popular girl in school, of course, Kate wanted to attract the quarterback of the football team, not the deep-fry, short-order cook. She could hear her mom's voice telling her she needed to find a rich Dick who could take care of her. But it didn't matter that he wasn't the most popular Dick in school, that he wasn't an athletic superstar, or that he didn't qualify as a brainiac. He was probably the sweetest Dick of all the Dicks she had met thus far. What she did notice was that he held a plebeian job at a chicken restaurant that probably would not amount to anything more than a chicken fryer. Even though it was a deal breaker for her, she still wanted him. For the time being, she was willing to turn a blind eye.

"Hmm," Little Katie said. "We both know he doesn't qualify. So why are you still pursuing him?"

"Shut up!" Kate reproached. "I like him a lot." Even though he did not appear to have a successful future, she saw something more that attracted her to him. "Look, he's kind, considerate, super sweet, and nice. And he really likes me."

"Well then, why are *those* qualities not part of your Fairy Tale List?" Little Katie questioned sarcastically.

It just made sense to Kate because she had been friends with this Dick all through junior high and high school. Their relationship was purely platonic until senior year when she felt she wanted more from him, and she sensed he felt the same way. For sure, this Dick was Kate's first love—or what she thought felt like love—so it was only natural to follow her heart. And without further ado, she kissed her first prince toadd.

Little Katie warned, "He's an infatuation, just a crush, Kate. This is a disaster waiting to happen."

Kate ignored her.

She knew very well what she wanted from him. Kate wanted love. So it happened in the back of Dick's car—the love, that is. He laid her down in the back seat of his midnight-blue Chevy Impala. They began kissing and groping like they always did. The popular term for it back then was making out. Except for this time, their make-out session was escalating and becoming more passionate. Kate could feel this weird stirring of emotion throughout her body that she'd never felt before.

Huh … Is this what love feels like? It must be! she thought.

Little Katie cautioned her. "Kate, don't do it. This feeling is not what you think it is."

Kate kept ignoring her.

She could not comprehend why he was taking her pants off, but Dick assured her everything was going to be all right. His touch made her weak at the knees and left her gasping for breath. *Oh yeah, this thing had to be love.*

"Kate, pull your pants back up!" Little Katie tried to stop her.

It was too late.

Dick entered her with huge enthusiasm as she shrieked in ecstasy. This curious pleasure lasted only a few minutes before Kate suddenly felt a slippery wetness between her legs. She knew it was not from her. It was from him. Then strangely, Dick apologized to her. She wasn't sure what for. She was still throbbing between her legs, trying to grapple with the flooding feelings and emotions taking over her.

Wait. Is this wet, throbbing feeling love? Oh, I think it is! That explains it all … I'm in love!

As Kate tried processing love, Little Katie queried with emphasis, "Seriously? You think that was love? No way, girl. That is what you call sex."

From a seven-year-old's point of view, Little Katie was pretty astute. Even though she appeared to be the voice of a seven-year-old, she was growing up with Kate and accumulating a wealth of wisdom along the way and serving it to Kate when she could.

"Why don't you understand the difference?" Little Katie asked. "Please let me explain it to you."

Kate continued to ignore her. *It is better to ignore her for now*, she thought. *I have my own rationale to contend with—like the fact that he has no money, but I am in love with him.*

Little Katie chimed in again with her words of childlike wisdom. "Are you kidding me right now? You are not ready for love. You don't even know what love is. Girl, we have serious work to do in that department."

Kate continued to ignore her.

The next day Kate got a call from First-Time Dick assuring her that his feelings for her were true and that it would not be the last time they would be together. And he was right.

But so was Little Katie.

Over time, it became obvious to Kate how inexperienced she was in the game of love and had no idea how to treat First-Time Dick. During their relationship, her head was spinning most of the time with thoughts of her future, and so she was always looking for something more—something better. They had great moments, but she was not ready to settle for what he had to offer her. Basically, Kate only wanted sex, which she thought was love, while First-Time Dick wanted love. She exhausted him with her demands for sex and the disregard for his emotions toward her, because in her mind, he did not live up to the fairy tale her mother professed constantly.

Kate could not get past the short-order cook detail and lost sight of what she had first seen in him. In the back of her mind, all she could hear was her mom repeatedly telling her to "marry a rich Dick." So ultimately, Kate wound up hurting First-Time Dick, taking with her the feeling of what she thought was love. She left him and moved on to a new Dick she thought for sure would provide her with the fairy tale she was looking for.

Not long after, ironically, First-Time Dick became one of the most successful import/export businessman this side of Texas, which meant tons of money for him and tons of remorse for Kate. It was too late, though. When she came to realize it, he had already moved on and married shortly after they broke up. This adventure left Kate with a throbbing between her legs and a broken heart longing for love—something that would constantly show up in her future.

Little Katie felt Kate's remorse over this adventure and tried clarifying a few things with her. Kate, however, didn't want to know. *Oh, that voice! Why is she talking to me all the time? Here she goes again—Little Katie, my inner chatter, the monkey on my back. Sometimes I just wish she would shut up! She's relentless in her quest to have me hear her.*

Whenever Kate did give Little Katie the okay to help her feel secure and supported, Little Katie opened up with sound advice to protect Kate's heart. And then in the same breathe, she would rip Kate a new one without hesitation when she knew something was not right.

Is it her that is keeping me from love? Kate wondered. *Or is she the one who keeps my heart protected?*

"What do you want?" Kate gave in to hearing Little Katie out.

Little Katie began with a rhetorical question. "Just answer me this: When is it appropriate to allow Dick to enter you for the first time? How about 'When your ass is grown up enough to know that love comes from the heart and not between the legs,'" she said. "Because when you have sex with someone, your head becomes clouded with feelings and emotions that are unrealistic and confusing to your heart. Instead of interpreting the red flags as a warning, you begin to rationalize them with those feelings and emotions. You say okay when what you really mean is it's not okay. You don't speak up for fear of losing him or hurting his feelings or scaring him away. It is a vicious cycle of crazy talk going on in your head, and the one you're talking to is me. This is not love, Kate. It is lust. Do you even know what love is?"

At that point, Kate realized she was confused about what Little Katie meant by love. *My heart? Huh? And what does she mean by grown up? And what is this* lust *word?* All Kate knew and cared about was that she got a feeling—that feeling of butterflies in her stomach.

"Well, your stomach is not near your heart. It's nearer to that place between your legs." Little Katie just shook her head.

Kate brushed Little Katie off whenever she tried to stop her from a mistake she saw coming. Kate didn't know any way to quiet down her broken inner child other than by ignoring her. She repeatedly asked the same hard questions about herself, trying to keep Kate from chasing love, or what Kate liked to think was love. Kate had to find a way to show Little Katie she was capable of navigating this daunting mission so she could quiet her down once and for all.

Kate headed back to the enchanted pond on a mission to fall in love. Little Katie, in tow once again, quietly trailed behind her while trying to stay out of her sight. Meanwhile, Kate prepared for the next Dick adventure, hoping this next one would bring her a windfall of love.

3

The Money Dick

REJECT HIS REJECTION AND MONEY

Kate was back at the pond to try her hand at picking a new Dick. The last one, First-Time Dick, left her feeling sad and somewhat remorseful. She never wanted to break his heart, but she wasn't satisfied with what he had to offer in their relationship. *I can do better*, Kate thought. And, lo and behold, she cast her sights on a toadd in the distance wearing a very shiny crown on his head. As she made her way closer to the pond, she could see his shiny crown was adorned with lots of diamonds and precious jewels. *Jackpot!*

Hmm, by the looks of his crown, he must have money! I'm definitely going for him, she thought, smiling at her discovery.

Her thoughts were rudely interrupted by Little Katie.

"Oh, but, Kate, just think about this. When is it appropriate to date a Dick for money?" asked the little one.

"Not you again. Did you follow me to the pond? Don't you have anything better to do?" Kate asked Little Katie. "Look at his crown. I have found my Prince Charming. Don't you see that? Will you just be quiet and let me fall in love? I'm just doing what mom told me to do. Don't you get it? I want to be rescued and taken care of. Isn't that what love is?" Kate argued back.

Kate actually left First-Time Dick for Money Dick—not that she was proud of it. It may sound floozy, but she couldn't pass up new Money Dick. He was a rock star—well, in the restaurant industry anyway. The point was, this Dick filled the bill.

Money Dick was the general manager of a very popular and swanky restaurant where Kate went to apply for a summer job during school break. Before setting her sights on him, her only interest was finding work in the summer to save some money before going back to college in the fall. So initially, she did not plan to hang around very long. He interviewed her and hired her on the spot as a hostess, a position that, coincidentally, Money Dick needed to keep a close watch on.

The spark with Money Dick was instantaneous. Kate felt a weird stirring of emotion similar to what she had encountered with First-Time Dick. In contrast to First-Time Dick, however, Money Dick was charismatic and handsome, had a big ego, dressed sharply, and, of course, had money. Kate told herself this must be love.

"Seriously, Kate?" Little Katie said, worried about where this would eventually lead.

"Yeah, seriously, little one," Kate responded sourly.

"Oh, you don't have a clue if you think this attraction is love! Here we go to the funhouse where nothing is what it seems." Kate could hear Little Katie mumble away.

Money Dick and Kate flirted outright at work to the point others began to talk about how she received favors they did not. Well, let's just say that those favors were in return for the favors she gave him.

One night, after the flirting crossed the line into heated passion, they secretly made their way into the bathroom stall of the men's room. Immediately, the gross smell of urine invaded her senses, and Kate could hear her shoes making cracking noises on the sticky floor with each wayward step she took. Of all things that could have appropriately crossed her mind in that moment, the only thing she could think about was, *How is this going to work?*

Money Dick was well practiced. He pushed her into the compact bathroom stall and brusquely bent her over.

Oh, that's how this is going to work, she thought. The flowy summer dress she was wearing made it easily accessible. As he performed the act of lovemaking, for lack of a better word, she was thinking, *Yuck!* The disgusting bathroom smell and the mere thought of fishy germs in the stall should've been a turnoff. But she rolled with it anyway because it was what *he* wanted, and she was happy to give him whatever he wanted from her.

Later that night, Kate recalled the moment Money Dick tried to enter her. His power was a bit flaccid, and he was lacking a forceful thrust that First-Time Dick had excelled at. She dismissed it at first, chalking it up to the awkward entry in that compact, smelly, sticky bathroom stall. She couldn't shake it, though, and the more she thought about it, the image of him going to the bathroom several times that evening came to mind—not with another woman, but several of his coworkers.

Each time he came out of the bathroom, he asked her if there was anything on his face. *Hmm, that is a strange question*, she thought. However, at first, she didn't think to ask why. Maybe he ate something and wanted to make sure he didn't have crumbs on his face. And, as far as Kate was concerned, she assumed he and the coworkers were having meetings where no one else could hear them.

Little Katie had other thoughts, chiming in with her withering little voice. "The writing is on the wall, Kate, and I don't mean the bathroom stall wall."

Kate ignored the comment.

Until … *Meetings my ass*! Kate soon found out she was right to be suspicious. She discovered Money Dick was a Coke Dick—and not the soft drink kind of Coke. He was taking drugs. She didn't want to believe it, let alone accept it. She tried to ask him, but he never gave her a straight answer. Wanting desperately to stay in the relationship, she kept quiet about it. After all, she believed this was love, and she was determined to make it work.

He never asked her to do drugs with him, and she never did. It became this weird routine day in and day out. He continued to do coke, and Kate continued to act as though everything was normal. And then there was Little Katie by her side, whose presence she felt staring up at her each time she saw him going into the bathroom with his coworkers, as if to say, "You see what he's up to?"

"So, what part of this do you think is love?" Little Katie's disparaging voice asked Kate.

"Well," Kate defended, "he says he loves me and wants a future together. I believe him, so I'm going to stay."

"What kind of future would that be, Kate? Think about it," she said, hoping Kate would reflect on that and open her eyes.

But Kate didn't want to think about it. She never complained to Money Dick, although her heart always sunk when she saw the change in his personality. One, it was so destructive to their relationship, and two, his dick could not perform. Kate learned in school that coke kills the dick—a slow, flaccid death. Money Dick transformed into Limp Dick more times than Kate could count, and the drug began to split them apart—well, that and his limp dick. It didn't make things any better that his money was going out the door or, more aptly put, up his nose.

They ended that summer on a challenging note. Kate and Money Dick supposedly were still dating when she left for college. She left him behind with his drugs, limp-dick sex, and rock 'n' roll chicks. He carried on partying, and word soon got back to Kate that he was seeing another hostess he'd hired. She was devastated because she wanted to believe they were still a couple—still in love.

"Oh, Kate, he's moving on. Get hold of yourself, girl. This has not been love, and it never will be. Can't you see that?" Little Katie tried to persuade Kate to wake up and cut her losses. But Kate continued to ignore her.

Kate begged Money Dick to visit her at the college one weekend.

"Bad idea, girl!" Little Katie called out.

Kate was still ignoring her at that point because Little Katie opposed her feelings. Her heart knew what it wanted, and she would find a way to get him back. Kate held onto the idea that she could change his mind by showing him how much he meant to her through sex, and Money Dick would fall back in love with her again.

"He'll come to realize that I am more important to him than his drugs and side chick. You'll see." Kate tried to convince Little Katie—and herself too.

Little Katie kept on supplicating Kate to reason and come to her senses, while Kate continued to ignore her.

The arrangement was that Kate would pick up Money Dick at the airport. Before the September 11 terrorist attack, people could still meet passengers at the gate as they walked off the plane. So there she stood, watching person after person as they exited the gate. She made eye contact with the faces of each passenger passing by her, hoping to recognize Money Dick. Her heart started to sink slowly as the passengers began to dissipate. She had a fearful feeling that something was not right.

Finally, the last person got off the plane. Kate rushed over to the attendant and asked about Money Dick, unwilling to accept that he was not on the flight. The attendant went through her roster and then returned her attention to Kate. Her look confirmed the answer.

"He never checked in, miss. He never got on the plane."

Money Dick didn't call Kate or try to contact her to tell her he would not be coming. She left countless messages and even tried getting in touch with his friends. No one answered her calls.

How could he do this to me? This is impossible and out character for him. Oh no … Maybe he's dead! Desperate thoughts turned to crazy thoughts, which then turned to angry thoughts. *Or, better yet, Limp Dick turned into Pussy Dick!*

When Money Dick finally did call Kate days later, he claimed his car had broken down on the way to the airport. She found it funny that he could easily explain why he missed the flight but not why he hadn't called to tell her. Kate came to find out that the newly hired hostess was fully satisfying his needs. Money Dick had grown tired of Kate being out of town and fell into the arms of another princess. When Kate went back to visit, he flat out ignored her. She felt like the talk of the town—the girl who was dumped for an even younger girl who, like Kate, worked for him.

Not surprisingly, Kate lost her mind and ended up embarrassing herself by begging Money Dick to come back to her. He declined.

Kate wallowed in self-pity. *What am I going to do without him? Who is going to take care of me? He is the best I've ever had. I know I won't find anyone better.*

〖◊〗

Little Katie desperately wanted Kate to come to her own senses about the lesson from this toadd, but she also knew how broken and rejected she was feeling. Instead, she did what she did best and dished it out for Kate in no uncertain terms.

"My heart is breaking for you, but I have to point it out to you again. When is it appropriate to date a Dick for money? Never!" Little Katie was determined to get this through Kate's head.

"This is the lesson we have to learn against Mom's will. Money is not the answer. It does not bring you love or happiness. It is just energy, and in this case, it's very bad energy. And frankly, Money Dick is quite irresponsible with his money. Do you want to live day in and day out with him spending money for a substance that is abusive to your relationship instead of securing your future together? It is time to look inside yourself and work on you to include making your own money. Money will not rescue you. *You* need to rescue you."

"But how do I do that?" Kate asked in a morose tone.

Little Katie softened her tone into more of a soothing voice as she became aware that it had a better effect on Kate when she spoke caringly to her.

"The best way to start is to reject rejection and, of course, lose the idea of a Money Dick. Get used to the idea that there will be a lot of rejection along these adventures, but don't give up. Just reject the rejection. Do not get stuck in your own fears and resentments. Instead, move on to the next adventure. Rejection can be seen as a wake-up call to not repeat the same mistake, and instead of retreating, pick yourself up and don't give up. Each rejection will uncover a lesson to learn and will bring you closer to the love you want—only if you heed the lesson. Just say, 'Next.' Don't let it destroy you; let it strengthen you. There is no other option if you are going to be successful in achieving what you want."

Something about Little Katie's words felt right and actually made Kate feel better this time, but she was still confused. It sounded easier said than done.

"Another thing," Little Katie added, but in a more serious tone this time, "don't get involved with someone who uses drugs!"

Yep, there was the reprimanding little voice Kate was so familiar with.

"Open your eyes and see that drugs will always be number one to a drug abuser, and you are the least important person in that relationship. You should never have to play second fiddle—especially to drugs. Think about taking care of you first. You need to feel worthy of finding a man who will treat you better than this Dick did."

Kate could not fathom what Little Katie meant by that. *Huh. Me? Worthy of better?*

Kate believed that Money Dick was the best she could get. He had so much potential. She could change him into the person she wanted him to be. She was worthy of him—that was all she knew. Kate could not wrap her head around what Little Katie meant by "taking care of you." It sounded good, but that was just weird talk to her.

Of course I take care of myself, Kate reasoned. *Well, at least I think I do. Although, in reality, what does that look like?*

"Oh, enough of this thinking crap! I know I can find another Dick to rescue me like I've read in all my favorite fairy tales," Kate said, trying to convince herself she knew best. It was too confusing for her to think of the alternative. Feeling devastated and dejected after Money Dick, Kate did the only thing she knew that would make her forget her latest toadd, and that included not listening to Little Katie.

"Little Katie, don't you know that the best way to mend a broken heart is to find someone else to heal it for me?" she asked while picking up the broken pieces of her heart.

Kate straightened herself out and headed back in the direction of Dickland, straight to the enchanted pond. She wasn't done searching for love just yet. After all, didn't Little Katie say not to give up and move on to the next adventure? For Kate, that meant moving on to another toadd.

As Kate disconnected from Little Katie, the little one stayed back a few steps and wept. She wasn't feeling so secure and loved, and it was a feeling that Kate had bottled up and left to her. Little Katie could start to see the path of pain that Kate would inevitably encounter and braced herself for the next Dick adventure.

4

The Gay Dick

PAY ATTENTION TO THE FEEDBACK

When Kate caught the trail back to the enchanted pond, she felt like a frequent passenger on Mr. Toad's Wild Ride. It's an amusement park ride that takes you on a dark, bumpy journey as you attempt to make your escape, crashing through different doors and being jerked around sharp corners while colliding with chaotic scenes of bizarre imagery. When it's all over, it leaves you spinning in a whirlwind of frenzy craving more. And Kate was craving fun.

Kate could hear commotion and excitement going on at the pond. Naturally, she couldn't resist the temptation to see what all the fuss was about. Frequencies of laughter and joy emitting from one of the toadds aroused Kate's curiosity. She spotted him immediately. This Dick's crown was dayglow, and it matched his metrosexual looks and personality perfectly—merry and fun, lighthearted and flamboyant. She was definitely ready for some fun and laughter in her life after crying so much over Money Dick, which made it decidedly easy for her to want to check this toadd out.

Little Katie, on the other hand, distinctly opposed the idea. She saw the colorful flags being raised, while Kate chose to see it as Little Katie holding her back from enjoying life. Little Katie attempted to admonish Kate's choice.

"Great, have some fun. But where do you draw the line on the appropriateness of dating a Gay Dick?" she chided.

Kate defended herself, "It's not that farfetched coming from the perspective of how a girl can easily become attracted to a gay man. It's no secret they can be a girl's best friend. They are a hoot and more fun than a girlfriend sometimes. They're always right on the money with fashion. They give brutally honest but great advice. They can see from a woman's point of view. On the emotional side, they listen to your sorrows and let you cry on their shoulder. On the physical side, they have a hard body, smell fantastic, dress to the nines, and are just plain hot!"

Little Katie saw the colors of the rainbow in Kate's aura as she described her enthusiasm for this toadd. "Kate, I think I'll let you draw your own conclusion with this one. All I know is that you'll soon find out who the real dancing queen is, and let's just say, it's not you."

༺༻

Yes, that's right. Kate did dabble in the gay man department. It happened when she transferred to a new college following her passion to pursue dance as a career—a passion that her father frowned upon and her mother encouraged. Whether she had made the right decision was not easy for Kate to determine at the time. She just wanted to do something that felt good to her without giving it a second thought about what it would look like as a lifelong career. Deep down, she mostly wanted to get away from her family, so studying dance at a school a few states away was enticing. It was also a great escape to leave Money Dick behind her. Immersing herself in her studies seemed like the best way to heal and recover from the pain.

As fate would have it, Kate met Gay Dick on her first day of study, and her love affair with him began. He was just what she needed at the time and couldn't help loving him to bits. Kate wasn't in love per se as much as she loved the companionship. It didn't help that Gay Dick was a triple threat. He could sing, dance, and act. Overall, the best part about a gay man for her was safety—meaning safety from the shitstorm of Dicks that she usually gravitated toward.

Gay Dick had never made a move on Kate until the night he asked her to go to a Prince concert.

He asked me out? I didn't see that coming, she thought. *In spite of my suspicions, it is a Prince concert,* she reasoned, *and I have the biggest crush on Prince. It would be more exciting going with Gay Dick. We'll have so much fun, and I won't have to worry about him hitting on me.* But then Kate began to second-guess herself. *Right?*

She dismissed her doubts and decided not to place too much emphasis on the asking out part, because she could see he was unmistakably gay. After all, he did call her up to say, "Hey, let's go shopping for outfits for the concert."

He wants to go shopping. Yep, he must be gay.

Little Katie had been kicking up an inner storm from the day Kate agreed to go the concert with Gay Dick. She was in Kate's head opposing her when she spoke to him, hung out with him, even just thought of him.

As expected, Little Katie emerged to forewarn her. "Kate, he has no money, and he's gay. Why are you hanging out with him? These qualities are not on your list. I see you going down in flames here. Are you listening to me?"

Kate pretended not to hear.

Because they both were on a college-student budget—otherwise known as the no-money budget—they took their shopping excursion to a funky thrift shop nearby. Kate and Gay Dick had a blast. They convinced one another other to buy crazy Prince-styled outfits with plenty of lace and purple. She imagined herself standing out in her purple velvet getup and hairspray-teased hair so high the security guard would notice and pull her up on stage to perform a song and dance set with Prince. She'd get the chance to tell him how much she loved him. *Oh my, there is that word!*

Yes, Prince did stir a bit of feeling down there in Kate. Realistically, she pretty much knew she would not be seen by security since their seats were likely nosebleeds. So instead, her reality turned toward Gay Dick, even more so after they were dressed up and ready to go. *Gay Dick never looked so great and gees he smells so good!* It had been a long hiatus since Money Dick and, well, Kate yearned to feel loved again.

They got to the concert, and as expected, their seats were located high up—way too far away from the stage. Kate wished she could jump onto the stage, grab Prince by the neck (among other parts), and pull him close to her. Except, Gay Dick was more within her reach, and maybe she would opt to grab him by the neck and go for his other parts instead.

She could hear Little Katie questioning that idea. "So there you go again, looking for love in all the wrong places, huh? Why is it you feel like you need so much attention?"

Kate didn't have an answer for her. She just liked it. Besides, she felt like he did genuinely dig her, and then there was that stirring feeling between her legs she couldn't stave off.

They were dancing and singing and just having the time of their lives. Kate glanced over at him a few times with doting eyes as the energy and the vibration swept her away into a purple-hazed fantasy. She was caught up in a Prince-fueled moment. Her thoughts went wild as she watched Gay Dick sway his hips to the music and move his lips to the lyrics.

So sexy! Damn, I know he is gay, but why? Maybe I can change him … She let her fantasy run away with her.

"What did you just say!" Little Katie shrieked.

"Pipe down. I'm on a mission. Don't blow this for me. I'm sure once he gets a closer look at me, he will see that he wants me."

"You must be joking, right?" Little Katie said in disbelief.

After the concert, they went back to Kate's apartment to chill out. They had been dancing so much their bodies were still clammy with sweat. Kate was feeling a little hot and bothered, and she wasn't ready for the evening to end. She put Prince on the CD player and had something more in mind as the song "Kiss" started to blare. Caught up in euphoria from the concert, they were laughing wildly and acting silly, collapsing on the couch and singing the lyrics to the song.

Then the song reached the part that said, "You just leave it all up to me / I'll show you what it's all about."

Kate thought, *How appropriate.* Oh yeah, Kate was gunning to show him what she was all about. On the couch sitting close to one another, she glanced over at him again in that same adoring way she did at the concert, but this time he was looking back at her. Kate could feel the throbbing intensify between her legs and grow increasingly stronger.

"Why are you looking at me that way?" Gay Dick asked.

A little embarrassed, Kate tried to look away, but she was stuck in a trance. She couldn't contain herself any longer and lunged herself at him, going in for the kiss. For a split second, she could feel him try to resist her. Just then, the song broke into the lyrics: "I just want your extra time and your kiss."

And Gay Dick gave into Kate. He leaned forward to capture her kiss. Bowled over but aroused by his action and reaction, she lusted for more. *I will convert him*, she thought.

The pair soon found themselves making out on the couch, and as things grew heavier, Kate started to feel the awkwardness of the kisses and the fondling. She removed her clothes as fast as she could, afraid to lose the momentum as soon as he became consciously aware that he was with a woman and not a man.

Little Katie rushed in as customary to ruin the moment for her. "I have to stop you, Kate. Genuinely consider what you're about to do. You can't possibly believe he's going to convert, much less fall in love with you. Kate? Kate, do you hear me?"

Kate turned up the song in her head even louder to drown out Little Katie's voice. Gay Dick entered her, and Kate knew instantly she was going to be less than impressed with the outcome.

"You've got to recognize the feedback you're receiving," she heard Little Katie say.

"Feedback?" Kate questioned. "What the heck are you talking about?"

"He's gay, Kate. He's feminine and not into you because you're a woman. How could you consider thinking this is what you want in a relationship?"

Kate ignored her as she tried to take charge so she could get some satisfaction out of this moment of passion, but Gay Dick pleasured himself and got there before she could. Kate laid there in anticipation of more, but nothing more happened.

The entire experience had been anomalous. His sexual moves mirrored feminine moves, and the sex lacked the passion of the other Dicks. But because he was with her, she expected that he'd be different with her. Worse, the result felt oddly familiar—she was left throbbing, unsatisfied, and still longing for love. They sat in silence as the strangeness of what just happened between them started to make itself apparent.

Prince's lyrics continued to play in the background: "You just leave it all up to me / We could have a good time …"

And that's exactly what this Dick adventure turned out to be—a good time and nothing more.

After all was said and done, Gay Dick broke the silence as he thoughtlessly blurted, "You know I just fucked you because you wanted it so badly."

"Uh … okay," Kate winced. "Thank you … I guess?"

She was shattered. Now what?

In the morning, he managed to plant a sweet peck on her forehead and left. She watched him walk away with a new version of Prince's lyrics playing in her head.

"I just wanted your extra time and your kiss."

And, well … maybe love too, she thought.

※

Kate sensed Little Katie looking up at her, tugging on what was left of Kate's heartstrings. Little Katie had another lesson to explain to Kate that started like all the others.

"When is it appropriate to date Gay Dick? Never. Just plain never! Gay Dick will always go back to his gay ways of being a gay blade. There is no chance he will change. If you want to be able to truly see a man for what he is and what he wants, you'll need to take a step back and take a good look at him before you leap at him. Sometimes what you want to see on the outside does not match the inside." Little Katie was seriously disturbed over this adventure and wasn't going to let Kate ignore her.

She tried to get Kate to reflect. "I think it's time for you to pay attention to the feedback you get from a man before jumping to your own conclusions and disregarding what is evident. Clearly, you could read the conflicting feedback from this toadd, and yet you were still thinking you could change him."

Little Katie launched her sound-bite advice, taking Kate by surprise. "When you know something isn't working in a relationship between you and a man, you can apply that awareness to find a middle ground in the relationship without compromising what he wants or who he is and vice versa. However, in Gay Dick's case, there is no middle ground and no compromises. Similar to Money Dick, you are consistently making this mistake, Kate, believing you can change a man.

"Learn to welcome and accept a man's feedback instead of taking it personally and use it so you won't keep going in circles. If you learn to consider the feedback, you will avoid painful situations in the future. It's a behavior change that requires you to pay attention to the response you're getting by listening to the feedback you're receiving from all your adventures. You must learn to interpret this with honesty and not twist it to adjust it to your liking. Doing this is crucial in helping you find the relationship you want."

Kate heard, but didn't fully comprehend the lecture Little Katie was ranting on about. It was going in one ear and out the other.

"I'm trying to help you improve your situation, and I'm seeing a pattern here to your behavior, although I can sense you are not ready to receive my input. Why do you choose to ignore me?" Little Katie sounded frustrated.

"Well, Little Katie, I am considering the source here," Kate retaliated. "What could you possibly know? I'm feeling a bit like a failure again, unloved and incompetent. I don't want to deal with the conflict that this so-called feedback is going to reveal. It's too painful."

Little Katie sighed. She was only trying to help Kate acknowledge this experience and not bottle it away with her other negative memories. The inner dialogue between them continued.

"It's better to acknowledge that you did the best you could in whatever experience you're currently engaged in. We're supposed to learn from our mistakes and grow from them so we don't repeat them. Instead, you're continually pushing away the feelings and emotions you have attached to each and every adventure and not learning anything from them. How do you expect to find what you are looking for in a relationship if you don't take the feedback, change the behavior, and not make the same mistake in the next adventure?"

"Well, that's easy." Kate pushed back. "I'll just head back to the enchanted pond and look for love in another toadd. I know I can make a toadd see how amazing I am. When I do, I know he will change his mind, want to be with me, and want a long-term commitment. You'll see, Little Katie. I've got this!"

Little Katie could not believe the feedback she was getting from Kate. Exasperated and not knowing what more to say or do, she followed Kate back to Dickland, hoping that something of what she shared would start to sink in.

"Maybe I'll get through to her in the next adventure," Little Katie sighed.

5

The Southern Dick

FACE WHAT IS NOT WORKING

Sometimes, depending on where Kate's last adventure dumped her, the road back to the pond might feel long, winding, uphill, downhill, even sometimes in circles. But after Gay Dick, Kate took the fast track with leaping strides to get back to the enchanted pond in a hop, skip, and a jump. The sooner she got over Gay Dick, the sooner she would be ready for love again.

As she entered the pond area, Kate heard a high-pitched screeching sound. *Or is that singing?* Her ears perked up. *That voice ... I know it!* At first, she couldn't tell why it sounded so familiar, but she could tell the voice behind the sound had a certain twang to it that she recognized. Sure enough, as Kate walked up to the pond, her eyes zoomed in on a toadd sitting on his lily pad with a cigarette in his mouth. He was attempting to belt a southern tune to a sad Eagles song—"Peaceful Easy Feeling." Yes, she definitely knew that voice and the toadd behind it. It was Southern Dick.

"Dear Lord," Little Katie emerged. "Have you not learned any lesson from the previous adventure? Is it necessary to have to ask you, when is it appropriate to date a Southern Dick?"

Kate's eyes stayed glued on Southern Dick as she rationalized with both Little Katie and herself over her choice of toadd.

"Well, at least I know who he is, so he's gotta be a safe choice." At least in that moment, Kate thought he would be. And so here began her adventure with Southern Dick.

Getting involved with Southern Dick was a tricky situation for Kate. They had met a few years back through her brother, whom he was good friends with and hung out all the time. Because Kate lived with her brother and was always around her brother, she was also inevitably in close proximity to Southern Dick. She was observant of him checking her out, but he shied away from making a move on her out of respect for her brother—or maybe it was out of fear that her brother would kill him if he did.

It didn't discourage Kate, though. She became attracted to him based on the stirring of feelings she got between her legs whenever she saw him shooting mysterious looks her way and then instantly dropping his gaze when he noticed she had caught him. With every flashing look, Kate became captivated even more. It got to the point where she decided to engage him in conversation past the idle, "Hey, how's it going?" chitchat they were used to.

One day, Kate's brother and his friends were all hanging out at the house as usual. His friends would ritually gather in the living room on the couch playing music or watching football. Typically, Kate would hang out on a chair across the room listening and keeping watch on the scene while they ignored her—except Southern Dick, of course.

In order to make her move, she had to catch Southern Dick's attention and make eye contact. The opportunity presented itself one day as he sat on the couch next to her brother. It didn't take long for him to glance her way. Their eyes locked. Now was her chance, and she couldn't lose her nerve. Heart pounding, she got up off her chair and headed over to where he sat. She could see him start to squirm nervously as she got closer.

Kate stood in front of him as he looked up at her with his penetrating deep-brown eyes. Her brother, still close by, made Kate aware she had to be careful how she started the conversation. She gulped before asking

Southern Dick if he had something he needed to tell her. She made it known that she saw him throwing odd stares her way.

Uncomfortably, he answered, "No."

Kate leaned in closer so only he could hear her.

"Hmm," she whispered. "Well, you look like you're trying to channel me a message. Maybe you want to step outside where my brother can't hear you tell me?" she teased.

He met her with a boyish smile and then got up and headed toward the door, expecting Kate to follow. Meanwhile, his smile sent her head spinning. She lagged a little bit, trying to be inconspicuous about following him outside. She could sense Little Katie's resistance cautioning her to stay put safely near her brother. Not bothered, Kate was defiantly more interested in whatever Southern Dick wanted to share with her. Oh, and damn that smile. She guaranteed Little Katie she was only going out there to hear what he had to say.

"Sure. I'll just wait here with your brother, and you report back to me on how that went," Little Katie grumbled.

Facing each other outside on the porch in awkward silence for what felt like an eternity, Kate finally drummed up enough courage to once again ask Southern Dick what it was he wanted to say. She gave him an inquisitive look, trying to be breezy about it. "What'd you want to say to me?"

She could tell by his demeanor that he was having a hard time putting his words together. She patiently waited for an answer, hoping he wouldn't lose his nerve.

Finally, with a coy, staggering voice, he asked, "Will you go out with me?"

Kate was momentarily speechless because she was not expecting him to ask her out. She visualized Little Katie peering at them through the window and shaking her head. Kate blinked and turned away to look back at Southern Dick, both surprised and moved. With wide eyes and a smile to match, she replied, "Yes, I would love to."

༺༻

Tickled pink that Southern Dick had asked her out, Kate wanted to look perfect for him on their first date. She recruited some of her girlfriends to help her glamour up. This was going to be a special night, and she wanted to look just as special. After a montage of outfits, hair, and makeup, Kate emerged sizzling in a formfitting mini dress and spiked black high heels. She felt a tingling sensation inside and out as she waited with anticipation for this magical evening to start.

Much to her dismay, the gods of romance must've taken the night off. Her first date with Southern Dick wasn't exactly what a princess might expect. The first disappointment was that he asked her to go to his house so they could walk to the restaurant he was taking her to.

Sensing Little Katie's suspicion, Kate actually considered agreeing with her. Walking was not in her plans. *Crap, I'm wearing spiked heels!* She imagined him picking her up in a car and driving to the restaurant like a real date. Little Katie didn't hesitate to plant the presumption in her head that this may not be a real date.

As usual, Kate ignored her meddling theories and went over to meet him at his house. She knocked on his door and waited anxiously for him to open. She waited long enough for her to consider letting herself in. Suddenly, the door swung open, and he was standing there at the doorway. They both stared at each other with eyebrows raised. Kate was clearly overdressed. He was in a T-shirt and jeans.

"Damn it," she said as her cheeks blushed.

He offered to change his clothes, but Kate insisted he didn't need to. Even though she wanted him to make the same effort she was making and show up for her the way she planned to show up for him, she kept her hopes hidden.

She heard a whisper from Little Katie. "Speak up, Kate …"

"Shhh, it's okay," Kate whispered back.

They walked to a nearby dive bar that served food. *How classy!* Kate caught the sarcastic remark racing through her mind. *Or was that Little Katie?* Never mind. Kate rolled with the whole scenario because she wanted to get to know Southern Dick better. Feeling fairly out of place, she promptly ordered a drink. She needed some liquid courage to get through this night. He ordered one too.

Good sign. He's right on track with me, Kate thought.

The conversation was dull at first, but after a couple of drinks, it finally started to get interesting. Once they dropped the small talk, Southern Dick opened up, and he was soon sharing the intimate thoughts he was having about her. He told Kate how he had fantasized about her from the moment he laid eyes on her and how beautiful and sexy she was. He confessed how he liked to watch her move across the room—how elegant and graceful she looked. All this came as a very nice surprise because before she made the first move, they'd hardly said two words to one another.

"It's all honky-tonk talk!" Little Katie wasn't buying it.

"The reason he never said anything before is that he felt like I was out of his league," Kate disputed.

"Well, that's true." Little Katie couldn't agree more with that remark.

Southern Dick kept on saying all the right things to Kate, and she continued to ignore Little Katie's pleas to make a run for it and get out of this rodeo show before he roped her in. Instead, Kate just caved with every sweet word he spoke to her. It's what she loved to hear.

When the check came, Southern Dick jokingly said, "Let's dine and dash!"

Kate could hear it coming from Little Katie. "Pause and reflect. First, he has you meet him at his place and walk to a dive bar. Now he wants to dine and dash. For heaven's sake, Kate, do you not see all the red flags?"

Kate snapped back, "Can't we call them yellow flags and consider your judgments in the morning?"

The dine-and-dash dare turned into an accepted challenge. With hearts racing and adrenaline pumping, they jumped the patio fence and ran off. A staff member came running down the street after them, bellowing for them to come back. They did stop and ended up paying their bill, but they laughed all the way home.

After that, Southern Dick invited Kate inside for a nightcap. She accepted his invitation to go inside his house for another drink, while Little Katie warned her to get in her car and drive away. *Of course, I'm going in,* Kate thought. She was out of breath, and her feet were killing her from all the running.

The other reason was that Kate didn't want the night to end just yet. She knew she could southern charm Southern Dick into a kiss. What she didn't expect was for Southern Dick to southern charm her pants off so fast. Shocker, right? Okay, maybe not at this point, but what was shocking to Kate were the requests Southern Dick had in the love department and the fact that she was willing to go along with them. She was floating on cloud nine and felt safe with him. As usual, she wondered if he could be her one, true love.

Kate ignored the little nagging voice coming from Little Katie, saying, "What about what you want?"

One thing led to another, and things in the sex department got precariously absurd when Southern Dick asked Kate to wear a strap-on dick and fuck him.

Alarm bells rang like a tsunami warning. "Say, what?!" Little Katie screeched.

"Umm, okay. If that turns you on …" Kate muttered hesitantly as she considered his request. She couldn't believe she was actually agreeing to this, but she didn't know how to say no either.

"Kate, no!" She heard Little Katie loud and clear, commanding her to stop.

Cutting right to the chase, Kate clumsily strapped on the strap-on and bent *him* over. She had no clue whatsoever how to insert the strap-on dick into the only backside hole he had and what she deemed as an exit-only hole. And, she certainly had no experience with how to thrust her hips back and forth like a man—she had never played that role. Remarkably, it resembled a scene from the movie *Deliverance*.

Maybe he took a tip from that movie, she wondered.

Little Katie was nowhere to be seen or heard. She temporarily disappeared because she could not bear to witness Kate's stab at reenacting out the scene. Did he squeal like a pig, one might wonder. No, not quite, but the strap-on dick might have been a tad too big for him because he squealed like a grown-ass man who just took it in the ass. *Ouch!*

To be perfectly clear, Kate wanted to believe he could be her one, true love. Aside from the wild and crazy requests in the bedroom, he was her brother's best friend. If her brother trusted him, so could she. During the period of their relationship, which was about five years, Kate became increasingly more in love, while it became more apparent that Southern

Dick was not following in her direction. In hindsight, Kate wondered if he kept the relationship going because he and her brother were friends, and maybe he felt a little guilty about breaking it off. Little Katie wondered the same thing.

The relationship turned somewhat awry when Kate suggested they move on to the next stage, which, for her, was marriage. The mere insinuation of making a commitment sent him into a tailspin. He would not commit to anything that would bind their relationship to a future together. The only thing he didn't have a problem with and would fulfill was sexual in nature, and for Kate, that was love, so she couldn't figure out why he wasn't ready. She tried to avoid the sore subject of marriage at all costs. She didn't like it, but she had put in her time into this relationship, and she was hell-bent on making it work—that is, until the clincher that marked their final year together.

Kate had been asking for a ring from Southern Dick for quite some time. So, when the holiday season rolled around, he contacted Kate's aunt who worked at a jewelry store and made the impossible move. He finally bought an engagement ring. Rumor had it he would surprise Kate with it on Christmas morning.

It was apparent Southern Dick was not a good gift hider when Kate came across the ring before he could surprise her with it. One day she went into his briefcase looking for pen and paper. When she opened up the case, she couldn't help but notice what was lying there on top—a pretty, little pink box. She gasped with surprise and delight. Her heart was skipping beats, and her thoughts were racing frantically. *He is finally going to pop the question!*

Unable to restrain herself, Kate opened the box to take a peek. The ring resembled exactly what she was hoping for—an absolutely stunning and perfect diamond engagement ring fit for a princess. Realizing he probably had a romantic surprise proposal all lined up, she had to pretend she had never laid eyes on the ring. Kate quickly closed it up and placed it back in the briefcase just as she found it. She didn't want to get caught and spoil Southern Dick's romantic surprise.

Kate was over the moon with excitement, imagining how he would propose. But for reasons unknown to her, he came home from work that day upset and miserable. Kate noticed that his moods did tend to change sporadically, and today was one of those days. She wanted to chalk it up to a bad day at work or him being tired, but he was acting contradictory to her, and his demeanor was wayward. There was no way for him to know she had found the ring, so it could not be that.

As customary, Kate chose to ignore his behavior like every other time he spiraled into a weird funk. It was inexplicable to pinpoint what set him off. Life was one big roller coaster ride with him. One minute she was elated as she planned the wedding and their future together, and the next minute she had to dodge the dark clouds looming over his head. She found herself very confused, trying to figure out what was going through his mind when he acted this way.

The night before Christmas, they went to bed, and Kate was restless. She couldn't sleep, as she still daydreamed about how Southern Dick would propose to her. *Will it be next to the brightly lit Christmas tree as he gets down on one knee? Will he keep me waiting until we get to my family's house and propose in front of them? Will he cook breakfast for me and ask me then?*

They woke up Christmas morning, and Kate's first instinct was to check under the tree to see if she could spot the little pink box. There was no sign of it. In its place, there was a larger box wrapped up for her. She smiled to herself. Maybe he was trying to trick her by wrapping the little pink one inside several bigger boxes.

"Go ahead and open the box," said Southern Dick, smiling ear to ear in a much better mood than the night before.

Kate didn't hesitate to rip it open. On the box cover, she saw a picture of a dartboard. She laughed because darts was one of their favorite games to play. *Smart*, she thought. *He put some thought and humor into wrapping the ring for the perfect presentation.*

As she fidgeted with the box's seal to get it open, Kate sensed Little Katie's dependable presence worrying that Southern Dick was about to dampen her spirits.

"You know, the box is kinda heavy," she hinted.

Kate reached into the box and pulled out what looked just like a ... *a dartboard!* She set it down on the floor and turned the box upside down, shaking it vigorously and emptying all its contents in hopes that a pretty, little pink box would fall out.

"No way! You gave me a dartboard?" Kate asked, bewildered.

Proud of himself, he replied, "Yeah, honey, and now we can play whenever we want. Isn't that great?"

Southern Dick didn't know that she knew he had the ring, so Kate sucked up her profound disappointment and held back her tears. She held on to a false hope that maybe he would still propose; he would tell her this was all a big joke, and he'd go down on one knee and ask her to marry him.

That evening at her brother's house for Christmas dinner, her entire family kept grilling her about Southern Dick's Christmas present. They all knew he had the ring because her aunt had spread it like wildfire within the family. Trying hard to keep a brave face, she relived the disappointment each time she returned the same answer: "A dartboard."

No one knew that Kate had found the ring and was expecting a proposal, so they kept their shock to themselves, while Kate pretended to be joyful about her dartboard. Her family just went right along with it.

Kate's wishful thinking was that he would still ask her to marry him before the night ended, but they eventually went to bed that night—no ring, no commitment. On the inside, Kate felt ashamed and humiliated that he never proposed that day, but what upset her more was that she didn't speak up or speak her truth. That night, the painful revelation hit Kate that her dream was never going to materialize. The pretty, little pink box that had given her a glimpse of a happy future with Southern Dick soon became the wedge between them that led to the demise of their relationship.

Kate eventually made the decision to leave Southern Dick, his dartboard, and all his noncommittal, sex-crazed ways. Love vanished from her like droplets of vapor dissolving into thin air. She didn't know what she was going to do next. Lost and empty, she took it a day at a time to recover from those five years she had lost. Little Katie was left to pick up the pieces of Kate's shattered dreams and broken heart.

A few months later, Kate found out Southern Dick tried to end his life after she left him. His family contacted her and told her he was a manic-depressive who suffered from mental issues and that she was to blame for his attempt on his life. It was an eye-opener for Kate that answered many unanswered questions about why it had not worked out and why he would sometimes turn despondent. *What a blessing in disguise that I never married him*, she thought.

Little Katie came to her with an epiphany. "Kate, that dartboard was a symbolic gift. In a way, it was a gift meant to reveal his true intentions and help you move past this hurtful situation. Southern Dick is the dartboard, and you are the darts—you were never going to hit the bull's-eye with him."

Strangely, it made sense.

Kate was over all the heartaches, but she still wasn't ready to give up on love. She moved on to someone else when several years later she got an unexpected message. Southern Dick found out her location and contacted her. A good span of time had passed after she had thrown him back into the pond to perch himself back on his lily pad of mental instability, and now he insisted on seeing her. Even though Kate was in a better place and happier, she agreed to see him again.

You can imagine the disbelief Kate felt when he showed up holding the pretty, little pink box she had found awhile back in his brief case. Even more astonishing was that he actually proposed to her in a sweet and romantic way. Caught up in the whirlwind moment and with an ambiguous heart, Kate said, "Yes!"

"Maybe he's changed. Maybe he can show me true love this time and be the husband I always wanted," Kate tried to reconcile with herself and Little Katie. But Little Katie's sixth sense knew something else was coming. It all would not correct itself that easily.

In the next breath, Southern Dick confessed something that he probably should have divulged prior to his proposal. "I haven't broken up with my current girlfriend … yet. But I plan on it."

And then the moment came to a screeching halt. Without wasting another second, Kate handed the ring right back to him—this time with a sense of relief—and told him to bugger off and never contact her again.

"Whew!" Little Katie was relieved too. "That was so close. I applaud your decision. This is progress. I think some of these lessons are sinking in, and you're wising up, Kate."

Kate reflected on what had happened in those five years with Southern Dick. They had not been a walk in the park, but they had meant something. In an effort perhaps to try to salvage those years from being a waste, she thought seeing him again would prove she had been wrong in leaving him. She discovered that she was, in fact, wrong, but not about leaving him—about thinking she had wasted those years. She matured emotionally in that relationship by coming to terms with the fact that he would never give her what she wanted, and in turn, she made a sane decision to leave. It was a step in the right direction.

Little Katie shed some light on Kate. "I'm not going to ask you when is it appropriate to date a Southern Dick, because I don't have any objection to you dating a Southern Dick. I think it's perfectly suitable. Frankly, they're quite the gentlemen and super sexy. Being southern has nothing to do with this lesson. Being Southern Dick is where the problem stemmed. He was a mixture of sexual dysfunction and mental instability. His issues were completely out of your control. People carry personal issues attributed to them that are not about you and what you are doing wrong. The responsibility lies in their hands too. Your responsibility, however, is to yourself and to stand up for how you are treated and regarded, and not less than you deserve. You always tend to blame yourself, but the reality is that a man has a role in the relationship too."

"Yes, Little Katie, you hit the nail on the head. There is responsibility on both ends. When he told me he was still seeing another woman while he was proposing to me, I saw right through him and the instability he portrayed. But what is that role? That's what I don't get." Kate scratched her head.

Little Katie went one step further to turn the light on in Kate's head and illuminate the lesson for her. "Your role is not to spend your time dependent on whether today will be a better day based on what kind of day a man is having and worried if he's going to be okay. In the case of Southern Dick, you always walked on eggshells, foolishly focusing on whether today he would act like a child or be the victim or want it in the ass or be a man. A man's role is his choice, and your role is your choice.

The choice here is to cut your ties and get away. Or rather, in this instance, cut the strap-on, lose the dick, and move on.

And this time, Kate did just that.

She had enough of the assorted men on this side of the States. She wanted to move away or, as Little Katie defined it, run away. It was time for Kate to get away from all the pain, turmoil, and bad men she kept attracting. Maybe on the other side of the country she would find a man who knew how to treat a woman. Whether she could find her true love so far away from her comfort zone was a challenge she would have to adjust to, but it was one she was willing to face.

Little Katie suggested Kate stay put and be alone for a while. Kate toyed with the idea, but she just couldn't bear to stay another day with the memories of her past failed relationships. The sad and painful memories were suffocating her mind. She decided to move away from her family, failed relationships, and everything else familiar.

"That is an audacious move," Little Katie expressed.

As Kate packed up her car, she reasoned with Little Katie. "I'll be on my own in the car as I drive across country. I'll have time to think about the role I've played in these relationships, plan for something better, and get ready for the next adventure. I'm not sure how much more my heart can take if I stay here. I am more than willing to try again, but I just have to get away from here."

"I agree you need time to process your disillusions, but running away from your problems to the other side of the country is not the answer, Kate. You're still taking the problems with you. They're not staying behind. At some point, you will have to face your gremlins head-on and stop holding on to your past patterns and failures. You should validate, eulogize, and release what you're feeling and learn from your mistakes."

Sometimes Kate thought Little Katie spoke in code. *What does she mean by* validate *and* release?

"And," Little Katie continued, "because you're willing to reflect on everything you've been through during this cross-country drive, while you're at it, you can think about your choices too. Doing so will help you not repeat the same mistakes in your next adventure."

Oh, Kate thought about them all right and cried a river in every state that she crossed. In spite of it all, she still held a glimmer of hope inside her that she took with her into the next adventure. Looking through her rearview mirror, she contemplated her past against the winding road with all the twists and turns she was leaving behind. Kate reckoned that if she was going to move past the heartache, she had to look ahead toward the future with restored faith.

She returned to Dickland and the enchanted pond determined to find another Prince Dick and get a new chance at love.

6

The Controlling Dick

TIME TO COMMIT TO IMPROVING YOURSELF

By the time Kate arrived at the enchanted pond, her battered heart had made room for a new love. Throughout the cross-country trek, she managed to convince herself all over again that true love was real, and somewhere out there in that big, wide pond there was a toadd for everyone, including her. Maybe she just hadn't met her right match yet. Feeling reinvigorated and confident standing at the edge of the pond casting her charm, Kate was certain that this trip would be her final visit.

I'll find my Prince Toadd Charming this time, she thought, *and show Little Katie once and for all that I'm on the right track.*

She had not been standing there very long before she noticed a toadd demanding her attention. He was jumping around in every direction Kate moved, edging closer to her with every step she took. He made it impossible for her to notice any other toadd. Unable to avoid him any longer, Kate reached over and lifted him off his lily pad.

Clink, clink, clink.

Kate could hear the delicate sound of metal as it bounced off the lily pad and rolled to where she stood. She looked down toward her feet and saw a shiny gold band topped by a radiant diamond. It was an engagement ring! She shrieked with delight, flashing a cheeky grin toward Little Katie.

"See, I knew I'd find Mr. Right on this side of the pond, and this ring proves it," Kate jeered as she bent over to pick it up.

"This ring doesn't prove a thing, Kate," Little Katie returned. "Don't forget that you've been proposed to before, and it didn't work out. Before you take that leap, I propose you find out why he is so prepared to put a ring on your finger. Don't you find him to be overbearing? Observe the feedback you're getting."

But the feedback Kate received was in the form of a shiny promise, and all she wanted was to be married and in love. "Can't you be happy for me just this once?" Kate begged. "Once we're married, he'll change his overbearing ways because he'll have me by his side."

Little Katie wasn't on board. She didn't feel secure with Kate's vision of love and marriage. Her narrative was that Kate needed to work on herself before considering this union—inner self-work that would shine a spotlight on her and her own behaviors that she needed to change first.

Kate preferred not to look at or fix her behavior. She thought she could adjust and be able to change him that way. It would all turn out fine. She was tired of thinking, tired of hurting, and tired of searching. All Kate could think of was *marriage … finally!*

"Think about this," Little Katie insisted. "Are you in love with the idea of being married and having a full-blown wedding ceremony, or are you truly in love with this Dick? More importantly, when is it appropriate to date a Controlling Dick?"

Kate did what she did best whenever Little Katie tugged at her conscience. She ignored her.

Kate met Controlling Dick after escaping her tumultuous relationship with Southern Dick within the first week of arriving in a new town—a fresh town where no one knew her. She left behind her past Dick failures, excited to embark on another Dick adventure. Something about this new place felt promising. Maybe it felt like that because of how quickly she found a job. The fringe benefit was having Controlling Dick as her boss.

"Oh no," Little Katie sighed when she figured out where Kate was headed. "Not again. You're repeating the same pattern as with Money Dick. He was your boss, too. Remember that didn't end well for you!"

Controlling Dick swept Kate off her feet by the extravagant good times he showed her at the beginning of their relationship.

"It's all fun and games when you first meet … all ten minutes of it!" Little Katie chided.

Working together was advantageous as they developed a friendship because Kate got to know him on a professional level and on a close, personal level. She loved how he handled his position on the job. He was so in control, and his confidence in decision-making was a big turn-on for her. When they enjoyed the perks of traveling together, Controlling Dick would handle all the arrangements to a T. Kate never had to do much in terms of planning, because he did it all for her. She settled into it, enamored with his directness, curtness, and constant attention.

However, those should've been signs of his controlling ways, and during their courtship, there were plenty of them that stood out as red flags. Little Katie picked up on them, but as usual, Kate ignored her rhetoric and chose to stick it out. She rationalized that him being in control would help her become a better person. Kate presumed that she had been out of control throughout most of her single life, and now it was refreshing to have someone who kept her on her toes, telling her what to do, how to do it, and when to do it—keeping her in line, so to speak.

And the sex … It was sexy, hot, and spontaneous because he was her boss and they were keeping their relationship a secret. Kate did notice he took the steering wheel in the bedroom, and at first, the move from strap-on-dick sex with Southern Dick to regular, controlled sex with Controlling Dick was a welcome relief. From work to home to intimacy, Controlling Dick took charge of it all for Kate.

Little Katie was screaming inside as she watched Kate sink into this relationship, letting go of every last shred of self as she fell deeper into it. When Kate accepted his idea to live together, she saw it as a step toward a proposal, but she missed the big picture—living together made it easier for him to control her.

One night, they invited some friends over for a party. Controlling Dick and Kate were in the kitchen together preparing appetizers and drinks and setting up before the guests arrived. She was in seventh heaven hosting their first party together as a couple. She couldn't help but wear a smile on her face as she thought about how everything was just as she imagined it would be—happy, blissful, and content. Kate baked a tray of her special cookies that she was excited for their guests to try, but more so Controlling Dick. She loved to bake and was eager for him to love her baking just as much.

Then out of the blue Controlling Dick flipped a switch. He got upset when Kate suggested arranging the cookies on the counter so they'd be the last treat for the guests. They were more of a dessert than an appetizer in her opinion. She sensed his irritation start to boil over as she rearranged the counter her way. His hot temper enveloped Kate like a dragon breathing fire down her neck. Suddenly, with one hand, he shoved her out of the way, and with the other hand, he swiped the tray of cookies off the counter, sending them to the floor.

She watched in shock as the tray flew in the air and landed with a loud crash. Kate stood there frozen in time, looking at her freshly baked cookies all crumbled on the floor, and in that moment, she could feel her spirits crumbling too. Stunned and hurt by his behavior, she fled to another room as he went dashing after her. Oddly, she didn't feel scared, even though intuitively she knew that something was terribly wrong. Not wanting to face this dark side of him, Kate chose to justify his behavior. *Maybe he is just having had a bad day, and he unconsciously took it out on me.* As he entered the room, instead of reacting to his outburst, she looked at him sympathetically and told him it was okay.

Little Katie was disconcerted by how easily Kate accepted what had just happened. She approached her gently. "Kate, no man should ever treat a woman like that—even if he did have a bad day."

"He apologized and promised it would never happen again," Kate implored.

Little Katie replied under her breath. "But it will."

And it did.

When Kate wanted to have a say or an opinion, Controlling Dick would sometimes lecture her until he mentally wore her out or patronized her until she was emotionally weak. He manipulated her to the point where she felt incapable of making her own decisions. He made snide remarks about her to his friends at work to undermine her intelligence. Still, Kate chose to wear the rose-colored glasses and remain within his confinement, wanting to believe that this was his way of loving and caring for her. She saw it as endearing the way he wanted to do *everything* for her.

Little Katie tried to reason with Kate and help her snap out of it. "There is nothing endearing about his behavior, Kate. He has you under his thumb. You need to realize he is controlling you. How much more of him discouraging you or putting you down are you going to take?" She reminded Kate of how much she had already accomplished in life and all the things she still wanted to do. Controlling Dick was always asking Kate to stop wanting more and be satisfied with what she had.

In her mind, all Kate could think about was how much she wanted nothing more but to be married and live happily ever after, exactly like those fairy tale princesses she read about as a little girl. They all seemed to be rescued by their princes, and it worked out great for them. *Why not me?* She was not about to listen to Little Katie now and risk losing Controlling Dick and giving up her chance at marriage. This was true love at last, and she knew she could make this work no matter what the cost.

A thought cloud hovered over Kate's head: *I do love him, right?* Of course she did. Or so she thought. Her next step would be to bug him for a proposal and make the suggestion he ought to ask her to marry him.

"You've been through this song and dance before with other Dicks, and neither one of them turned out to be the Prince Dick you're looking for because you are not ready for marriage yet." Little Katie tried to dispel Kate's fantasy.

Kate saw it differently. She had been through several Dicks by this time, so it seemed natural that she felt ready for marriage. "I've met my match, Little Katie. The previous Dicks could never stack up to this one. What about the fact that Controlling Dick also matches about three-quarters of my Fairy Tale List? Especially the sex portion—he has a generous libido, similar to mine."

Little Katie pressed on. "Think about at what cost you're willing to marry this Dick. It's not all about sex. Marriage is not built on a foundation of sex, and great sex is just part of your list. It wasn't even in the top five. You might want to check back and refresh your memory. Tell me: since when is 'in control of me' on your fairy tale list?"

"True, but maybe it should be. I feel like most of my life has been out of control, and it's sorta nice to have his direction," Kate snapped back.

"But, Kate, it's not *your* direction. It's his. Whatever he says goes."

Kate was adamant she had found her Prince Dick Charming and tried to pull the strings to get him to propose. On a few occasions when she tried to prompt him into asking her, he would burst out in a fit of anger. "I don't know, and stop asking me!" That fiery red flag is one she should have heeded.

Eventually, the day came when Controlling Dick decided marriage was in his best interest, and he finally decided to propose. However, it came nothing like Kate's fairy tale version. She had envisioned it taking place on a beach with a breathtaking sunset on the horizon. She would be standing in front of him as he got down on one knee while looking up at her. Haphazardly, he would pull out a pretty, little pink box (yeah, like Southern Dick's pink box) and open it. Kate's eyes would then fall upon a big, fat, shiny diamond engagement ring. She would rush to say yes, tearfully full of joy as he placed it on her finger. *Just like Mom said it would be.* Then they would celebrate that magical moment drinking champagne and making love until sunrise.

Zzzzip! We can close that curtain. That's definitely *not* how Controlling Dick asked Kate … uh, erm … *told* Kate to marry him.

One thing was for sure: Controlling Dick did manage to surprise Kate with his proposal. The timing of it all caught her totally off guard. More aptly put, she totally got caught with her panties down. In fact, that's exactly how it went down—with her panties down. Well, at least they were pretty panties for such a memorable event.

As Kate was getting ready for bed one night, changing into her pajamas in front of the closet, he charged into the bedroom like a lightning bolt. His big hands were suddenly in her face and holding a little pink box. He stared at her with eyebrows raised in a questionable look as he blurted out the words, "Marry me!" It wasn't even a question—just, *"Marry me!"*

With her panties down around her ankles, shirt halfway off, Kate was confused for a split second. Should she shout for joy or scream in rage? In her mind, she fumed. *Is this how you are proposing to me? Are you fucking kidding me? I have to tell everyone this is how you proposed to me?!*

And that's how Controlling Dick finally decided to propose to Kate—when it suited him, under his time and control.

Kate was devastated. She wanted to rip every page from the fairy tale books that described the magical moment when the prince asks the princess for her hand and throw them into a burning furnace. *This is certainly no Cinda-fucking-rella story!* she thought.

Little Katie could see the despair in Kate's eyes through the looking glass, and she was just as devastated as Kate. She tried to stop her and help her see that he was not the Prince Dick she was looking for.

Maybe he'll make it up to me with a nice beach wedding. Kate wanted to believe. Only that would have transformed this story into a fairy tale, so no, that's not how it took place. Instead, the ceremony took place very, very inland—in a city that embarrassed Kate too much to disclose on her wedding invitation, far away from the beach resort she had wished for. She didn't even get a horse and carriage to carry them off into the sunset. The closest thing she got to horsepower was his Ford truck, which drove them to a chain hotel where he did not even bother to display the romantic tradition of carrying her over the threshold.

Kate's heart was heavy with doubt that night as she tried to fall asleep after having controlling honeymoon sex. *What have I just done?* she thought. Controlling Dick always got what he wanted, how he wanted it, including her—she was now his wife.

During their marriage, Kate became more and more subservient to his needs. She began to realize that she cast all her needs aside in order to fulfill his. He demanded kids when she wasn't even sure she wanted to have kids with him. These little lives would only demand more of her time and more control from him. Nevertheless, she let herself be carried away and had two beautiful children with him.

Kate's once uninhibited and free spirit was disappearing as rapidly as his control was growing. After kids, he completely threw romance out the window. It got to the point where she had to do exactly as he wanted, or there were consequences. But Kate shrugged it off because she thought they were not abusive consequences. The biggest consequence to her passive behavior was losing sight of herself, her self-respect, and her dignity.

"Maybe that is abusive," Little Katie gently posed.

Kate eventually did start to question if this was what marriage was about. *Am I supposed to love a man who controls all aspects of my life, including sex and children?* Still, she couldn't bear to end their marriage for fear of being alone, not certain whether she could take care of herself and two children after years of being under Controlling Dick's restraint. So she endured it for as long as she could keep up the charade—twelve whole years to be exact.

During that time, Kate kept her silence and fell into a deep depression, but she hid it from Controlling Dick so he wouldn't be angry at her. She got pretty good at playing the part of happy wife, happy life. Then sex eventually came to a halt—death for Kate. They became roommates, carrying on like robots and nothing else. Even though Controlling Dick controlled every aspect of her life, she felt like her life was spiraling out of control. She couldn't take it anymore and wanted to be released from the marriage. The time had come for Kate to take back control of her life.

"What am I going to do, Little Katie? *Please* rescue me!" Kate begged.

Those words to Little Katie were like music to her ears. Relieved, she resurfaced to come to Kate's aid.

"I thought you'd never ask!"

Over the years, Little Katie had been saving some questions for Kate. She had avoided asking them because they were the kind of questions that required some deep thinking, in solitude, on Kate's behalf, and Controlling Dick never allowed her time to do much of that. Little Katie's first question was all too obvious, and so was the answer.

"When is it ever appropriate to date a Controlling Dick? Never!"

The next several questions were tougher than Kate wanted to face.

- ☐ Are you allowing yourself to be in this relationship because of how you feel about yourself?
- ☐ Are you allowing him to make you believe that you could not live without his control?
- ☐ Are you allowing him to regulate what your needs and desires are?

☐ Are you allowing him to set limitations on what you want in the relationship and, more importantly, what you want out of life?

But the last question really stung:

☐ Why are you allowing him to crush your spirit?

"This is going to be a bare-all, feel-all lesson," Little Katie began, "so let's look at where you are now."

"I feel like I'm tied up to a heavy rock and sinking deeper and deeper in a sea of misery," Kate described. But there was much more to it.

It was an eye-opener to hear Little Katie talk about the reality of Kate's life, making her confront her true feeling. "It's plain to see you've fallen into a depression. You feel unworthy of a better man or even a better life. In the process, you've developed your own limiting behaviors, like not making decisions without Controlling Dick's influence, needing his approval for even the smallest of details, and not being involved in anything that doesn't include him. Your whole life revolves around him and the children—the children you adore but who he wanted you to have."

Little Katie then talked about Kate's self-talk, which were the negative thoughts she had about herself. At first, Kate could not understand what she meant, because she believed everything she thought about herself was in line with who she was.

"Wrong, Kate! This marriage is placing a shroud over who you are in reality. You have been smothered under his control, and you've lost sight of *you* and what you want out of life. You compromised yourself so much that we're back to being insecure and sad little Kate. And you want to know what else? The way Controlling Dick treated you and how you responded to what he told you—believing him—was the demise of your relationship. And even worse, in the course of it all, it was also the demise of your spirit."

Little Katie was aware Kate needed someone to tell her how to fix this. She didn't trust her own decisions. Strangely, even though Little Katie lived somewhere inside her, Kate could trust Little Katie's guidance, but not her own.

It was apparent the marriage was heading for divorce. Some people may think divorce is the easy way out. To Kate, divorce proved to be the most difficult, life-challenging experience she ever had to face. In her case, it was inevitable. To remain in the marriage the way she was feeling, and after Little Katie helped her realize how depressed she was, would only have caused more damage to not only herself but the children. Kate became overwhelmed with emotions of guilt and lament because of the divorce. She felt like it was all her fault and naturally took all the blame.

"It is not your fault completely, Kate. It takes two in a relationship. Your relationship was never going to fit you because of the suffocating pattern it was cut from. You had an inkling of this on your wedding night, so own it. You are free now—free to take care of yourself and your children. Relish being out of his control."

Little Katie tried to encourage Kate with self-empowering words and had her look at the way she spoke to herself. "*Now* step into *your* control and get back your power. Take responsibility for your life. Take responsibility for changing your self-talk. Out of the fifty thousand things you say to yourself every day, about 80 percent are negative. Let's work on the negative thoughts you have about yourself. We can do this with some positive affirmations. Stop judging yourself, and start to love yourself again. You were like a lion living in his cage, and instead, he treated you like a mouse. It is time you step out of that cage, take charge of your life, and roar like the lioness you are! This can be a powerful change for you if you do what I ask and consistently do it."

Intrigued, Kate asked, "Positive affirmations? Like what?"

"How about talking to yourself from a place of love instead of a failure? For instance, when you start to put yourself down respond to it by thinking this way: *Thank you for bringing this up. What exactly is my fear of feeling this way? What can I do to change this negative thought? How will changing this thought serve me better?*

"So, if you say this to yourself: 'I will never find anyone better than what I have now.'

"Your response to that negative thought would go like this: 'Thank you for this awareness. My fear is that I will be alone, but now I can change this thought by believing that I'm able to enjoy being alone in my own company and open up space to find someone better than Controlling Dick. I am free to be me and attract the right partner.'

"What do you think?" Little Katie asked.

Kate didn't quite get it yet. "Honestly, I think it's a load of crap. I get the whole positive talk stuff, but how is it supposed to change my behavior? I'm so far gone in my head that I'm not sure there is a way back to my sanity. I wish I could believe that your positive affirmations will help me make a 180-degree turn and be happy again, but your suggestion doesn't make any sense. It sounds just as insane as I feel. I want to go back to the enchanted pond and try again."

"This will buy you time, Kate, so you can examine your behavior to see why you are attracting the wrong Dicks." She was asking Kate to take responsibility and make improvements on herself now in order to avoid hard lessons ahead, but Kate was still resisting.

"My time is ticking, Little Katie, like a bomb ready to explode in my head. Let's just head back to the pond, and on the way, I'll try saying this positive thought to myself: 'I am worthy of a better Dick. I am worthy of a better Dick. I am worthy of a better Dick.' Does that work for you?"

Little Katie sighed. "Well, I guess it's a start."

Kate felt her proposition was simple—a lot simpler—than trying to figure out what Little Katie was talking about. *Blah, blah, blah … positive affirmations and loving myself. Isn't the man supposed to say positive affirmations to me and love me to make me feel worthy? I just don't get her. Whatever!*

"I'm not going to watch you become shark bait, Kate. You are heading into some treacherous waters ahead. Yet I know you are onto something because you called out for me and asked me to rescue you. I'm here now, and I'll be there for you when you come back up on the other side. Always know that you can count on me." Little Katie was the reason Kate didn't completely unravel.

Kate headed back to the pond, carting all the heavy baggage she'd collected from her failed marriage and past relationships on her shoulders. Her idea was that once she arrived at the pond, she could unload it in the murky water where it would all sink to the bottom where she'd never need to deal with it again. Free from her past, she would choose another toadd for her next adventure. She still had hopes of finding true love with the next Prince Dick Charming.

The affirmation must be working, she thought. *I am worthy of a better Dick!*

"Kate, I appreciate your tenacity and drive to find the Dick of your dreams, but little do you know that unloading your baggage won't be as easy as you think. I see you carrying it into your next adventure and adding onto it. Let's see what happens with the next toadd, but remember that it's important to continually commit to improving yourself and to taking responsibility for your actions and decisions."

It was an uphill battle for Kate getting out of the marriage, and she felt the weight of it all as she tried to have a normal life after the divorce. Just because she was starting all over didn't mean she was starting from zero—quite the contrary. As Little Katie had counseled, Kate had a long way to go before she learned to reset.

7

The Married Dick

Are You Willing to Pay the Price and Take Responsibility?

After the divorce, Kate wasn't eager to get back to the enchanted pond, as enticing as it sounded. Emotionally, she was still in pretty bad shape. The pain of all her past adventures got in the way of being able to see anything beyond the failures, obscuring the meaning of true love. She made flunking efforts to recite the positive affirmations Little Katie had assigned to her, which Kate found annoying. Coming to terms with the pitfalls of her divorce was still too difficult at this stage. Rather than taking the remedial steps to mend her broken heart, she half-heartedly resumed her quest to unearth Prince Dick Charming. Surprisingly, Little Katie appreciated her drive in finding the one after divorce. One thing was certain: she was determined.

Kate perused the pond, hoping to attract a toadd capable of rescuing her from her misery. There were several loud, croaking toadds willing to jump to the task, but she'd heard that kind of croaking before. Kate walked around looking for a safer area of the pond where the toadds weren't as threatening. She came to a section where the pond glistened with shiny objects that blinded her view. She tried to divert her sights to another spot because of her awareness that toadds with shiny objects had the propensity to end up becoming poor relationships. Then, as she passed by, she saw one toadd frantically jumping up and down on his lily pad. So at the risk of repeating the same fallible actions that kept her visiting the pond, she let her curiosity wheel her toward the toadd fetching for her attention.

Little Katie fretted the direction she was headed. "Just keep looking the other way, Kate. This toadd is in disguise and has trouble written all over him. He's full of a whole lot more baggage than I think you can handle."

Kate identified the shiny object he was wearing on his left ring finger as a wedding band. *So if the ring is not for me, why does he want me?* she wondered. Intrigued, Kate decided she was going to find out for herself and not listen to Little Katie. *Shocker!*

✦

Even though in Kate's newly single life she was introduced to lots of Dicks everywhere she went—places like the grocery store, mall, events, kids' parties, school functions—she typically would hang around her married friends instead. Her interest for toadds had diminished postdivorce, although she had not given up on finding true love altogether. Romantically jaded, she was still figuring out what to do with her life and working to regain love and self-respect. She lacked feeling any sense of worthiness—a constant soul reminder from Little Katie and the focal point for her positive affirmations.

Whenever Kate could drum up the energy to go out, it seemed safer to seek the company of married friends because they were all attached with kids and had seemingly stable lives. Sometimes she did think they felt sorry for her, but frankly, Kate felt sorry for them as well. In her view, she could see the exhaustion in some of her girlfriends' eyes reflecting their lamentable feelings for having succumbed to this life. Their fairy tale ending had turned out to be anything but. Yet, they would still pretend to be in one.

Marriage seemed like a lie to Kate after hearing their stories behind their lives inasmuch as she presumed to be a survivor of divorce. Kate became cynical, swearing off marriage. No way would she fall into that trap again. Instead, she fell for a married man.

✦

Kate met Married Dick through mutual friends. At first, Kate would avoid a certain husband within the group of married friends she hung around at all costs. He had an ego that clearly exceeded the size of his dick. Kate could not figure out what his wife saw in his swollen head. He would brag about his job, the money he made, and all the good fortune he had acquired. His conversations were all self-centered and self-aggrandizing. Every chance Kate got, she left the room whenever he started boasting about himself.

Then she started to notice something odd. He would pay more attention to her than she was comfortable with and would follow her out of the room. Kate couldn't figure out why he would search her out. She tried to get away from him, but he kept trying to catch her alone and strike up a conversation any chance he could get. He started with small talk such as asking Kate what she did for a living.

Gradually, the small talk turned into inappropriate personal questions considering he was married. Their conversations evolved into discussions about what their likes and dislikes were, what was happening in their lives, and even their kids. It was a complete surprise to Kate that he was even the slightest bit interested in her life. Without warning, his attentions awakened her interest in him. She changed her initial opinions of him because for the first time in a long time, here was someone attentive to her and concerned with what she was doing or how she was feeling.

At first, Kate cast away the thought of this being anything other than friendship, maybe because she was still emotionally distraught, feeling less than attractive and much less worthy of his attention. Or maybe, somewhere in the depth of her soul, part of her knew the ramifications of what could possibly follow. Only, this guy was resolute on trying to get her to pick up on his signals. It soon became apparent that Married Dick had become smitten with her.

One night while attending a party at his house, he made his move. He carried a camera with him and followed Kate around to take pictures of her. She politely allowed him, but it did make her feel uncomfortable. He made the excuse of asking for her phone number so he could text the pictures to her. The pictures then turned into text messages.

Initially, he sent indiscreet texts saying things like, "You are so beautiful and sexy." From one day to the next, they turned into unabashed sexting. "I want you, and I want to fuck you!"

So, Married Dick wants to have sex with me. I should have guessed, Kate thought as she zeroed in on what was happening.

Here he was with the same attention and love offering that she craved from other Dicks and that had gotten her into trouble. Married Dick said all the right things to push her sex button. In the same pattern as before, she fell hard and fast into this fairy tale adventure. *Maybe he will leave his wife to be with me,* she thought wishfully.

"Oh my gosh, Kate," a little voice interrupted. "Did you seriously just let that thought cross your mind? You know he will never leave his wife for you. Married Dicks never do!" Little Katie exclaimed.

Kate knew Little Katie's two cents were true, but she didn't want to accept it. She loved the attention she got from him. It felt like a drug—a love high that she did not want to come down from. Never had Kate felt this way with anyone before, and the feeling kept her going back for more. She reached a point when she didn't want the affair to end, and she didn't care if they got caught. Like a drug addict, she was a love addict to Married Dick's emotional attention. She craved the love buzz every day.

There was an instance when Kate should have been able to see right through him. Following the sexting, Married Dick made an off-base sexual suggestion that involved a threesome with his wife. He asked Kate if she would be open to it. Appalled and disgusted, the idea turned her off and admittedly made her a bit jealous.

What kind of jerk would think I would go for such a thing? she wondered.

Kate theorized it was his way of getting permission from his wife to have sex with her. In a perverse sort of way, he could have his cake and eat it too—or, in this case, have his wife and eat Kate too! Even after that, he still managed to keep Kate interested. Although she turned him down on the three-way, she did let him have the cake part.

Kate's affair with Married Dick was strictly emotional up until the day they took the indiscretion to the back seat of his car. They could no longer contain the urges and feelings of desire boiling over. He madly searched for a place to park and barely pulled over when the ardent kissing began. Then Kate's clothes started to come off. Body temperatures rising, their breathing became heavier and fogged up the car windows. He groped and kissed her all over in that one steamy moment, and Kate reached down to unbuckle his pants. Suddenly, he stopped her in her tracks.

"We can't do this," he grunted over his breathless panting.

"Oh yes we can, and we will," Kate vehemently breathed back.

It was ballsy of Kate to rise in arms, but she wasn't good with rejection, and in that moment, she wanted what she wanted. She continued to advance with gusto, removing his pants and began to go down on him when he stopped her again.

"Really, Kate. We need to stop this," he insisted.

"Are you fucking kidding me?" Kate declared with shocking disbelief. "You're the one who has been pursuing me relentlessly. And now all of a sudden you're feeling remorseful?" She felt gutted by his abrupt copout. Not to mention she felt rejected—again.

That is as far as Married Dick and Kate came to going all the way because he decided he couldn't handle the guilt. And it was also the only time they were together because after that incident, they got caught. Not in the car, but via technology. Yes, technology can be a nice means to carry on a secret love affair, but it can also help uncover that very same deceit. His wife discovered their texts on his phone and went ballistic—rightly so. The affair drove her so crazy she threatened to kill Kate.

That was it. They never saw each other after getting caught. Kate never heard from him again. She did not know whether his marriage survived that indiscretion, but moreover, he never even knew that Kate barely survived it. The end of their affair felt like having teeth pulled and left to bleed. Kate went from full elation to full depression as quickly as a text message sends. And then she knew she had hit rock bottom.

"Not yet, Kate. Close, but not yet." Little Katie rushed in to break her fall.

※

It was not Kate's proudest moment. She'd had an affair. As scandalous as the story sounds, before jumping to judgment, let's just say that when you're at the bottom of a dry well and someone reaches in with a bucket of water, you take it to survive. All Kate wanted was to be loved and appreciated. She stubbornly ignored all the obvious signs that the affair was destined to fizzle out like a moth drawn to flame. She wanted to believe with every bone in her body that he would leave his wife for her. In reality, all it amounted to was a fling that had an expiration date stamped on it the day it started. She should've listened to Little Katie and saved herself from playing the scarlet woman in a scandalous affair.

Little Katie's voice of reason interjected. "Kate, it was highly improbable you could have avoided this mess or the pain you and Married Dick put so many people through, including each other, because you were stumbling across unchartered territory. You didn't know how to stop yourself, and then when you found yourself wrapped up in the affair, you didn't know how to handle the situation. This is why you need to start collecting the right tools and resources that show up for you along the road of hard lessons."

It sucks to have an affair, and it sucks even more being left all alone when it reaches the end. Kate was wallowing in guilt and remorse while dealing with the painful ramifications from it that she had subconsciously foreseen. She clung to Little Katie's advice this time. *Maybe she is onto something, or maybe I'm just so desperate to get out of pain that I badly want to believe her. I never want to do this to anyone again. I want to change!*

But the real trick was the recovery and healing in the aftermath.

Kate conceded to Little Katie's call that she needed a lot of work to make sure she rose above this. Little Katie tried to paint the starting line for her. "The reality is that both you and Married Dick played a part in the affair, which makes both of you responsible for owning up to the deliberate behavior that created the affair and that led you both to stray. You must forgive yourself first. If you accept that, you can stop agonizing and apologizing and start living again."

Little Katie knew how desperately Kate wanted to change, so she descended with some tough love. "I don't expect you to answer this next question, just like all the other dating dick questions. But I'm still going to ask it, so just sit back and listen. When is it appropriate to date a Married Dick? Never! For obvious reasons."

Kate listened as Little Katie spoke to her openheartedly.

"What he's not getting at home, he'll want from you. And if you give it to him, be forewarned—he will not give anything of substance in return except for his empty promises. He will never intend to leave his wife or his family. Even if you come across a Dick who does, remember that you are the rebound girl—the other woman wearing the scarlet letter on your chest. Everyone will dislike you on his side of the fence, and your respect and integrity will be on you to fix. It's a vicious cycle of guilt, shame, and regret. It's not worth the price of bitter pain that's caused by this choice of behavior."

Then Little Katie softened up. "But after all is said and done, there is still hope."

It took a lot of inner soul chatter and heart-to-heart conversations with Little Katie to cleanse the wounds of the affair. Most of the time Kate ignored Little Katie's warnings when her impractical actions were headed in the direction of yet another destructive outcome because of wanting to feel in love. But Kate was ready to listen this time. She knew it was time for her to weigh all the factors involved in this adventure.

Married Dick was not worth the loss of balance in her life, not to mention the damage to the other people involved. Only Kate could decide what is right for her and what price she was willing to pay for her choices. The chance of repeating this dangerous dating faux pas was high if she didn't take responsibility for her actions.

In Kate's quest for love, she collected a lot of baggage from her past adventures that did not serve her, but she ignored the weight of them. The question remained: Would she be able to do whatever it took to forgive herself, get back on her feet, and jump back into the pond once more without the baggage? And was she committed enough not to pick up any new baggage?

"It is crucial that you to take responsibility for yourself and for your personal happiness!" Little Katie desperately tried to shake some sense into Kate.

"What does taking responsibility look like?" Kate asked.

Little Katie shared a reminder for Kate to take with her and use as a tool for recovery.

"Acknowledge your mistakes, pick up the pieces, and put yourself first."

With the help of Little Katie, Kate was able to explain why she fell into the arms of a married man. She felt entitled to having an idyllic relationship after not being happy for so long. She programmed herself to expect someone else to rescue her and make her happy after losing her confidence and having her self-esteem splattered on the display of her vibrant relationship wall.

It was a mechanism to save herself from the responsibility of caring for herself, loving herself, and creating her own happiness because she didn't feel worthy of it. She was to blame for making poor decisions; therefore, she found someone who could make it right for her instead. These were the feelings that made Kate cross the thin line between love and hate. At first, she couldn't stand Married Dick, and then she couldn't get enough of him to make up for what she couldn't stand in herself.

Little Katie carefully wove together words of advice into a blanket of encouragement.

"It's time for you to be responsible for the quality of relationship you want. You can't blame your parents or anybody else for what you do not like in yourself. You alone have the ability to change your destination so you don't have to end up like your mom who dreamed of a fairy tale life but did not get it. Take control of the paintbrush to create with careful strokes the romances and friendships you seek and replace your relationship wall with a new display. That means chucking all the excuses for why you can't be happy, removing the victimhood outfit, and no longer blaming your mother and father.

You have always had the power to obtain what you want. Ignorance, lack of awareness, fear, the need to be right, the need to feel safe, or whatever the reason you are choosing not to exercise your power, from this point forward you must make the conscious choice to change this and take responsibility for creating what you desire. When something does not turn out as planned, you can self-reflect on meaningful answers to this list of questions:

- ☐ How did I create that?
- ☐ What was I thinking?
- ☐ What were my beliefs?
- ☐ What did I say or not say?
- ☐ What did I do or not do to create that result?
- ☐ How did I get the other person to act that way?
- ☐ What do I need to do differently next time to get what I want?

A loving and healthy relationship does not come by without going through a few heartaches, but the pain is only a temporary by-product of the valuable lessons you acquire if you are able to identify them and use them as a resource for future growth and self-improvement. This is how you will persevere in the face of setbacks, disappointments, and downfalls, whether they are in a relationship or of a personal nature. Be willing to take time for you to heal your wounds and not simply find another Dick to use as a bandage for mending your broken heart. Last but not least, remember to check the price tag—make sure you are willing to pay the price for your choices."

Little Katie's intuitive heart-to-heart talk prepared Kate for the inner work she was finally ready to undertake before she headed back to the enchanted pond and takes another shot at Prince Dick Charming. She needed to do the work, starting with self-recognition. With caution and more optimism than ever, Kate was eager to take a step toward a healthy relationship—but more importantly, a step toward an emotionally healthier self.

In the end, Kate came to realize that there were life choices that cost more than you wanted to pay. There would always be consequences for her actions, so she needed to be prepared for them before recklessly jumping into relationship decisions that may leave her for broke.

8

The Drunk Dick

CLEAN UP YOUR MESS, NOT HIS

Kate thought long and hard about the questions Little Katie had posed for her to consider before getting into another relationship. She reflected on the advice about accepting her share of responsibility for the awful adventure with Married Dick. All that stuff about processing the pain, blame, and shame and turning it into self-forgiveness and positive self-talk and so on. Only, there was one problem. She didn't know where to start. Evidently, with herself would be a good starting point, but the know-how was not evident to Kate. Even though she had all the materials and outlines from Little Katie's lectures, figuring out the study work and putting it into practice … well, it was a bit overwhelming for her to process. Besides, it was probably too late to learn and act on because Kate had already made headway toward Dickland and back to the enchanted pond.

When Kate got there, she heard the sound of clinking glass and loud chatter. Curious, she walked toward where the noise was coming from and found a large group of toadds perched around one peculiar toadd. The toadds each had a drink on his lily pad.

It is a little early in the day, but what the heck, thought Kate. *It must be five o'clock somewhere.*

Before she could turn back around to walk away, the one peculiar, yet sociable toadd was already handing her a drink.

Little Katie's eyes grow wide. "No, no, no! Not this one, Kate. You'll end up falling back into some of your old patterns again. This certainly isn't part of the working on yourself that you're supposed to be concentrating on."

Kate tried to avoid the warning look Little Katie was giving her because she was more interested in what this toadd was drinking. And how rude would it be of her to leave him hanging by not accepting his drink?

"Your inquiring mind will not bode well in this situation. Let's just skip this one and move on. You're in the wrong place. Let's get back on track," Little Katie suggested prudently.

"But, Little Katie, this guy looks *fuuuun*!" Kate childishly squealed.

Little Katie shook her head back and forth like wobbly Jell-O. "Fun?! He's nothing but a Fun Bobby. Besides, fun is the shallow portion of your Fairy Tale List. Let's be real here. When is it appropriate to date a Drunk Dick?"

Kate decided now was not the time to get into it with her, so she ignored her and happily accepted this toadd's yummy drink, knocking it straight back into her next adventure.

※

Kate actually met Drunk Dick at a gym. She was waiting in line to check into the fitness club when she heard a car screech up to the valet parking outside the lobby. She turned to look out through the tinted glass walls and noticed Drunk Dick drive up in a Porsche. *Hmm … okay, this guy must have money.* Big *check mark*, Kate thought.

With her eyes glued to him, Kate watched him glide in through the glass doors, pass by her and everyone else standing in line, and walk right up to the check-in desk like some sort of VIP. Taken by surprise over his lack of courtesy and total disregard for the people waiting in line, she was secretly somewhat glad he did. Now she could size him up.

At first, Kate was a bit timid to look his way, but when he opened his mouth and gave the staff behind the counter a very cocky sort of I'm-the-shiznit hello, she swapped her shyness for boldness. There was something sexy about the blithe, albeit dickish, manner he tendered his animated hello that gave Kate the impression he was harmless and amusing. He was an attractive Dick, no doubt, so she continued to take notes on him.

He is taller than me. Okay, that'll work. Mmmm, nice legs and in shape. Check, check. Uh-oh, I can tell that he has a big *ego. Well, there's a red flag for me. Oh, but wait. He is making the manager behind the desk laugh. Check for sense of humor.*

I wonder what size his package is. Her mind began to stray. *Did I just think that aloud?*

"Oh my gosh, Kate. You did not just go there," Little Katie scolded.

Whew! Only Little Katie heard that. "What? It's just part of the assessment," Kate remarked.

Oh, one more thing. Kate glanced down at his left hand. *No ring on his finger. Check!* She needed to confirm he wasn't married, as she was gun-shy about guys with rings based on her last encounter with Married Dick. *Green light goes before I lose the nerve,* she thought as she made her move.

"Hello! Excuse me. Would you mind moving over so I can check in? I believe I was here first," Kate said with a coy smile.

He turned around and saw Kate standing behind him. He had the most amazing sea-blue eyes. Her stomach started to churn nervously.

"My apologies," he answered in a deep, husky voice as he stepped aside and looked away.

Hmm, what's his problem? Kate wondered.

Two seconds later he turned to look at her again. "I didn't quite catch your name."

Bingo!

"Kate," she stated. She looked into his striking blue eyes, which immediately sent an electric shock running through her that set off that all too familiar throbbing sensation in motion.

"Well, hello, Kate. Nice to meet you. Do you come here often?" he queried.

She let out a chuckle that resonated in her throat. Trying to be fresh, she remarked, "Do you use that pickup line often?" Little did he know he had her at "my apologies."

Both came to the discovery that they attended the gym around the same time every day, and they flirted relentlessly every time. There was just something Kate couldn't figure out about him, though. He would joke around a lot, keeping clear from any serious conversation or anything too personal. He was very private and closed off when it came to talking about himself.

Tucked away in the little corner of her consciousness was Little Katie. She couldn't understand why Kate even wanted to suss him out when she was still reeling from the wounds of her last adventure.

Kate's reason was simple. This guy appeared to be the whole enchilada. He was nice to her, he sounded smart, he seemed to be well-to-do, he looked sexy from every angle, and he clearly took good care of himself. He was at the gym working out, which seemed normal. He was someone Kate could definitely see herself with.

Little Katie had already done her own sussing out. "Oh boy, are you in for a rude awakening. Not to mention the fact that you still need to work on yourself before contemplating someone new and getting involved in another relationship. The little bit you know about him up to this point has been from a gym setting. You don't actually know whether he's with someone else. Just because he isn't wearing a ring doesn't necessarily mean he is not in a serious relationship. I'm cautioning you not to move quickly with this one. Get to know him better."

Just when Kate thought Little Katie had finished her ranting spiel, she threw in her last jab. "There's a reason why he's not telling you about himself, and there's nothing *fun* about it."

Kate was done listening to Little Katie blow smoke. How bad could he be? After all, she saw him always showing up for his classes and into his workout. She admired his level of commitment to stay in shape. Something about this one felt good, and Kate's interest in getting to know him better grew. Sure enough, the opportunity presented itself.

One afternoon after finishing their workout, they stayed to chat. She found out they had something very much in common: divorce. And neither one of them was dating anyone. The path was clear. Then they got down to the nitty-gritty. When he asked Kate a bunch of questions about her divorce, she tried not to play the part of the victim in all of it. But she did. Why? Because she couldn't help it. The truth was that Kate was still hurt and felt ashamed from all that went on with Married Dick. Drunk

Dick played into the emotional game for the time being. He heard her out, creating a sense of trust in Kate. Yes, she began to trust him.

As they became more acquainted, the attraction grew. They exchanged phone numbers and talked to each other several times a day. He called Kate on one particular day when she felt just exhausted from dealing with divorce, kids, bills, etc. On a whim, Kate took a chance and asked, "Hey, do you want to go out and do something? I feel like I just need to escape."

Before he could even reply, Little Katie was already interjecting. "Interesting choice of words. So you just need to *escape*? Haven't you been doing that all along? I want you to be present right now and *think* about what you are saying and not use a man to escape. This avoidance nature of yours is what gets you into trouble—just like with Married Dick. You chose not to weigh the consequences and escape. But instead, disaster happened."

Except in that moment, Kate didn't want to think. Thinking was more work, and what she needed was a break from all the stress she was under. She rationalized with Little Katie, and herself, that he was the perfect kind of guy to take a break with. *I'm allowed to have a little fun occasionally to de-stress myself.*

Drunk Dick graciously responded with an invitation to dinner and a movie. Later that evening he picked her up in his sporty Porsche dressed in scrubby clothes. Kate, on the contrary, chose to dress up nice. Clearly, he wasn't too concerned with making an impression. Oh, she should have seen that red flag too. *Oh well*, she thought, shrugging it off. *Technically, we aren't on a date—we're just hanging out.*

Sitting beside him in the theater, Kate was excited just to be out with him. His shoulder grazed against hers; he was close enough for her to feel his body heat. Her heart started pounding, and her loins began throbbing. She could just straddle him now and get started on her escape. *Okay, I have more discipline than that. I'm not going to fuck him in the theater.* Although, the film actually sucked, and it was more fun to fantasize about fucking Drunk Dick than pay attention to it.

After the movie, they went for dinner and drinks. As the night drew to a close, he still had not made a single move on her. He had not encouraged any physical contact in the theater either. The attraction was there because she could feel the sexual energy between them. She couldn't understand why for the time being he kept his sizeable package under lock and key. How did she know it was sizeable? She peeked and sized it up while in the theater. There's no shame in that and no reason why there should be. Desire is human nature, and checking out the goods shouldn't just be expected of men.

Inherently, the night was over when he dropped Kate off at home. There was no kiss—not even a hug, nothing. *What was wrong with him? We had such a good time. There was definitely chemistry, and we had fascinating conversation.* Kate found herself wanting more of him—no, not just tending to her throbbing loins. She wanted to connect on a deeper level. But he just told her he thought she was a "really cool chick." *Hmm, that's an unusual sentiment from someone who is trying to come on to me.* So for a moment, Kate thought, *I guess this is* not *love after all.*

If Kate had really believed what she thought, the adventure would have ended here. Because if it didn't look like love, didn't talk like love, and didn't smell like love, then as far as Kate was concerned, there was nothing to pursue. Except this was not the end of this adventure. Kate should've listened to Little Katie because it was time to brace herself. This toadd ride was just getting started.

The cool-chick rapport turned into a hot-chick connection when one late afternoon Drunk Dick called her. They started having the usual sort of chat, but this time he sounded different to Kate. He spoke in a low, husky voice, telling her how beautiful she was, how sexy he thought she was, and all the things she had been hoping he was thinking and feeling. He pushed all her sex buttons like he knew her program well. She felt like she was skydiving a thousand feet in the air in an atmosphere of love and lust.

Kate had wanted this man to make a move on her for months. She finally let her guard down and spoke back to him with the same implication. "You're sounding quite sexy yourself."

No response, just silence from the other end of the phone.

Uh-oh … There. I said it. I shared my feelings, and he stayed quiet. Kate couldn't tell in that dreaded still moment if his silence was consenting or if he didn't want her to reciprocate. The moment of silence became unbearable, but she didn't say a word after that. She waited to see how he would reply.

He took her out of the dark when he finally spoke up after what seemed like an eternity and asked provocatively, "What are you doing right now?"

She could barely breathe, sensing by the tone of his voice that he was ready to make his move.

"I'm sitting on my back porch … reading a book … sipping on a glass of wine. Want to join me?" she asked as she raised her glass and wet her lips with the ruby-red liquid.

Then he asked her what she was wearing. Kate started to play into his game. She described a distressed pair of hip-hugging jean shorts and a thin, formfitting tank top clinging to her silhouette … no underwear, no bra. In the dead of summer, the humidity was hot and sticky with a light drizzle coming down from the skies, making it just bearable enough to be outside. He would join her he said.

Kate heard the sound of his Porsche come barreling down the street, and as he arrived, he revved up his engine before turning off the car. Her internal engine was revving up as well. The sound of his Porsche turned her on just as much as his ego. The car was an extension of his persona, and the two had an interchangeable effect on her.

Pacing while nervously waiting in anticipation for the doorbell to ring, Kate took one final breath in preparation for what was to come before letting him in. She got a delicious waft of his white, musk cologne as she opened the door. Her thumping heart felt like it was going to tear through her chest, and the throbbing between her legs began.

She pulled herself together and invited him in. He smiled as though he knew she was holding back. He fixated his eyes on her with a look that pierced her soul and made her feel faint. He'd never looked at her that way before. She had to control the urge to pounce on him and jump his bones right then and there.

Kate offered him a drink and led him to the back porch where they sat on the couch and started small talk. She just wanted him to reach over and kiss her. Instead, he got up, walked to the opposite side, and left her sitting alone. *Why is he sending me confusing signals?* She knew what he was there for; there was nothing confusing about that. She began to undress him with her mind.

The rain had increased from a light drizzle to bouncing raindrops, and the temperature had cooled down. Seeing the goose bumps on her arms, he walked over to her and suggested they move to the warm, dry indoors. Kate could feel his energy the same way she did when they were at the movies. She was getting increasingly wet—not only from the rain but in between her legs as well. He leaned over and reached for her hand to help her up. They were face-to-face and finally touching.

Tracing each other's bodies with their eyes, he leaned his head close to hers. With one finger, he lightly tipped her chin toward his face and placed a soft, gentle kiss on her lips, parting her mouth. She moaned, feeling a shock of sexual energy shoot through her body. He grabbed her by the arms and pulled her into him. They kissed passionately, their bodies intertwining, until they fell onto the couch behind them.

They never made it into the house. They pulled each other's wet clothes off and made mad love like never before. It virtually felt like the sexual tension they built up amassed into a supernova. The explosion was pure ecstasy. They could not get enough of one another, and he made sure to take care of her several times over. Kate felt so in love afterward. She wanted to know everything about this man. She was already thinking she was going to marry him. They fucked like rabbits for days, weeks, months …

And then she noticed he started to change.

※

Drunk Dick slowly opened up to Kate. At times, he was still vague about his story. He told Kate he retired very young, a detail confirmed by the fact that he never worked while they were dating. He stayed home a lot except for the occasional errand he needed to run or when he decided to play a round of golf. He rarely hung out with friends, which Kate found strange.

They kept in touch by phone constantly, and as time went on, they met once in a while for a drink and sex, but not as often as they did in the beginning. He got to a point where he stopped working out. Kate grew increasingly wary about whether he actually took time to play golf or whether he had any friends at all. One other strange and curious factor that crept up stemmed from the fact that he still had not asked her over to his house. They were always meeting up at hers. He saw how she lived, and she wanted to see how he lived.

Then one day out of nowhere, he invited her over. Kate was thrilled that he was finally opening up more by welcoming her into his personal space. But her joy was short-lived. Kate was surprised to discover his place was pretty trashed and littered with all of his ex-wife's shit. When she left him, she left her stuff behind, and he never cared to clean it out. Kate asked him the obvious questions: "Why are you keeping these things? Why are you not cleaning stuff up? Why can't you take the time to get your house organized?" He was home night and day; surely he could find the time to clean up his home. Much to Kate's disenchantment, he saw nothing wrong with how he lived—he thought it was fine.

Kate found herself judging him more than she realized. It became a habit to critique him constantly. When she noticed he stopped going to the gym, she asked him why, and he just clammed up. She just wanted to help him, but perhaps it was hurting him instead. Drunk Dick withdrew from Kate. When she would go over to his house, she noticed he'd been drinking before she got there. That's when the real truth behind his behavior became exposed.

One night after making love, Kate stayed awake while he slept. She went into the kitchen to get some water and accidentally spilled it on the counter. She grabbed some paper towels to clean it up. When she opened the trash can to throw away the clump of wet paper towels, she saw it was full of empty wine and liquor bottles. Kate was shocked. Not knowing what to think, she grabbed her smartphone and looked up the signs of an alcoholic. As she read through the list, she noticed his behavior corresponded with most of the signs. Her heart sank. *This can't be true!*

Kate believed the man she was dating would one day become the man she would marry and live with for the rest of her life. After her failed marriage, she fell in love hard with Drunk Dick. She wanted this relationship with all the good parts of what he brought to their union so badly that she lived in denial about his problems. They went beyond alcohol. He was dealing with depression and other mental health issues that she buried away and ignored.

"I believe that is called codependency, Kate," schooled Little Katie.

Kate knew Little Katie was right, but they continued this abusive alcoholic/codependency relationship for three debilitating years. Like all the previous adventures, this one also reached that one pivotal moment that would stigmatize their relationship and mark the slow, winding, downhill plunge. Kate could no longer disguise this codependent relationship as a healthy one.

They had planned to go out for dinner one night when she showed up at his house and he wasn't ready to go. He had changed his mind and decided instead to go to a bar and play pool. He made the excuse that he didn't know how to play the game well and wanted to learn. He wanted Kate to teach him. She wasn't dressed up for a dive bar, and she made him aware that she wasn't happy with his change of plans. She could also tell he had been drinking—a combination that made her feel like the night would not end well.

Nevertheless, Kate went along with it to please him because she didn't want the night to go to waste. Little did she know that Drunk Dick was effectively putting her on display. He watched how she carried herself around all the men with eyes on her whenever she bent over to shoot a ball on the pool table. As soon as Kate caught wind of the whole scenario, she began feeling uncomfortable and decided not to drink that night just in case she had to drive.

Drunk Dick was getting lit up, and his manipulative temperament was rising with every shot Kate made. After hitting and missing the first few shots, he grew impatient with his own game, and then, one by one, he proceeded to shoot every ball into the respective pockets. Kate watched completely dumbfounded because she still wasn't aware he had lied to her about his low skill level. He turned to look at her over his shoulder as he guzzled down another beer.

"You passed the test," he said coldly.

By this time, Kate had taken about as much of his erratic behavior as she could. She put the pool stick down and told him she would be in the car waiting, which sent him into a tailspin. He blew up at her and started yelling as she made her way to the exit, spitting fire, being disrespectful, and calling her lewd names across the bar for everyone to hear.

The cool night air hit Kate's face as she darted through the parking lot to the car, her heart racing. She could hear footsteps coming up behind her. It was Drunk Dick running after her. In her hurried attempt to get out of the bar and into the safety of the car, she scrambled into the passenger seat when she should have gotten behind the wheel. Although giving it a second thought, she feared his reaction because he was already out of control.

Drunk Dick climbed into the driver's seat fuming and sped recklessly out of the parking lot, driving like a bat out of hell. In a split second, he stopped in another parking lot at a nearby high school. Kate didn't understand what was happening and was terrified of what he was going to do next. He screamed at her to get out of the car and walk home.

"But I don't know where we are," she cried with tears streaming down her face as she stepped out of the car shaking.

"Figure it out," a demonic voice yelled back.

He sped away, this time leaving Kate in a dark, empty parking lot all alone in the middle of the night, not knowing where to go or what to do. She was scared, humiliated, and too embarrassed to call anyone for help because she did not know how to explain what had happened.

A few minutes went by before his car came tearing back into the parking lot and pulled up next to her. He got out and walked toward her. As she braced herself for more of his erratic behavior, he leaned over to open the passenger door, made an apologetic remark, and politely asked Kate to get into the car.

"I would never leave you like this," he said calmly. "I only wanted to teach you a lesson."

Kate was mortified. Her emotions were all over the place. She didn't know what the fuck had just happened or what lesson he was trying to teach her. She felt afraid, anxious, and panicked and just wanted to run away and escape. But she didn't want to react for fear of him leaving her stranded again.

She got into the car and remained silent all the way back to his house, baffled by his manic behavior. She made the excuse she had work early in the morning and couldn't stay. He spewed more degrading words at her as she left his house.

Drunk Dick had exposed his dark and volatile behavior to her, which didn't stop there. One minute he was fine, and the next minute he was losing it with her. He would use intimidation, guilt, or threats to gain control of her emotions and manipulate her. He would say hurtful things to her under the influence of drugs or alcohol. He always blamed Kate for how unhappy he felt or how mad he acted, never taking any responsibility for his actions toward her. All the abuse he gave her was his wacky way of teaching her a lesson, or at least that's what he called it.

Little Katie stood behind the scenes, observing it all and wondering how much more Kate was willing to take. "Why are you putting yourself through this? I heard you use the word *escape* again, but this time it was from him. And yet, you're allowing him to control you."

Kate could sense exasperation in Little Katie's tone. Emotionally depleted, Kate confessed, "Because most of the time he makes me feel like the most beautiful woman in the world … and, by the same token, the worst woman in the world."

Kate spent so many days thinking over their relationship, considering whether she should stay in it or not, and then she would rationalize her reasons for staying. She convinced herself that he loved her like no other man ever had. According to him, she was the best thing that had ever happened to him. Kate needed to feel loved and special, so she chose his flattering words over self-love.

Yes, he had a dark side to him, especially the verbal abuse that came with his drinking. In Kate's need to feel loved, she convinced herself that she deserved the negative things he said about her. Why? She didn't know. On several occasions, she did try to leave him, but she kept going back. She was dependent on a belief she had constructed: *I can change him.* There it was. Change him. Because of the good she saw in him, she felt she could change him for the better so that they could live happily ever after.

Kate was still under the misconception that she could change a man she loved if she loved him enough—if she loved him more than she loved herself. *Why wouldn't a man change for me?*

"Why in the world do you think he would change for you, Kate?" Little Katie tried to open Kate's eyes once more, but Kate was ignorant of the answer to that question.

Little Katie hesitantly let her experience the painful adventure for a long time. She knew it was something Kate had to go through, and inevitably, she would reach her breaking point. Until then, she wanted Kate to get everything out of this experience she needed to in order for her to reach the point Little Katie was waiting for—for Kate to wake up and come to her senses.

In the meantime, Kate tried her best to hide the turmoil in her relationship from anyone who would tell her that Drunk Dick wasn't good for her. She did not want anyone to know his secrets, because if they knew, they would judge her for staying with him. She only confided in friends who supported her in this relationship even though they knew about his problems and worried about Kate getting hurt. Or perhaps they only pretended to support the relationship when, in fact, they were supporting Kate so she wouldn't push them away and they could stay close if she needed their help.

Deep down, Kate felt ashamed and embarrassed because she was aware that the life she was leading with Drunk Dick was not healthy for her or her children, and it took away from her sanity, which was a huge distraction from everything else in her life that could potentially be positive.

Whenever she became drained and depleted, Kate would hear Little Katie's whispers come over her like a soft, warm breeze hoping to save some of her self-esteem. "You cannot live when there is that kind of draw on your energy and your self-respect, Kate. You cannot live when inside you're fighting with yourself to hide, even from yourself. Look at the damage you're doing to yourself by being with Drunk Dick." Her words were sinking in subtly.

The final straw came when Kate attempted to put a bandage on their wounded relationship. She could see Drunk Dick had taken a turn for the worse. They went on vacation and spent a lot of time alone together. But at night when she went to bed, he would stay up and continue to imbibe. In the morning, she woke up to countless empty liquor bottles and a very grouchy man. Sometimes she witnessed him getting sick in the bathroom and then come out and hit the bottle again with disregard as though it were a normal thing to do.

Needless to say, they fought that weekend. Kate had enough of the torment fueled by his alcoholism. She was no longer willing to let this man continue to bring her down. She opened her eyes to the fact that he was sick and had a disease. Even scarier was her premonition that he was dying. She couldn't stand by someone who didn't want help and refused to get better.

Kate made a decision to live and love in a healthy manner. She was worth more than this trauma, and once she truly embraced this thought, she broke free. She crossed the bridge and broke the cycle. That time, she did not go back to him.

※

After they parted that fateful weekend, Kate never spoke to Drunk Dick again. Sadly, a few months later, one of his neighbors contacted her to share some tragic news. Even before the words escaped the neighbor's lips, Kate could already predict what she had to say. He had died of liver failure. Even though she had the premonition he was on the path to an early grave, the news was no less shocking.

Kate's heart ached so much for him and always did whenever she thought of him. He died alone, depressed, and with nothing to live for. As she mourned for him, she also knew that she did the right thing by disengaging from the relationship. Kate could not save him. Only he had the power to do that. She had to save herself.

Alcoholics Anonymous defines *insanity* as "continuing the same behavior and expecting a different result." That was their relationship—insanity for both of them.

※

Once Little Katie got wind of Kate's decision to leave Drunk Dick, she knew what was coming next. There was so much Kate had to come to terms with, and Little Katie made sure of it. She had let Kate live this experience her way without much interference as part of the learning curve. Sometimes people have to experience the bad to learn a good lesson—not like the lessons Drunk Dick tried to impose on Kate, rather a life lesson that made her a stronger and wiser woman. However, the revelation of the lesson didn't happen overnight. It was definitely a process.

Kate's session with Little Katie began immediately.

"When is it appropriate to date a Drunk Dick? Never! You both hit rock bottom. I'm relieved you have finally reached this point of self-reflection. You spent all that time living in denial, preoccupied with making Drunk Dick's needs and desires more important than your own. I keep seeing a pattern in every one of your relationships. If you continue doing what you've always done, you'll keep getting the same results. He is gone now, and you're out of his grip, so you can start picking up the pieces of your broken heart. It's time you dig yourself out of the swamp of low self-esteem this adventure swallowed you up in and move up in the direction of positive light. It is time to take responsibility for yourself."

Her words were harsh but true. Kate was able to make some sense of what Little Katie was saying. She just couldn't take another ounce of pain. On a scale of 1 to 10, Kate had surpassed it feeling depleted, lost, anxious, disappointed, confused, and hurt beyond what anyone could fathom. First, she cried for days on end for all the loss suffered in this relationship. She had been in love with a man she could not change, and even though it was a dysfunctional relationship, she kept going back for more.

If the saying "What doesn't kill you makes you stronger" was true, Kate would rather have been dead than endure the pain of Drunk Dick. But she was blessed with two children who gave her the will and strength to keep on living. She pulled herself up once again.

"Little Katie, I'm listening now. Where do we start?"

She took Kate by the hand, and they began with taking responsibility for her self-care by cleaning up the past in order to embrace the present. They collaborated on putting together a checklist of personal goals to work on in order to initiate a new beginning where Kate's well-being was first and foremost. If she could achieve them, she could create a healthy space in her life and attract other healthy relationships into her life. Kate would work toward finding a true match. Her list of goals looked like this:

- ☐ loads of self-care
- ☐ believe in yourself
- ☐ speak impeccably about yourself
- ☐ positive affirmations daily
- ☐ put yourself first
- ☐ *love yourself*

Kate started with clearing negative behaviors to make room for nouveau love—dumping the past hurts and hang-ups. She believed she was indeed worthy of so much better. It was time to stop living in the past and realize that the past was not a life sentence; it was a life lesson. She took the reins of responsibility Little Katie handed her. She was responsible for nurturing a state of love for her and her children. Just like Kate knew Drunk Dick was the only one who could save himself, Kate too realized that only she had the ability to save herself.

The lesson she learned here was that when she didn't take the reins of responsibility into her own hands, she was essentially saying she didn't trust her ability to create her own happiness. Instead, she ended up creating a need for someone else to make her feel safe and secure and happy and loved.

Kate was thinking with clarity. *The revelation is that I don't feel safe and secure because I fell into the belief I had been consistently abandoned and not loved by the men I loved. This belief made me dependent on someone else's love.*

Little Katie had finally gotten through to her. Kate sought to take responsibility for changing the way she looked at her life. The phrase "If you change the way you look at things, the things you look at change" became a customary reminder for Kate to switch off from the blame she placed on her past for the bad experiences in her present.

"In order to move forward, you have to be willing to do the hard internal work. Accept that you are safe and secure and that you are loved, taken care of, and supported by a higher power that exists within you—a power only you can reclaim. But in order to reclaim your power, you will have to start with loving yourself, because the secret to attracting true unconditional love is to love yourself first. If you don't love you, how can you expect another person to love you?"

Kate was speechless in response to what Little Katie revealed in that single question. After thinking about it, Kate replied with another question. "I have to love myself before another can truly love me? What does that look like?"

"You have to do the work. The lesson will take as long as you need to accomplish the final goal on your list: loving yourself. The goals listed before this one lay the groundwork for building the foundation of self-love," Little Katie replied.

Contemplating this, the process of loving herself intrigued Kate. She decided from this point forward she would, and possibly could, play with the idea of loving herself. Little Katie watched as Kate's eyes filled with hope once again. She was on the right path now.

Kate discovered that the first step to loving herself was to be open to making the effort. She wished she could say that at this point she learned all she needed to learn about self-love. Unfortunately, said questions would resurface a few times more in the future. It would take time and a few more adventures before she identified what loving herself really looked like. But at least now Kate believed it was something she could learn to do.

As Kate and Little Katie made the journey back to Dickland and the enchanted pond together, Little Katie witnessed Kate move into her personal power—a power that she helped Kate find within, A power Kate would need to develop and embrace, and one that she was excited to explore and start moving into.

Little Katie set Kate's sights to an even greater lesson. "When you reach the final goal, you'll go from expecting someone to give you what you think you need to manifesting what you want."

Manifesting what you want. That one sounded tricky, and Kate changed the subject.

"Little Katie," asked Kate, "why is it that some of us decide rightly to save ourselves and pursue the lives we long to live, while others choose not to?"

Little Katie answered, "The answer to that is coming, and it will be revealed. For now, I love that you're willing to go for the life and the love that's right for you!"

So off to the next adventure they went with Kate embracing the discovery of her personal power.

9

The Porn Dick

Ask for What You Want or Don't Want

Kate was sick of trying and tired of crying. There was no more escaping. Kate had discovered that escaping was only an illusionary solution that took her around in circles. But the grim thought of being alone always stuck out in her mind, and so she chose to return to Dickland and go back to the pond much sooner than she should have. In reality, she wasn't ready for another adventure. The slow, dreary return to the enchanted pond was like walking through quicksand. Every step she took toward it felt like she was being soaked up by the mushy marsh as she sunk deeper and deeper into the earth.

Maybe I've fallen into a booby trap. Maybe the enchanted pond is actually a swamp, and these toadds are bait. There has to be some sort of trickery going on because there is no reasonable explanation why every adventure so far has left me in the dark like some lost soul searching for a glimpse of light, Kate wondered.

Meanwhile, Little Katie continued to review Kate's adventure history with her because Kate scrawled through the homework of loving herself in a hurry to get back to the pond. Perhaps she deserved more than Drunk Dick, but Kate wasn't sure she truly believed she was worth more. Little

Katie's chatter in her head was loud, though not loud enough for her to make a complete 180-degree change.

It took some time to get over Drunk Dick, and even though she missed him, she comforted herself with the knowledge that he was no longer suffering. Neither was she. Sadly, it took his death to free Kate from codependency and the underlying agony of their relationship. She was not sure she could have fully released him otherwise. She believed he felt he could not let go of the addiction either, so he chose death. Kate chose life.

Drunk Dick once prophetically shared a quote with her from Friedrich Nietzsche: "That which does not kill us makes us stronger."

The irony of those words after his death provoked Kate enough to want to dig out the swamp she had fallen into and inspired her to want to work toward cleaning and clearing her heart, soul, and mind for the next Dick adventure. Reluctant to sink into further darkness, Kate pulled herself up by the string of hope she found in that line.

But Little Katie did not agree with Kate's purpose for doing so. She stood in front of her with widespread arms to stop her from going past her without first hearing what she had to say. She couldn't let Kate approach the pond feeling like this.

"It's not about doing it *for* the next adventure, Kate. You're definitely on the right track with the cleaning and the clearing, but I'd like to see you clean and clear for yourself first. Then, and only then, will you be strong enough to build a healthy relationship. It needs to start with you. Remember what I've been telling you? You need to love yourself first."

"I know. I know. I remember," Kate replied in a drab tone.

"You need to be alone to sort out yourself. That is exactly what you need!"

"But what's the joy in that? How will that make me feel better?"

"It can be … All you need to do is create joy for yourself doing all the things you love to do."

The notion was inconceivable to Kate. In the first place, why would she want to be alone to remind herself of all the past mistakes she made, inundating herself with negative thoughts and emotions of failure? *Being alone is intolerable and drives me to want to escape again*, she thought.

"Let me go, Little Katie. I need to get back to the pond and find companionship."

"No. Wait!" Little Katie tried once more to get her to hold off. "Hear me out before you go down that road again. It's precisely the reason *why* you need to be alone because you should first deal with your past mistakes so you don't keep repeating the same patterns. Face your demons and all the things that are blocking you from what you want."

Little Katie was adamant she would drill her rubric of self-love and positive change into Kate's head. She kept stopping her in her tracks every time she went to take another step. For a moment, partly because Kate truly was exhausted, she decided to sit back and listen. She didn't have enough energy to fight Little Katie even if she wanted to. Kate scribbled on her mental notepad as Little Katie arranged her words in the best form she could for Kate to gobble them up. Admittedly, they did sound tempting to Kate.

"What if, from this moment, you could love all your mistakes and acknowledge them as lessons in love and life? What if you looked as these adventures as positive steps leading you to the right person at the right time? You can accept everything that has happened to you so far as a lesson in love instead of a loveless defeat. You have it in you—the love for yourself because if you didn't, you would not have been able to rise above these challenges. You just don't recognize that love yet. The promise is that once you do, with just a change of mind, you will be able to promote a healthier mentality that brings you joy and love."

If only it were that easy. How brilliant it would be if I could be at peace with myself, living without regret and weathering each plight like a bird who flies free in harmony with all the seasons of Mother Nature. But the past always comes to wreck the dream, crashing in like a brick through a glass window. The window to a happy future shattered.

Little Katie interrupted Kate's drifting thoughts. "Identifying the harsh relationships and the circumstances that lead you to the wrong Dick is necessary, but hanging onto the memory with blame and regret is not. That is how you get caught up looking for an escape. Your definition of escape is turning to a man and using sex for your strength and identity. Sex has been your identity and your way of love, but that has not served you in any of these adventures so far. When you lack self-confidence, you are powerless, which is how you have managed to become overpleasing in order to get attention from your partner—the wrong attention. This behavior has resulted in you landing in one of two roles, overly dependent or codependent."

Little Katie had Kate reflect inward on some difficult questions: Can you be alone and love Kate? Ask yourself. Who am I? What are my strengths? What can I do to stay connected to myself and maintain a sense of individuality and independence when I become involved in an adventure?

She asked Kate to allow herself alone time to save herself from further trouble and pain. The explanation was that with a bit of time to herself to get her head straight using the resources Little Katie had put together for her, she could ultimately fall in love with herself. Every day she would get closer and closer to find what her soul was looking for by practicing and preparing until the day came when true love showed up and Kate was ready to embrace it.

Little Katie was on fire, wanting to bring everything out on the table for Kate to nourish her mind and soul before going back out there. She explained to her that there should not be any expectations placed on relationships. A partner should love you for who you are and not just for sex. The same went for Kate when it came to giving in. Compromises are healthy, but not to the point of losing your identity and looking to your partner to figure out what you need or want.

"This time, before you get to the pond, let go of any expectations for love. Instead, embrace the notion of you loving yourself and not the idea of looking for love in another fairy tale adventure. Can you love like that, Kate?"

Kate pondered that single question as they continued their journey back to Dickland. *Can I?*

Kate heard some unusual musical sounds as they came closer to the pond unlike any type of music she heard before. No, this wasn't pop, rap, or soul music. In between the music were sounds of moaning and laughter. Kate's natural curiosity sought to identify the source toadd. Following the sounds, she reached a clearing, and within close proximity, she saw a very good-looking toadd who appeared to be extremely withdrawn sitting on his lily pad. He immediately caught Kate's attention with his semblance of boyish innocence. She also sensed a bit of mystery surrounding him, and this toadd felt different to her.

"I want to go on an adventure with this one," Kate said emphatically.

Little Katie proceeded to caution her. "Go ahead and pick this Dick, but beware that innocence with a mixture of mystery can prove to be a toxic concoction. Don't let the strange music catch you off guard. You might find yourself dancing to the beat of someone else's drum."

※

Kate first met Porn Dick when she and her husband were married. They had moved into their new home as Porn Dick moved in downstairs from them at the same time. He was incredibly hot and sexy. It was hard for Kate to contain herself from drooling over him, but she was married, and so was he. And he was a very quiet and secluded neighbor—friendly from a distance, but very private. She never got to see much of him, although she would hear him rumbling about in his garage in the middle of the night.

Because their bedroom was above his garage, more often than not, the squeaking garage door opening would wake her right around two o'clock in the morning. It irritated her so much and pissed her off to no end. *What the hell is he doing in his garage so late?* So many times Kate wanted to sneak downstairs to see what was going on, but she held back, not so much for lack of guts as for lack of impropriety. And so her curiosity grew.

The neighborhood got together and held block parties and holiday events so the residents could mingle periodically. Porn Dick did attend some of these events with his wife and their young child; however, he was never very sociable. He would show up for a few minutes, have a substanceless conversation, and then disappear. Even Kate's husband commented on how rude he came across, but they dismissed it because, after all, it was none of their business. Kate put it down to him just being a dick. Although, she still wanted to know why his garage door kept opening in the middle of the night and waking her up. It remained a mystery.

Kate and her husband moved out of the neighborhood into a larger home after the birth of their second child. She never saw or thought of Porn Dick after that. That is, until she got divorced, and one day, out of the blue, she ran into a Chatty Cathy at a local grocery store. She was from her old neighborhood and lived across from Porn Dick. Kate updated her with news of her divorce, whereupon Chatty Cathy didn't stutter to divulge that Porn Dick was divorced as well.

"Oh, is that so?" Kate replied with attentiveness.

"Yeah, can I give him your number?" asked Chatty Cathy.

And so it came about that Porn Dick would ask Kate out on a date. She felt a little nervous going through with it. She remembered back to when she was attracted to him but also how much of a dick she thought he was for ignoring the rules of social moral conduct, not to mention for waking her up at two o'clock in the morning most days. After all this time, it still spiked Kate's curiosity. Now she finally had a chance to find out about his middle-of-the-night shenanigans in the garage.

Porn Dick picked Kate up at her house to take her out for dinner. The reencounter was awkward at first because even though they both knew each other from the old neighborhood, they still had past preconceived notions of one another. In the car on the ride over, they spoke about kids and exchanged small talk, and once inside the restaurant, Kate couldn't wait to order a drink. On the other hand, he was hesitant about ordering one, which immediately raised questions in Kate's mind.

He paused for a moment and then disclosed that alcohol was to blame for his divorce—his wife was an alcoholic. Kate shared her Drunk Dick story with him, breaking the ice as they discovered they had both gone through similar experiences. The only difference was that Kate got out from under the torment because Drunk Dick was dead, while Porn Dick still had to deal with his ex-wife because they shared custody of their child. Kate empathized with him and was very sympathetic to his situation as well.

After talking about their common ground for a while, they hit it off talking about each other's likes and dislikes. Throughout the evening, even though she felt like they were enjoying themselves, for some strange reason, she felt that something was a bit off.

"Great intuition, Kate. Go with that gut feeling," Little Katie intruded.

Kate sensed some pain in his voice, but there was also something about his demeanor that was off, and it made her wonder if he was not yet over the divorce. She wanted to bow out of the date gracefully and end it with a handshake. She decided to politely end the date when he dropped her off at home.

In the car driving back to Kate's house, Porn Dick unexpectedly placed his hand on her leg. She let out a nervous laugh because she was definitely not in a space of wanting anything more than a friendship at that point. She liked him, yes, but she assumed he was still dealing with the pain of his divorce.

How can I let him down gently? Kate wondered. *He appears to be vulnerable, and I don't want to hurt him.* She was feeling guilty about wanting to let him down.

He drove the car into the driveway and parked it. As Kate turned her head toward him to say thank you and good night, his face was already in her face. Kate froze as she watched his mouth targeting hers. It happened so fast—his tongue was in her mouth, swirling around in it the way a kid licks ice cream. She couldn't move. It was so sloppy and awful. *My good-looking, mysterious, sexy neighbor doesn't know how to kiss!*

Trying to catch her breath, Kate pulled away from him in a jolt, gasping for air. He was caught off guard and asked her if everything was okay.

Wiping her sopping-wet mouth with the back of her hand, Kate kindly replied, "Yes, thank you for tonight." And for unknown reasons, she politely added, "Let's get together again soon."

With that, Kate quickly grabbed the handle to open the car door and got out. As she bolted up the walkway toward the front door, she looked back at him with a smile, making sure he wasn't planning on following her. She dashed into the house and closed the door behind her as she leaned her back against it. Kate sighed with disappointment. Her perception of her neighbor when she lived above him was different from what she had just experienced. Kate wasn't particularly sure if she wanted to go out with him again, but within minutes, she received a text from him.

"How about brunch tomorrow?"

Against her gut feeling, she agreed to go out with him and then again a few more times after that. During the course of getting to know him, every time became less awkward and more interesting. Chemistry started to work its magic, and Kate started to like him.

Since their weird first kiss, he had not tried again. They would meet up somewhere to eat, talk more about their lives, and go their separate merry ways afterward. Kate soon changed her mind about him being the dick she thought he was before. Instead, she saw a man with a big heart, but a broken one. And naively optimistic, Kate believed she could be the one to help him mend it.

"Kate, it's not your place to fix his heart. The past lessons have taught you that he needs to be the one to fix his heart, just like you are the one who needs to fix your own," Little Katie pointed out.

"But I feel like I can help him, and then he'll see that I'm the one for him." Kate was hopeful.

"There is more to him than you think you know. His heart is broken for a reason, and it doesn't only have to do with his divorce," Little Katie said with concern.

"Well, the more I get to know him, the more he's becoming attractive to me. I want to explore more of this relationship, and our fondness for each other is growing. I haven't felt this way in a long time," Kate argued.

Little Katie's concern grew. "I can appreciate how you've been taking your time getting to know this Dick before having sex with him, but there is still more to learn about him. Remember you had a gut feeling in the beginning that you should be following."

Kate ignored her the same way she ignored her gut.

One day, Porn Dick invited Kate over to his house for dinner. She felt comfortable with their relationship at that point, so naturally, she accepted his invitation. He greeted her at the door when she arrived with his captivating gorgeous looks. The mixture of his sexiness and the mouthwatering smells from the apartment—a combination of cologne, candles, and dinner cooking—put Kate in a hypnotic trance as she walked in. She knew that this night was going to end well—that is, end well as in S-E-X.

Porn Dick offered her a glass of wine, which she didn't hesitate to accept. They started off talking about how their day had gone as he continued to cook. Kate couldn't stop gazing at him with vampish desire as her longing to get into his pants welled up inside. And he couldn't avoid noticing the seduction in her eyes.

"Why are you looking at me like that?" He grinned.

"Well, I'm quite turned on by this display of affection," Kate said bluntly.

With that, Porn Dick put down the spoon, grabbed a glass of wine, and walked toward her. Kate felt her body temperature rising as she floated off her chair and across the room to meet him. She couldn't help but recall that awkward kiss on their first date, hoping to god it wouldn't be like that again.

She held her breath as they locked lips.

Pleasantly surprised, Kate promptly discovered it was 100 percent better. His kiss was soft and supple. As he gently pecked her lips and face, he used one hand to gently palm the side of her cheek, while the other was still holding the glass of wine. His touch sent pulses throughout her body. Kate felt the familiar throbbing sensation and a longing for *love* that she has not felt in a long time.

"Love? Really?" Little Katie interrupted.

"Hush! Go away," Kate snapped, blowing her off.

Porn Dick paused the kiss to hand Kate a glass of wine. He then grabbed her other hand. "Come with me," he said, pulling Kate out of her trance as he led her to … *The garage?* Kate silently thought.

"What are we doing?" She was so confused.

He pointed to the garage wall. Kate glanced over in the direction of his pointing finger where she saw it there hanging on the wall. *A fucking dartboard!*

"We're going to play a game of darts," Porn Dick said, raising his eyebrows at her.

Confusion set in. *What the fuck?! Are you kidding me right now?* Kate had a flashback to Southern Dick, which may have been a premonition alerting her to where this was heading. But in that moment, more importantly, she thought they were on their way to having sex.

"I'm … guessing … this is foreplay?" Kate stammered.

"Kate," he began explaining, "I just want you to know that I am very sexual."

He had Kate's full attention as he continued to say in a seductive voice, "I *reeeeally* love sex, and I love doing it as often as possible."

"Oh, okay. I'm listening." Kate was on board with that. "I do too."

"No. I don't think you understand … I would like to play darts with you, but let's play naked darts." Porn Dick gave her a sly look. "Whoever loses the game has to take off an item of clothing that the winning player suggests."

Now, this is getting interesting, Kate thought.

Being super competitive herself, she soon found out he was even more so, and as luck would have it—or maybe not—Kate lost over and over again. She wound up completely naked, while he managed to keep his clothes on. The only thing he had succeeded at by the third round was making her extremely embarrassed and not a teensy bit turned on. But the cherry on top was when he recorded a video of her.

Kate noticed he flipped his phone out during the game, but she thought he was just texting someone. A little too much wine had distorted her perception. That is, until he howled with excitement and hollered, "And I recorded it!"

"What?!" Kate shrieked.

She shook her head in humiliation as he jokingly laughed at her. She didn't know what else to do except gather her clothes off the floor. She headed back into the house to get dressed. She would have fled in that instant if she'd had her clothes on.

Fumbling to get her underwear on, she felt the air of a blanket envelop her. Porn Dick placed it over her naked body to cover her up. He walked her over to the couch and sat her down next to him with his arms around her. Half-heartedly joking after what had just happened, Kate asked, "So what are you going to do with that video of me?"

He told her he was going to replay it whenever he was alone because it turned him on.

At a loss by the thought of his suggestion, before Kate could surmise a response to it, he did something even more questionable. He switched on the television and told her that he also liked to watch pornography.

Now Kate was not opposed to people watching porn, but it wasn't her sort of turn-on. So here she was—drunk, hungry, naked, and unwillingly subjecting herself to watching porn in Porn Dick's living room. She felt extremely uncomfortable watching because the people on-screen were acting, and everyone looked perfect. At that moment, she felt less than perfect when all of a sudden, he took the moment to lock his mouth to hers with a hot, drawn-out, ardent wet kiss like she'd never experienced before.

Little Katie interjected. "Why are you not speaking up, Kate?"

Honestly, for Kate, it felt like the wrong time to say anything in the heat of the moment. If this is what he liked, maybe she should be open to it. Then insecurity surfaced and stopped her from fully surrendering to him. What if what he wanted were the actors in the porn movie and not her? She could see how turned on he was by watching, which made Kate question whether his passion was erected by her or the porn.

Then he led her to the bedroom.

"Uh-oh, Kate, this is not going to be good," Little Katie remarked as she covered her eyes.

They were at that stage where they were so far into it, kissing and groping, all hot and bothered, that it didn't seem right to turn back. In his bedroom, he switched the television on again to porn. The gaudy swinger music weirded Kate out. It was hard on her ears, not to mention distracting while she was trying to get turned on.

Why can't we just enjoy good, old-fashioned sex, man on top of woman, room quiet and dark, both pleasuring each other's bodies instead of needing porn for external stimulation to get turned on?

And what happened next was the final episode for Kate.

They got into bed, and he made an outrageous request. He wanted her to go down on him *and* bite his dick. That's right, he asked her to bite his dick, and not with just a gentle nudge. No, he wanted to feel Kate clench her teeth into it.

Alarmed, Kate sat up on the bed. "What the fuck did you just ask me to do? Did you say bite my dick?! Ugh, I'm good, thank you. I'm open to a lot of things, but I'm not open to this. I'm outta here."

"Wait, Kate," Porn Dick implored. "We don't have to do this. It just seemed like you were into all this."

"Well, I thought I could be open to it because I like you a lot, but I have to draw the line somewhere."

Kate whipped her clothes back on and marched herself out the door.

"Whew!" Little Katie said with relief, keeping up with Kate.

Porn Dick came running after her half naked and caught up to her outside next to her car. Kate turned and looked him straight in the eyes with a stern glare. With her finger pointing at him, she politely instructed, "Please delete that dart game video of me from your phone. You won't be needing it anymore."

His head, and probably his dick too, hung low as he affirmed with a nod.

On the drive home, Little Katie and Kate could not stop from laughing their asses off at the entire experience.

"Did he really ask you to bite his dick off?" Little Katie roared as Kate's eyes teared up with laughter.

And what made it funnier was now Kate knew why she would hear his garage door constantly open in the middle of the night: Porn Dick had to pull out his car in order to play darts. Apparently, Kate wasn't the only target in his dartboard of women.

Kate kept laughing as she wondered how many others he might have tried to seduce the same way. *Did they succumb to biting his dick, or did they go running for the door like I did? Wow, I'm just glad I dodged that bull's-eye!*

※

Even though Little Katie and Kate got a good laugh out of the adventure, Little Katie still had some wise advice for Kate.

"Kate, I'm sure it's safe to say after this porn deal that you already know it is *never* appropriate to date a Porn Dick, and so I'm not even going to ask you."

"There is no question about it, Little Katie."

"So why did you go along with his sexual requests that you felt uncomfortable with?"

Kate thought about it carefully and was able to get to the nitty-gritty of why she went along with what Porn Dick wanted sexually. It was because she was afraid of rejection. She initially pictured herself having a relationship with him, so she just rolled with his antics in the beginning because she wanted to be with him and please him. But Porn Dick pushed for more until Kate came to realize that his sexual tendencies were way too far out of her comfort zone. It came down to either she had to give in to him or find herself alone again.

"Kate, you should learn to face the music and ask yourself the hard questions in the beginning to avert the uncomfortable moments that might arise later on. If you had just told him early on that you didn't want to play naked darts or watch porn, you might have been able to sidetrack the whole biting-his-dick thing and avoid the humiliation. You could have told him you were only interested in normal sex and mainly that you want a normal relationship. And in doing so, you would have discovered that a normal relationship was something you couldn't pursue with him because he likes something that makes you feel uncomfortable about yourself: porn.

"Think about it. A relationship with Porn Dick would either be compromising what he wants, or you would be compromising what you don't want. It's also possible he would never have been sexually satisfied and, worse, probably would have compared you to his past conquests, the porn movies, or who knows what other weird fetishes he dabbles in—needs that are driven from so deep in his psyche that you would never be enough to satisfy him completely. Imagine, early on when he introduced you to the naked dart board game if you would have rejected playing. He would've known you didn't share any interest in his sexual game. If you would have rejected watching porn, you probably would've discovered he couldn't be turned on without external stimulation.

"The sexual fantasies and desires of a Porn Dick will always outweigh your own needs, and so there will always be some sort of disconnect. That's not what you want in a relationship. It seems like we're identifying another pattern here. In your future adventures, start asking for what you do want and similarly what you don't want without assuming rejection. Take the risk to ask for what you do or do not feel comfortable with. You will only benefit in the end from taking this stance because you're clear on what you want and how much you will tolerate. Communication is the key to any relationship.

"The opportunity to dodge that entire fiasco existed there if not for your fear of rejection. The rejection is a creation in your head, not his. Simply because he likes to engage in sexual tendencies that you don't agree with doesn't mean he rejects you. It just states the fact that you're incompatible sexually. That is on him, not you. The situation only gets worse when you feel guilty about your decision so you accept what he wants instead of communicating your honest and true feelings. Do you see where the responsibility lands? It is on you to ask for what you want or what you don't want."

Kate was intrigued. The picture was becoming clearer to her as all her words began to fall into place.

Little Katie added, "When you begin to trust in the feeling of what you want, you'll learn to filter through these toadds and adventures in order to make a suitable selection for a more compatible toadd and adventure without wasting your time on the wrong ones. The path to finding Prince Dick Charming will be easier if you can start by asking for what *you* want in the next adventure."

Kate made an important discovery here after analyzing this adventure with Little Katie. For the first time, she put her wants before a Dick's because she chose to risk being alone again rather than play bite the penis. Even if it took her awhile to get there, Kate was catching on.

"Yes, I can see what you mean and how a lot of this could have been avoided had I listened to my gut sooner. I believe I can ask for what I want or don't want and be more discerning in choosing the next toadd."

With that said, it was back to Dickland for the next adventure. Kate couldn't recall the last time she was this excited to get to the enchanted pond. Little Katie couldn't recall the last time she saw Kate take one giant leap in the right direction.

10

The Sexting Dick

DECIDE WHAT PAIN YOU CAN TOLERATE FROM A RELATIONSHIP

Kate was keen on visiting the enchanted pond, again feeling self-assured and unshakeable in terms of not settling for less than what she truly wanted. En route, Little Katie refreshed her mind with tips and advice on being clear about what it was she desired. Kate practiced by envisioning the course she hoped her next adventure would take with herself in the driver's seat this time.

Yet, as old patterns tend to repeat themselves, Kate quickly became distracted by a noise she heard coming from the pond. Naturally, it aroused her interest. Making her way nearer, she heard the sound of a camera's shutter. Little Katie was quick to sense Kate's attention span disintegrating as she veered away from the focus of her mental vision and toward the focus of the clicking camera. It wasn't that she didn't want to listen to Little Katie, but she just had to check out what that flashing was all about.

Kate arrived at the pond where she scoped out a toadd holding up an iPhone that obscured his face. He was taking pictures with it, but she could not figure out what he was taking pictures of. As she got closer, she presumed he was taking selfies. *Okay, cool,* she thought at first. *This toadd doesn't look harmful.* But as her view of him came into better focus, she noticed he was actually snapping pictures of her. *Aw, that's so sweet of him to want to photograph me*, she thought, flattered by his attention.

"But why are you taking pictures of me?" she asked him.

The toadd leapt into her arms and replied as one would expect a Prince Toadd Charming to reply. "Because you are so beautiful."

"Oh crap," Little Katie's voice interjected. "It's a catchphrase, Kate. Don't fall for it again. Buyer beware: he is not the merchandise you're looking for."

"How do you know that? He happens to be tall, dark, and handsome, which are all qualities on my list," Kate assured her.

"It's not his looks. It's the smartphone that is sending out the red flag," Little Katie cautioned.

"Don't be ridiculous. It's multifunctional and not just for communicating but also for connecting socially nowadays. Let's just give him a chance and see what he uses his for," Kate proposed eagerly.

Little Katie just shook her head from side to side. A tall, dark, and handsome toadd who was a smartphone aficionado! She had a hunch something was terribly wrong with this picture.

※

Kate met Sexting Dick on Facebook—the social app of the century created by a college student. Kate only joined Facebook to keep in touch with family and friends. Never once did it ever occur to her that it could be used as a dating scheme—that is, until Sexting Dick came into the picture.

"For crying out loud, Kate, you can't be serious," Little Katie said with distaste. "Why would you friend this guy in the first place?"

"Well, he popped up on my wall as a mutual friend, so I added him. There's nothing to worry about. I would never date anyone on Facebook," Kate said, trying to cover up her hesitation by sounding nonchalant. She assured Little Katie that she had no motive in getting to know him beyond Facebook.

"Is that so? Then why do I sense a hint of hesitation in your voice?" Little Katie asked presumptuously because she knew Kate so well.

Kate took in stride what Little Katie said next.

"He's a voyeur. Look at how he prowls women by scouring Facebook and making unsolicited comments. He is going after you. Men like this are only after one thing. Sex!" Little Katie was sounding the alarm.

It's not like Kate was going to take this guy seriously. She could see right through him commenting on her posts and liking everything she shared. She just enjoyed the online attention she was getting from him, even if he did come across as kind of creepy.

"Kate, please. I urge you to stop and think about what you're considering doing and save yourself from engaging this ogler on Facebook. Ask yourself, When is it appropriate to date a Sexting Dick?"

"That's the million-dollar question. You never know until we find out." Kate replied, sounding melodramatic. Then she softened up her tone and said, "Let's see where this goes. Everything happens for a reason." Kate was trying to be optimistic and think positively.

"Well, this most definitely is happening for a reason, but not for the reason you might be thinking. I suppose I'll have to sit back and watch this adventure unfold the way I know it's going to. Don't think I'm going to sit quietly, though," Little Katie said with hands at her waist.

It certainly was not the blessing Kate was hoping for from Little Katie as she signed onto Facebook and her next adventure.

One day Kate received a private message from Sexting Dick:

"Hi Kate … Just wanna say that you are Gorgeous … U look great in all the pics you post. Hope you accept the compliment."

She didn't immediately respond. She was used to getting creeps messaging her all the time. This one was no different. He continued to like and comment on her posts on Facebook, and then, finally, a few days later one of his messages intrigued Kate:

"Kate, you are seriously an unbelievably Gorgeous Lady … with the most beautiful smile ever … hope you accept the compliment. How is your week going?"

His words kept drumming through Kate's mind. *Hmm … Something about him feels different. He seems to say just the right thing to fire up my interest.* She decided to have a look-see into his Facebook page and do a little investigating on him. As she scrolled through his page, she concluded that he looked fairly unoffending, but moreover, he was smoking hot. No further encouragement was needed to reply to him.

"Thank you! You are so sweet to comment all the time. My week is good so far. How about yours?"

He wrote back almost immediately.

"Well, I find it hard not to every time I see your pics and you're welcome … mine is going well so far too but really busy as I'm opening a new vape shop in town."

"So what's a vape shop?"

"A vape shop is an e-cigarette and liquid tobacco store. I'm sure you never tried it before. I can tell it is not your thing and it's better for you that you don't. I don't like it that much either but it's a good business that's why I got in it."

Little Katie shrieked. "Ew! That sounds disgusting. A real winner, Kate," she slammed sarcastically.

Kate rolled her eyes and ignored Little Katie because why wouldn't she want to get to know this person who was relentlessly messaging her with showers of beautiful thoughts about her? Little Katie, however, wasn't throwing in the towel just yet. She wasn't kidding when she said she wasn't going to sit back quietly.

"Kate, by now you should've learned that these types of comments are the ones that lead you down a path of pain and destruction. They all start out like this—complimenting you and flattery. It's plain these men only want one thing from you, and so they'll stop at nothing to say whatever it takes to get it from you. This guy is no different."

"And what is it that they want, Little Katie? Because I'm *still* figuring out this thing called love," Kate replied, feeling irritable.

"Sex, not love. Don't fool yourself into believing they want something more serious at this stage. They might fancy more down the line, but ultimately, they decide if they choose more or not. So I'm just saying, don't be too quick to give into sex. Right now, this guy is trolling you, and if you're not careful, you *will* get hurt again."

Kate knew Little Katie shared a good point about not jumping into sex with this one. And while it was unusual to meet a guy on Facebook, an air of mystery surrounding him lured her in, and his sweet comments and compliments drew her in. *Maybe he will turn out to be different. One date would be harmless*, she convinced herself.

Little Katie was convinced Sexting Dick was not right for Kate, but she was fully aware that, like every other adventure, Kate needed to find this out for herself.

Sexting Dick turned up his messaging a notch.

"I would love to invite you out for a drink one day."

Even though this was what Kate hoped for and wanted, she still had some reservation and had to clear something up with him before accepting.

"Well, I'm flattered, but I'm quite a bit older than you are."

She had seen his Facebook page publish that he'd recently celebrated his forty-first birthday.

"Kate, I swear I'm not just saying this, but I've had you as a friend on Facebook for a long time, and every time I see a pic of you, I say wow … you get more beautiful every time, and you don't look a day over thirty-five. So how old are you?"

Kate hesitated for a moment, unsure of whether her true age might turn him off, but honesty prevailed.

"Forty-eight," she sent back.

There was a momentary pause from his end. Just when she was thinking, *Uh-oh, he's turned off*, his lengthy reply popped up on her screen.

"Oh wow, you must be doing a great job of taking care of yourself because like I told you, you look like you are in your thirties. You definitely get more beautiful as you age. Since you said you were flattered, I still stand with my invitation to buy you a drink. I'd be honored to be with a Gorgeous Elegant Lady like you."

Kate took to his words like bees do to honey.

"I just might take you up on your offer," Kate typed back, feeling gushy.

Little Katie could not take it anymore and spoke up. "Kate, does the phrase 'flattery will get you nowhere' run through your mind? C'mon, admit it. He's excessive with it, and it's apparent that he knows what he wants and won't stop till you drop it. He's nothing but a ladies' man, a Lothario."

"I'm open to being that lady, and I totally can't wait to meet him personally," Kate told Little Katie with complete resolve.

For their first date, as a precaution, Kate chose to meet Sexting Dick at a local restaurant that her friends and she frequented in case the evening took a dive and she might want to make a break for it. She figured it was always smart to meet someone for the first time in a public place. She wasn't sure whether he'd turn out to be a creeper like Little Katie warned, so she wanted to keep him at arm's length until she had a chance to feel him out personally.

Kate arrived before he did. *Could be a red flag,* she thought. Not to panic, though. She wasn't thinking he would be a no-show, and even if he was, she could quickly delete him off of Facebook. *No skin off my nose.* Just when she was considering several deluded scenarios, he texted her that he was nearby and apologized for being late. There were butterflies in her stomach as she read the text and let out a nervous sigh. Yes, she was a little nervous because the what-ifs started to cross her mind. *What if he doesn't like what he sees? Or worse, what if I don't like what I see?*

She sat waiting for him in the lobby of the restaurant as she fiddled with the strap from her clutch. She watched as people walked in and out of the restaurant and then turned to look out the front window. That's when she caught sight of him in the distance. He was dogtrotting across the parking lot. The closer he got, the more she could see how good-looking this guy was in person. He was positively tall, dark, and handsome. *Check,* she thought.

He walked through the door, looked around the lobby, and saw her sitting there. He recognized her right away from the pictures on Facebook and approached her. He leaned over and whispered into Kate's ear, "You are even more beautiful in person."

The warmth of his breath, his dashing looks, and the lingering scent of his cologne mesmerized Kate. As he straightened back up, still gazing into her eyes and flashing his Colgate smile, Kate could almost feel Cupid's arrow go straight through her heart.

"I guess that does it," Little Katie said. "You're already falling for this one."

"I sure am, Little Katie," Kate replied, entranced in the moment.

They sat down across from each other at the candlelit table. It felt like it was taking the server forever to bring their drinks, and Kate started to feel a bit uncomfortable because Sexting Dick wouldn't stop staring at her. She needed to break the ice. With nothing better to say, she decided to confront him.

"Why are you staring at me?" she asked, wishing for a drink to help quell her throbbing nerves among other parts.

She told herself she didn't want to have sex with him … yet, anyway. Little Katie's reference to her past adventures reminded Kate it didn't bode well to start off with sex on the first date, although she couldn't deny the chemistry between them was already brewing.

"I can't keep my eyes off your angelic face," he wooed her, gently sliding his hand across the table before touching hers and caressing it with his long, thickset fingers.

Kate melted like butter on a hot steamy roll and giggled at his comment. *He is good.*

They talked about business and work first, eventually getting onto the subject of relationships and divorce. That's when he dropped a doozy on her. He still lived with his ex-wife, but in a separate bedroom—a living arrangement they settled on for the sake of their kids. The idea of it was strange to Kate. It seemed a peculiar thing to do. Was he following the celebrity trend of Gwyneth Paltrow's whole "conscious uncoupling" thing or Ben Affleck and Jennifer Garner's separated-but-still-living-together deal? It wasn't something that average ex-partners did. No, this didn't sound right to Kate, so she continued to press.

"So, why aren't you *really* moving out of the house?"

"Well, it's not quite convenient for me," he answered unflustered.

"Oh, I see," Kate said with a raised eyebrow.

Then he added that he also stayed at his uncle's house occasionally, as if to assuage her wariness.

By this time, Kate, wasn't the only one raising eyebrows. "Very suspicious, don't you think?" Little Katie challenged.

Yes, it was suspect, but Kate wanted to give him the benefit of the doubt. While she was leery of his home situation, she justified it because she was still interested in getting to know more about him.

"Maybe he's just going through a hard time financially, and maybe it's hard for him to part with his kids." She tried to convince Little Katie, as well as herself.

Kate and Sexting Dick talked for a while longer about all sorts of things. She was keeping it as casual as possible, trying not to steer things in the direction she wanted them to head—intimacy, kissing, and much more than that.

"Good call, Kate. I am proud of you," Little Katie remarked regarding her attempt to stay on course.

They came to the end of their dinner and started winding the conversation down to the typical niceties that come at the conclusion of a first date. Sexting Dick offered to walk Kate to her car. She saw it as a nice gesture, so she took him up on it. They walked in silence most of the way, every so often commenting on the meal or about the restaurant. When they arrived at her car, she leaned in close to give him a hug and thank him for dinner.

Get in the car, get in the car, Kate told herself. But a whiff of his cologne, and the throbbing began.

She felt his warm breath on her neck as he reached over to give her a hug and what she sensed was an incoming kiss. Her mind was still telling her to get in the car when she quickly pulled away from him and turned to open the driver's side door.

Accurately sensing Kate wasn't going to take things any further than a hug, he gave up. "Hope we can do it again soon," he said. He then turned and slowly walked away, pulling on Kate's heartstrings like passing by a puppy dog in a store window. It was hard to let him go.

As Kate drove off, she immediately heard a ping from her phone. It was a text message from him.

"I really wanted to kiss you."

Kate was surprised not only by how quick his text came but by his desire to kiss her. She drove off, not replying and feeling proud of herself that she got away from him without kissing and much more than that.

The next day he sent her another text about how he was so bummed that she got away without so much as a kiss. She thought it was cute and endearing that he kept on expressing how badly he wanted to kiss her.

Little Katie, on the other hand, didn't find it so cute. "He wants more, Kate, and you're not ready."

"Unfortunately, I want more also, but … You're right. Not yet. I want to get to know him better first. I would like to see him again and deem whether there is potential for a relationship," Kate thoughtfully replied.

To which Little Katie affirmed, "Good idea!" she quickly added a warning. "Because it's more than just a kiss that he's looking for, and it's not a commitment, because he hasn't even gotten himself out of the last commitment he was in."

Kate went on a second date with Sexting Dick about a week later. This time she let him pick her up at her place. They went out for dinner again, and their conversation revolved around the texts they had been exchanging. His sultry brown eyes were fixated on Kate, gazing deeply at her across the table. She had seen that look before in other men—a look of wanton desire that electrified her body and sent a tingling sensation up her spine. She saw what was coming, aware of the sexual tension rising while she hung on every word he spoke to her. It was more intense this time, leaving no room for small talk just sweet talk.

He commented on how sexy she looked and reminded her of how much he wanted that kiss. He kept going on with comments about how gorgeous she looked in that dress, a vision of beauty, and how attracted he was to her. He was coming on so heavy that it started to make her feel uncomfortable. She somehow managed to maintain her end of the conversation as light as possible, though she too really wanted that kiss. Temptation was for resisting, and the throbbing feeling from the sparks he ignited in her, along with his looks and his voice, made it that more difficult for Kate.

Little Katie, sensing Kate's uneasiness scooted in to dissuade her. "Remember—be clear on what you want."

"Oh, I know what I want, and I know what he wants. I'm certain it's the same thing," Kate sighed with thirsty desire.

Surely, Sexting Dick picked up on Kate's body language because he lightened up on the flattery, redirecting instead to ordinary conversation. Kate was relieved as the tension between them dissipated, and they resumed the small talk until, at last, they finished dinner.

Now came the hard part—the end of the evening and the ride home. As soon as she closed the passenger's side door, he lost no time. All of a sudden, Kate felt his puckered lips pressed to hers, moving them with circular motions. The kiss was so unexpected and awkward it fell short on passion. He apologized for kissing her so boldly but admitted that he had been dreaming about it for a long time. There was an upside to it, though. Kate wasn't aroused by it—no temptation to resist.

The awkward drive home consisted of more small talk, while Kate's head raced with thoughts of what she should do next. *He is taking me home after all. I could easily invite him into my house for another drink,* she considered.

"Which would be a disaster, Kate. Seriously, think about the consequences. He only wants one thing from you," Little Katie harped.

"I'm not going to argue that, but ..." Kate replied, unable to finish her sentence as she pulled her thoughts back to the present moment, realizing this could actually end badly.

When they arrived at her house, Sexting Dick placed the car in park with the motor still running. At first Kate was relieved because it was a sign that he wasn't simply assuming she would invite him in. Then he went into action again, seducing her with the same piercing look he'd given her at the restaurant. He leaned over to kiss her, and Kate caved, yearning for a kiss better than the first one. *Damn it ... it was!*

The mood in the car started to heat up. Kate became more aroused as they kissed harder and deeper. She could feel him gently grasp her hair with his fingers, pulling her closer to him. Their lips adhered, parting only to taste one another with their tongues. The passion intensified as the pleasure increased with each kiss. Just when Kate was about to reach the point of no return, she felt a tap, tap, tap on her shoulder. Little Katie was summoning her to stop and go in the house.

While it felt good to keep making out, Kate realized this was exactly what she wanted to avoid. Stopping herself, she gradually pulled away gracefully with a smile on her face. He asked if he could come in with her.

She cocked her head to the side and gave him one more kiss, said good night, and got out of the car. Trying to compose herself, she walked up the sidewalk toward the front door, using every ounce of willpower not to look back. She would have given in had she turned back to look at him.

Once safely in her house, Kate locked the door behind her and leaned against it. Narrowly escaping the inevitable power of his seduction, she cried out into the darkness, "Fuck! Yes, babe, I want to fuck you too."

Little Katie praised her. "Well played, and good job getting away. Now, don't you feel better that you controlled yourself? When your head is clear, I want you to think about whether this relationship could stand to work. So far, he has been a gentleman, but there is something a bit off, and I want you to start recognizing the signs."

She was right about something being off because that night the sexting began. Kate's phone lit up with his message: "I really enjoyed kissing you and I can't wait to touch your body. Please send me a picture of you naked."

Little Katie was confused about what sexting meant.

Kate tried to make it sound innocuous. "Well it's in the dictionary."

"Oh, is it a smartword, like a smartphone?" Little Katie mocked.

"Since you're going to find out anyway, I'll tell you what it means. It's when someone sends sexually explicit photos, images, or text messages with a smartphone."

"Oh my gosh," Little Katie gasped. "And you're going to engage in this?"

"I'm just as uncomfortable with doing it as you are imagining it," Kate replied.

Sexting Dick insisted on knowing what Kate was wearing and asked whether she would be willing to send him a picture of her in pajamas. She wasn't feeling very sexy; all she wanted to do was go to sleep. Kate paced the bedroom floor as she undressed to get ready for bed. His sexting became extremely arousing. He was explicit in his sexual requests, and his attention fired her up. Intrigued, she wondered where this might lead if she did what he wanted. Kate decided to snap a picture and send him one.

"Wow, you just gave in, and now he knows that he has you," Little Katie said, shaking her head with disappointment.

Kate's sending that photo only led to his sending more lustful photo requests and sexting.

"I would love to be doing some things to you! Wish I could show you my hard cock. Can I send you a picture of it? I am putting myself out there saying I want to FUCK YOU!"

By this point, Kate was a willing participant in his sex game. She played along for quite a bit until he remarked he was tired and ready to go to bed. Before signing off, he suggested they get together again. She was still feeling a bit too hot and bothered to wind down for bed, so she did the unthinkable and suggested he come over so they could fulfill their sexting fantasy.

"Kate, no. Don't do it," Little Katie commanded.

It was too late. She had already asked, but surprisingly, Sexting Dick declined and then quickly assured her that they would get together soon. He proposed that next time he'd come over to her house with wine and dinner. *A romantic gesture*, Kate thought.

"See, Little Katie. He is into me."

"Oh yeah, he lured you in with his sexting," Little Katie declared, pointing out his strategic yet irresistible move to suggest another date but at *her* home this time. "He saw you get away at dinner without scoring with you, and now that he's aware the sexting aroused you, he knows he has a chance of having sex with you if he gets into your house. Your bedroom will be his target."

Kate tutted back at Little Katie, sounding appalled. "Surely he's not that manipulative!"

Kate agreed to have Sexting Dick come over after work one evening.

"How convenient for him," Little Katie said. "That means he has an excuse not to sleep over with you because he has work in the morning."

"Maybe that's the case," Kate said, although she didn't want to believe it, "but I want to see him again, and I know he's got a busy schedule. So if it's better for him during the week, I'm good with it."

Kate was anxious and nervous with a buildup of sexual tension from all the sexting. When she opened the door to let him in, her first impression was to strip him down and devour him. He stood in the doorway in all his tall, dark, and handsome glory, smelling so ravishing. She quickly collected her thoughts, realizing he had his hands full with sushi and a couple of her favorite bottles of wine. She greeted him warmly and had him follow her into the kitchen. She could feel the energy of his gaze as he admired her physique up and down with his eyes.

He opened the wine while she fetched the glasses. They said cheers and took a sip. No sooner had Kate's lips and tongue tasted the full-bodied ruby-red liquid than she already got a taste of his full-bodied ruby-red lips and tongue. Taking her wineglass from the clutch of her hand, he placed it on the counter without releasing his lips from hers. He pulled her body closer into his. She became weak at the knees, and the scent of his skin disarmed her of her last shred of resistance.

Kate could feel his strong, muscular arms around her and his thick hands caressing her curves. He delivered slow, passionate kisses, his lips making their way down her neck, an erogenous zone for Kate, inducing a soft, sexy moan from her lips.

Nervously, she interrupted the moment by gently whispering into his ear, "Are you hungry?" She was referring to dinner.

He stopped, looked into her eyes, took her hand in his, and led her toward the bedroom. "Yes, I'm hungry for you," he professed in a low, husky voice.

"Clever," Little Katie balked with sarcasm.

Annoyed, Kate answered back, "Could it be that he's just being romantic and loving, Little Katie? Do you always have to be so skeptical?"

"We've been down this road before, Kate. Think about it. What kind of relationship could this possibly be? He is still living with his ex-wife. Why are you bothering with this guy?"

It was way too late to give consideration, let alone credence, to her words. Kate ignored her and focused on the moment of seduction.

They both stood in front of the bed with enough light beaming in the background to illuminate their eyes dripping with desire. He erotically undressed her and laid her down on the feathery-soft duvet. The power of his seduction was mesmerizing. Kate reciprocated his power by stroking it beneath his clothes. She was hot to feel his naked body on top of her. She noticed that his dick was as tall, dark, and handsome as he was. He slipped his power inside of her, and she let out an erotic moan.

He kept pushing his power inside her, roughly penetrating her as Kate thought, *Oh my gosh. You are huge and—ouch!* Her focus was interrupted. A few strokes later, Sexting Dick became Express Dick. He lasted all of about thirty seconds … and, well, so did the relationship. Every time the Midnight Express came, it left her throbbing between her legs, while he got his rocks off with speed and then went on his way. He never once tried to please her—not that night and not any other night.

The shape of this so-called relationship took form through weeks of sexting and excuses from him about why they couldn't get together. He never took her out again. They hooked up at her place if, and when, he had the time to see her. Interestingly enough, in the beginning when he was looking for sex, he could make the time to court her. But once he got it, their time together became something else—strained, almost like a second thought, except whenever it was on his desired time, not hers.

He didn't stop asking Kate to text pictures of herself, and the sexting continued. She was so confused because it sounded like he wanted her all the time, but whenever she mentioned them getting together, he always had a reason why he couldn't.

One afternoon he finally came clean. He had texted her to apologize that he had been missing in action and asked if he could come over. Because Kate had not had the opportunity to see him in person in a while, she thought it was perfectly adequate to vocalize her feelings. So she let him. She wasn't in the mood for sex at that point. She just wanted to know what was going on. How had it gone from so much wooing in the beginning to just sexting? Their conversation—their entire relationship, really—was taking place over a smartphone and texts.

"Are you ready, Kate? You should brace yourself for this moment," Little Katie said to prepare her.

Sexting Dick paid Kate a visit. They sat at the kitchen table, which reminded Kate of their first date when they sat across from each other at the restaurant. This time the feeling was a far cry from what she'd felt that night. He began by telling her what an amazing, beautiful, and sexy woman she was. Kate half-heartedly managed to smile at him, finding it difficult to reciprocate his affections. Her mood probably made it easier for him to say to her with such casualness that even though he was still very interested in her … "I am dating other women."

In that moment, Kate felt as dumb as a doorknob. "Dating other women" equated to taking them out, sexting, and fucking them too, at the same time he was doing it with her. Disappointed and hurt, she wondered how she didn't realize before that he was seeing other women.

Little Katie interjected with an I-told-you-so spiel. "Remember, Kate, I said he was a Facebook voyeur and an ogler. But now he's moved down a level to dick scum!"

Meanwhile, Kate's heart sunk as everything started to fall into place. He didn't have time for her because he was juggling other women and conveniently kept her interested with his sexting ways.

"Okay, I see." Kate summoned the courage to reply with clarity. "You can go now. I don't have anything to say, and furthermore, while I appreciate you telling this me in person, you can now go fuck yourself and all the other women you're sexting. Please don't contact me again."

She could see in his eyes and in his demeanor that he was confused and upset, which was probably just a wounded ego, but she didn't care. He had made her feel duped and dumb.

As she ushered him out the front door, he still had the audacity to tell her he wanted to keep seeing her.

"What part of 'go fuck yourself' did you not understand?" Kate flared back and then slammed the door behind him.

She turned around and leaned her back against the door with a tear in her eye. This time she said, "Fuck! Yes, babe, I really just wanted to love you."

※

Kate couldn't hold back the tears from streaming down her face or stop the melody from "Everybody Plays a Fool" strumming through her mind. Little Katie felt her pain.

"Maybe 'there's no exception to the rule,' Little Katie interjected, "but, Kate, you clearly knew this time around that the path you were heading down would be a treacherous one. After all, when is it appropriate to date a Sexting Dick? I believe you know the answer to that. You even tried to stop yourself several times."

The answer was as clear as day. Never. It was also clear this toadd was not into pleasing Kate for one minute—just pleasing himself once he caught her in his little sexting trap. And it involved not just her but other women, not forgetting his supposed ex-wife.

Little Katie spelled out the lesson for Kate. "When entangling yourself in a relationship with unhealthy elements that make you uneasy or are difficult for you to tolerate, it is probable that it will never get better, easier, or satisfying. Toadds like this one don't change, which is why you need to be clear with what you want. You are deserving of true love, so stop settling for less than what you want, and go after what is right for you—what feels right to you."

Kate tried to sustain a relationship with a smartphone via text and sexting. When it didn't work out, her judgment became clouded. She began to fixate on trying to get him to spend physical time with her. Her downfall was ignoring the telltale signs and making his needs and desires more important than her own. Just to be clear, the telltale signs were living with the ex-wife, sexting, pleasing only himself, disappearing behind a phone, and, the final and intolerable one, being indifferent about being with other women. The combination of Facebook with all the above, or even just one of those, was a lethal concoction for any relationship.

Once again, Kate had signaled acceptance to a situation she wasn't comfortable with by trying to be okay with it and going along with Sexting Dick's relationship conduct—maybe because she thought she could change it. The light bulb in her head went off as she realized this was still a recurring pattern in her adventures.

Little Katie ironed it out further for Kate. "You can break this pattern by deciding to make your needs and desires known right away when you feel something getting out of alignment with what you feel is tolerable. If the relationship is not in agreement with what your desires are, then that person is not the person for you. Break it off when your vision of what you want becomes muddled with uncertainty. Don't be fooled into believing you have to go through a great, painstaking decision to break up a relationship that isn't satisfying you. It should be the easiest decision you make. You need to be happy too.

"Remember the line from *Dirty Dancing*. 'Nobody puts Baby in a corner!' And the sooner you recognize that, the less painful the relationship will be."

Little Katie's advice helped Kate pick herself up quickly from this wobbly fall and got her to see this adventure from a mature and wise perspective. Kate was beginning to form her own hypothesis on dating curriculum drawn from the conclusions in each adventure. Sure, she'd started with baby steps alongside Little Katie, but she was walking with more confidence toward more successful adventures in the future. The upside was that this adventure was only a quick quake and Kate was able to handle the outcome and recover with a healthier outlook than what she'd had on past adventures.

"Now, in order to regain your power and go after what you honestly want out of a relationship, it's essential that you become more present with the signs, signals, and surroundings you are confronted with," Little Katie advised.

Even though Little Katie could foresee there was still some rocky road ahead, she was at ease with where Kate had arrived mentally and emotionally. She was much stronger, and she had a positive reaction to this outcome that made Little Katie optimistic about Kate selecting the next toadd. Not because of whom she would choose but how she was prepared to handle the situation much better than she had in the past.

"It's not going to be pretty," Little Katie said with caring concern, "but I have confidence that you will survive and come out on the other end ready to handle more adventures with less pain and more clarity."

Kate held on tight to her bonding thoughts of Little Katie. She was aware that it was always Little Katie at her side, or close by, walking with her back to the enchanted pond to get her through the next adventure. As annoying as she was, meddling in her affairs, Kate knew that Little Katie's guidance and support was stellar in her progress. Little Katie's presence made her feel safe, secure, and self-assured that she was on the right path. A much better path to a healthier relationship.

And then this happened …

Update

Sexting Dick came sexting back a year later:
"I know it's late and I'm sorry to text you right now, you just crossed my mind and wanted to check on you and say hi."

Kate's immediate interpretation of his text: "I'm horny. Wanna fuck?"

It was so out of the blue that confusion and uncertainty took hold of her, but curious Kate naturally wanted to know what he had up his sleeve. Guided by her gut instinct, however, she decided not to reply straight away. She needed some time to figure out how she should respond to him, if at all. She knew more or less what he wanted, but she was prepared to play his game this time. So twenty-four hours later, Kate texted him back, mirroring his text from the night before.

"I know it's early and I'm sorry to text you right now. I'm great. Why did I cross your mind?"

"Lol you are so funny. I saw someone on TV that looked like you and thought of you. But she was not as sexy as you."

"Oh, nice … and thank you."

Kate was already beginning to feel uncomfortable with where this was going.

"So I see that it is your birthday tomorrow. My god and have you looked any better."

Clearly, he was still following Kate on Facebook if he was aware of her upcoming birthday.

Hesitantly, Kate replied, "Thank you, feeling great."

She couldn't believe his brazen response, but she knew not to expect anything less from him.

"I'm glad you're feeling great and you still look sexy as fuck."

Kate was instinctively aware that he was seeking arousal, so she continued to tease.

"Thank you again. I feel sexy as fuck."

"Ha Ha, good answer cause you are … Last night I started imagining you laying down on your tummy completely naked and me giving you a full body massage, every single inch."

By this time, Little Katie was on alert. "Oh boy here we go—"

"I know. I know what you're thinking, but I have to play along because I have a good final reply," Kate reassured Little Katie. "Trust me."

Kate heckled Sexting Dick.

"Well happy visualization."

"Ha ha, you are so cute but I really want to do that to you."

"I understand and am flattered that you do but we have crossed that road before."

If he was going to be brazen, Kate wasn't going to tiptoe around the pond either. He avoided her upfront comment.

"Ha ha, I know. So how is dating life going?"

She wasn't laughing with him. Her response to his shameless and flagrant talk came across strained.

"My dating life has been discriminating and discerning. Being very careful these days."

By now, she was actually ready to shut him the fuck up when he sent another text before she could. Kate refrained and decided to wait for the right moment to land her punch.

"Oh that's good for you. You know what you want," he texted.

She and Little Katie both thought at the same time. *Yes, and that certainly does not include you!* But Kate let him slosh in his swamp for a minute until he sent her another text.

"I have not been going out lately at all. It's been some time."

Kate's immediate interpretation of his text: "I'm horny and lonely, and I want to fuck you."

She couldn't render a sympathetic response to that. Fueled with sarcasm and utter annoyance, Kate commented.

"Oh bummer. I have had great adventures dating Dicks."

"I hope I'm not one of them."

"Well, you are …" Kate now had her chance and she would take it unapologetically.

She continued outspokenly. "Yes. You were the ten-inch dick, painful and quick."

Maybe she should have gone with express dick instead. But she went with that description even though it was every man's ego builder for a woman to tell him he had a big dick. Reason being, Kate wanted to prompt him into further conversation, setting the stage for what she was prepared to tell him. She was going to be honest and forthright with him about something she wished she had the courage to say during their time together.

"Did you really like my dick?" he asked.

Sexting Dick had no idea what Kate was going to say next.

"I'm saying this with love but you were too quick for me. I was always the one pleasuring you each time. There was no consideration for me not only in bed but in our relationship."

He appeared to be so confused with his next text. "I don't understand. You mean I was quick cumming?"

"Uh, yes," Kate admitted, somewhat remorseful.

Cleverly, he shot back.

"Yeah, honestly when I'm sleeping with a very sexy woman like yourself this happens. I'm sorry."

"No worries, but don't you only sleep with sexy women?" Kate asked with sarcasm.

"I try lol, you are so funny. Can I tell you something and I swear I'm telling the truth?"

"Sure."

"I never enjoyed someone sucking my dick as much as I did with you, and you were definitely one of the best fucks too. I'm serious."

Was that supposed to be flattery? Kate didn't fall for it.

"Thank you, I think? Yes, I do enjoy sex but learning that there is more to a relationship than that is what's important. Remember I wanted more."

Kate was trying to convey to him the pain she actually went through. But he sidestepped that remark too and continued with his gaudy interpretation of what he thought would be arousing.

"Just looking at your gorgeous face while you're sucking me is something else. Not to mention I really enjoyed diving and eating your ass."

"Okay …" Kate texted back. She was ready to land her knockout punch.

"We are done here. I appreciate the acknowledgment, but I am more worthy than your ridiculous texts and sexting. I want a real relationship with a real man. Not a man who hides behind his phone. I'm sorry to be so frank, but we will never be together again. You had your chance and you decided at the time that there were things in your life, including other women, who were more important than me. That may be okay with you, but it is not okay with me. You should know I have forgiven you for how you treated me. I had to in order to move forward and I am not looking back. So, thank you again for reaching out, but we will be nothing more than friends. Ever!"

She did it. Kate stood up for what she wanted and spoke her truth. And it felt great. Little Katie clapped her hands with joy, jumping up and down as she praised Kate's poise and confidence.

"You stayed in your power, and that is what a year of work on yourself looks like. I am proud of you and your accomplishments. You were able to stay present with him in the moment and stay clear on what you wanted and what you did not want. When you choose to take the stance of forgiveness, love, and honesty, you remain true to who you are, accelerating the healing process. Keep up the good work because this will get you closer to what you want."

Who knew how far I'd come, Kate thought. *I finally won my first round.*

11

The Yoga Dick

BE CAREFUL WHO YOU BEND OVER BACKWARD FOR

It's true that male toadds come in all different shapes, sizes, and levels of machismo, but they all have one thing in common. They all croak for the same reason: to attract a mate. And just like a real toad, croaking is a toadd's game for calling on females to come see what they have to offer. The only difference is that in the animal world, by nature a real toad will scope out an unsuspecting female, lure her with his croak, and hop on her back without asking. The very clever toadd, also by nature, does the same thing, but with a pickup line to woo the unsuspecting female into lowering her guard when she feels he might definitely be the one—that is when he jumps into her arms.

That's how Kate went wrong with Sexting Dick. *Maybe* she'd been naive about him at first, but in the aftermath, she gained a sort of female power when she stood up to his smooth-texting Casanova ways and cut him loose. Doing that had transformed her. Kate gratifyingly stepped into her goddess warrior power, and it felt good. She took this power with her as she returned to the enchanted pond with high-spirited, valiant strides. Perhaps this newfound power was why she felt confident she would be writing the last chapter on her final love affair.

But this time, it would not be the toadd's croaking she would fall for. Instead, the next Dick captivated her with something more than the appeal of his voice. What she saw him doing got her all tangled up in his game. There he was: a cute, adorable toadd on his lily pad involved in a most curious position—a headstand—unperturbed by anything or anyone around him.

"Wow, look at that!" She was in awe watching. Kate had never before seen a toadd do that.

"What the heck is he doing?" Little Katie was not impressed.

Kate was fixated on this toadd as he flipped around, landing in different poses until he eventually lost his balance and fell into the water. She couldn't help laughing out loud as she watched how cute he looked hopping back up on his lily pad dripping wet with embarrassment. It was at that moment, feeling bad for his flopped performance, that she leaned over to pick him up.

Little Katie took one look and immediately had the inkling that Kate would eventually be the one 'bending over backward' for this toadd.

Kate pleaded with the little one to try to get her to see what she was seeing. "Come on, Little Katie. I like that he has a healthy attitude and the way he moves like he does. He's a far cry from the past Dicks I've been with. None of them cared about their health, and remember that being fit is a criterion I put on my Fairy Tale List. I want to take a chance on this toadd to see what position he lands in with this relationship."

Little Katie knew exactly what position that would be. Anyway, she let Kate go on this adventure without opposition to learn her next lesson in love.

"Okay, Kate. It's your call. Let's go," she sighed.

※

As one might naturally guess, Kate met Yoga Dick at a yoga class. She noticed him standing behind the counter when she arrived at the yoga studio and couldn't help notice what a good-looking guy he was—not that she was necessarily looking at him in any way other than as a yoga instructor.

Kate was actually the first student to arrive. She walked into the room scoping for a good spot to place her mat far enough away from the instructor so she could close her eyes and be to herself, yet still near enough where she could watch him do the poses. She was there to be present in mind, body, and soul without caring about what anyone else was doing or what anyone else thought.

She lay there in a calming silence on the floor, enjoying the stillness and peace of the room. But as time ticked on without anybody disturbing the silence, Kate realized she was the only one there. *Crap. Where is everyone?* She began to panic because she didn't want to be the only one in class and have the instructor's sole attention on her.

Suddenly, the peaceful sensation turned into heart-pounding anxiety. She just needed one more person to show up to relieve her of the anxiety. Kate had come to enjoy her class, to lose herself in the moment immersed in yoga—not to have a one-on-one interaction with her good-looking yoga instructor. Before she could muster up the courage to grab her mat and leave, he walked into the room.

"Well! You are it." He clamped his hands together. "And we are going to have a great class," he added with enthusiastic energy.

Feeling uncomfortable being the only participant, and trying hard not to let it show, Kate replied, "Oh … no, I understand teaching for just one person isn't an appealing class from an instructor's point of view, so I have no qualms if you want to cancel the session. I could come to a later one."

But she could tell he was a committed yogi when he cheerily answered, "We're here now, so let's do some yoga."

Still feeling self-conscious, Kate managed to close her eyes, taking long, deep breaths to calm herself down as he began the class with a cross-legged position pose. His voice was soothing as he guided her into the next pose and the next. She could sense she was in good hands by the way his energy and presence commanded her attention. His physical skill with each pose was methodical and precise. Even though she was somewhat new at this, he didn't make her feel awkward. Instead, he personalized each sequence to her ability while still challenging her with a good workout. Within minutes, he had calmed her anxiety about being the only one in class.

At the end of class, Kate couldn't thank him enough for staying committed to teaching her the entire time. She was truly grateful for the experience and the lesson of presence she took from it. She connected with the best version of herself in that yoga class.

He was awesome, Kate thought as she left the studio.

As soon as she got home, she sat down and penned a very heartfelt thank-you note. She wanted him to know she acknowledged his professionalism for teaching her when he could've easily gotten out of it. She jotted down her phone number with a note to drop her line with his class schedule so she could show up and support him at another time. Kate dropped the note off with the studio manager that same day, and it was only a matter of hours before she received a text.

"I appreciate your thank you note. You know, you're the talk of the studio."

There was a three-second pause.

"Would you be interested in going out sometime?"

Huh. Is my yoga instructor asking me out? This could be interesting, Kate thought for a second.

"Uh-oh ... no. He is a yoga instructor. This type isn't on your list for several obvious reasons," commented Little Katie.

"Little Katie, I don't see any harm in possibly meeting him for just a drink and conversation. Besides, he was such a doll teaching his yoga class to *only* me this morning."

"This one is going to teach you more than just yoga, Kate! Why would you want to fall for him?"

"Well, for starters, he is ridiculously charming, speaks intelligently, teaches a pretty sexy yoga class, is hot as hell ... oh, *and* he looks just like James Dean, American cultural icon of the fifties. Ugh, c'mon! How could I resist?"

"Yeah, that's what you always see first in a Dick—irresistible, sexy good looks until he charms your pants off. Hold your pose, and check out what he does for a living: yoga teacher to a majority of women. Don't you think he has probably hit on other women in class besides you? Plus, don't forget 'makes good money' is on your list. How much money do you think he earns doing this?"

"Okay, maybe you have a point about him teaching to a majority of women, but maybe there is more to him than you think. And, to your second point, it's not always about money, Little Katie, is it? I've decided

I'm going out with him, and I'll find out for myself if he's what I'm looking for … without your interference, please."

Without any further hesitation, Kate texted back. "I'm interested!"

"Okay, great. Looking forward to it. Your place or mine?"

"What?!" Little Katie cried out.

Kate also thought this guy was being presumptuous for a first-time date. If she'd learned anything from Sexting Dick, it was once a Dick makes it into your house, it was game over. The pursuit ends in nothing but a booty call.

Playing it safe, Kate texted him back. "It's probably best if we meet somewhere neutral. If you drink coffee we can meet at a coffee shop down the street or if you drink wine there's a wine bar next door."

"Let me be clear about my proposal to you," he replied. "I have a six-month rule."

Kate stared blankly at her phone, thrown off by his response.

Little Katie snickered. "Is he trying to be funny? What the heck is a six-month rule?"

Another text came through. Maybe he read their mind because he answered their question.

"I date someone for six months—no kissing, hugging, touching, sex, etc. until we really get to know each other. At the end of the six months, if we like each other without the externals, then we can move forward."

"Hold on, Kate. Sounds more like this is his rule for you," Little Katie said with apprehension.

"It's definitely a different approach," Kate said, weighing the idea. "Imagine not worrying about having sex right away. Starting slow would give me a whole new perspective on falling in love without sex being the focal point of a relationship. I could learn an important lesson about how to fall in love without sex. You should be ushering me out the door to meet this one."

"I'll admit I do like where you're going with this. But what I don't like is that he's introducing it as his rule and following his timing. Love doesn't work that way," Little Katie countered.

"Well, guess what? I do want to test out his rule."

"You know what I am starting to see here? Another pattern. You date Dicks who have their own agenda with a set of rules and time lines for you. Not to mention all his communication is texting, in case you hadn't noticed. Didn't you learn this sign from Sexting Dick? And whatever happened to the traditional telephone call? Men these days are too afraid of a woman's power. That's why they hide behind text messages instead of having the guts to engage in verbal communication for fear of rejection so they won't have to face it. It's saving self-pride. Doesn't that say something to you about a man who does this? And regardless, I'm just forewarning you of a pattern I see," said Little Katie.

Kate ignored her. She had her own theories, even though Little Katie did raise a good point. Intrigued by his six-month dating rule, she answered back. "I'll go to your place." She didn't want him to know where she lived, and anyway, it gave her chance to see how he lived.

Kate drove up to a condominium complex. Even though she was not impressed, she tried not placing too much judgment based on where he resided. After all, she wanted to meet him on his own turf. Kate told herself this would serve as good practice for learning to keep an open mind. But she threw all her preconceptions out the window when he opened his front door. *Damn, he looks good!* Out of his sweaty yoga clothes and bathed in alluring cologne, he actually cleaned up well. Kate had to snap herself out of a momentary trance as they greeted each other.

Stepping into his lair, she did the quick scan around the room to get a glimpse of what it looked like. Even though it had the undertones of a bachelor's pad, which was a good thing, the place was put together, nice and tidy. She was actually impressed with how it looked. Over on the kitchen bar, he had a bottle of wine, two sparkling empty wineglasses, and a small sampling of appetizers laid out ready for them to enjoy. *Hmm*, she thought with a smile, *he put some time and effort into this.*

"They always do in the beginning, Kate," Little Katie interjected.

"Not now. Let me enjoy the moment. I just got here," Kate replied sternly, tuning her out.

Yoga Dick offered Kate a seat in front of the bar. Trying to make herself feel comfortable, she smiled and sat down. *Just enjoy the moment*, she repeated to herself. The conversation began with small talk as she responded seemingly interested. He lightened up the mood by joking about first-date nerves. He picked the moment to explain to her in more detail about his six-month rule.

"So the reason I came up with this rule is that after going on so many dates with different women, I realized that the moment we ended up sleeping together, all of a sudden these women had new expectations of me. The sooner sex came into the relationship, the sooner the expectations made an entrance," he stated, sharing a story about one woman who became crazy when he didn't comply with her expectations.

"Well, what type of expectations do these women have?"

"A relationship," he chuckled. "They just start to get too emotional and want more from me than what I can give them."

"And what is it that you can't give them?"

"My time." He paused and looked at her matter-of-factly before continuing. "Look, I'm an instructor." He then proceeded to list his reasons for not being able to give the women he dated what they wanted. "But I also have a second job and have kids part time from a failed marriage. I have to work all the time in order to make ends meet, leaving me little time to spend with anyone else in my life."

To Little Katie, these were not reasons. They sounded more like excuses. "He sure does make himself seem like he's a busy man, but I'm still not buying his excuse of not having time. If he legitimately had wanted to be with any one of those women, he would have adjusted his schedule and made the time."

"Well, I'm the woman on his mat now, and I know he's going to want to make time for me." Kate felt positive. Little Katie begged to differ as Kate prepared to win over Yoga Dick's time and affection playing by his relationship rule.

<hr>

They took it slow during the first three months of dating, going back and forth from each other's houses whenever he had time, just talking and getting to know each other. Kate didn't let it bother her that they didn't communicate more than once a week because of his busy schedule. He would text her the day of to let her know he was available, typically on a

Tuesday. So it got to the point where she would save Tuesdays just for him so they could spend time together. He kept it very respectful—nothing would happen between them, meaning every time they met up, he would sit opposite her, preferably separate seating, never trying to make physical contact.

Kate appreciated that he never made or even attempted to make a sexual move on her. He was *so* disciplined. She thought this six-month rule was so great because it took the pressure off whether they would end up having sex when he called on her. He already told her it would be six months.

"See, Little Katie, this relationship has been going so well. He's such a gentleman. It's so nice that I'm getting to know him better in an uncomplicated way that has nothing to do with sex, just good, old-fashioned conversation," Kate boasted. No doubt, a part of her did want to engage in some hanky-panky, but, like him, she too could respect his space, and she did.

"He's a grown man, Kate. He'll want sex with you before six months is up." She heard Little Katie's words ring with confidence.

And damn it if she wasn't right!

One night, Yoga Dick asked Kate if they could watch a movie together.

"Sure. Come over to my place. I'll make us dinner."

He arrived with a movie and a bottle of wine as she was putting the final touches on dinner. This time he greeted her a little differently—with a smooch and a tight squeeze. Over dinner, they talked mostly idle chitchat, but she was aware of how intently he looked at her. When they were finished eating, Kate went to get the DVD started, while he grabbed their wineglasses.

As the movie began showing, he walked over to the sofa Kate was sitting on.

"Is it okay if sit next to you?" he asked.

Kate looked over at him and saw a sultry glow in his eyes. She scooched over to let him sit. *Hmm.* She paused for a moment while she did the math in her head and thought, *Wait a minute. I'm pretty sure it's only been three months since we've started dating.*

He took her hand in his then asked, "Would it be okay if we lay on the couch together?"

A longer *hmmmm* reverberated in Kate's head as she checked her calculations again. She was right. Hesitantly, she verbalized what she was thinking. "I'm not sure. It's only been three months, hasn't it? We shouldn't chance it."

"It's fine. We're going to stick to the six-month rule. You have nothing to worry about," he calmly replied.

Kate was trying to understand what was happening as he slid his arms around her waist and lay her down on the couch.

"So just to make sure ... Snuggling and watching a movie does not constitute anything else, is that right?"

Ignoring her, he inched himself closer to where they could feel one another's body heat. Kate was becoming a little uneasy. She could sense Little Katie was too.

"Could I lay you down on your side, and I'll lay down behind you, holding you?"

Kate found herself nervously agreeing to him spooning her. Was this going to lead to sex after all, or could she trust that nothing more would happen? She was still relying on his word and his six-month rule.

"Really, Kate? You think this is just an innocent cuddle?" Little Katie interjected sarcastically. "He's cornering you like *Neptune's Daughter*, she scolded as she played the tune in her head: "Mind if I move in closer? ... What's the sense of hurting my pride? ... Baby, it's cold outside."

"And you're the prey for his pride," she barely heard Little Katie exclaim while Yoga Dick wrapped his arms snug around her waist.

Kate tried to keep her head on straight by telling herself that he wouldn't break his six-month rule by going any further. Although his warm breath on her ear as he nuzzled his face on the nape of her neck sent her body tingling. She let out an uncontrollable moan. *Ugh, my erogenous zone. How does he know it?* she wondered.

"Because all horny toadds know it!" Little Katie quipped. She was now very irked by the scenario playing out, never mind the movie playing in the background on the DVD player that neither of them was watching.

Kate could feel Yoga Dick's power growing. Her body, provoked by his arousal, slowly wriggled with every touch as she moaned with pleasure a little bit more. His tender lips were slowly kissing her neck, while he caressed every inch of her body with heated desire. Her conflicted mind still could not settle down its racing thoughts, switching back and forth from sexual yearning to percolating confusion. Kate couldn't take it anymore.

"But hasn't it only been three months?" she blurted out loud with sexual tension detectable in her voice.

And with that, he flipped her over onto her back and straddled himself gently on top. There was no answer except for the sound of his breathing growing heavier. His parted lips searched for Kate's, tasting her along the way. Their bodies became entangled as the wet kisses and groping grew with intensity, as did his power, while she was quickly being stripped of hers. There was no resisting him anymore. Kate felt his body rise and fall on her the more turned on they became.

In her head, she heard the echoing of the words 'What about the rule?' while her body moved in sequence to his sexual commands. He slowly rose up off of her, examining her body with lust. Feeble and yearning for more, Kate raised her eyes up to meet his sexy James Dean look. He reached down to take her hand, guiding it to his lips, kissing the tips of her fingers. He then asked, "Can I stay the night?"

Little Katie shot in. "Kate, snap out of it! Remember what he said about his six-month rule? If he can't keep his own rule, you can't trust him to keep anything else he promises."

"Oh God, but he's passionately into me. Just let me see it through," Kate prayed.

The voice of reason continued. "Don't go down this route. You're only going to end up hurting yourself. When you give into sex with a Dick, they get what they want for a moment in time until they're off on their next conquest. You rarely ever get a commitment from these types of Dicks. And this Dick is no different."

"This one *is* different. We waited longer than three dates … We waited three months! That has to be worth something."

Little Katie knew she was starting a battle she wasn't going to win. Done with trying to convince Kate, she sighed. "I will be here when his time runs out."

Yoga Dick led Kate into the bedroom, locking her with his gaze as he looked passionately into her eyes. Even though she had seen that familiar, electrifying look before in other men, in that moment, she felt his eyes pierce straight through her heart into her soul. He leaned down to taste her lips, and her body automatically rose to his.

He removed her clothes first with a seductive gentleness and then his. Kate traced the outlines of his naked body with eyes of desire as he climbed on top of her. He said her body was like a playground as he ran his fingers over her naked flesh. The passion rose with his whispers of what he wanted to do to her. He began ravaging her playground with his mouth, finding every erogenous zone and causing her to swell with anticipation, wildly crazed for him to enter her.

Kate was at the peak of sexual desire, and all she wanted was to rock his world in the same way he was rocking hers. She reached down between his legs to play her part in this passionate venture. Then, without any warning at all, he stopped everything—just like that. He rolled off her body and lay right next to her. Kate's breathing was still heavy as she tried to grasp for a thread of insight into what was happening.

She looked at him bewildered and gasped, "Is everything okay?" In her mind, she was thinking, *What the fuck just happened?! Is he going to leave me completely in the dark with a throbbing desire in between my legs like all the others do? No, this can't be happening.* She started panicking.

Yoga Dick assured her everything was fine as he reached over to hug her the way he did on the couch. He snuggled up, wrapping his body around Kate's and lay his head on the pillow next to her. Within minutes, she could hear him snoring.

Kate's ego was about to throw a tantrum. She had to force herself from letting the rant in her head boil over and voicing it aloud.

You have got to be kidding me! What the hell was that all about? Is this part of your six-month rule—to tease the shit out of your subject and see how she reacts? Did you adopt your rule from a scene in the movie 9 1/2 Weeks *and think I'd be willing to play along? Well, no! I am not consenting to this six-month scheme of yours—not like this.*

She kept all her anger and frustration inside. She knew in that moment she should have promptly kicked him out—out of her bed, out of her home, out of her life. But her wounded ego wanted to find out what the hell had happened. So instead, she decided to let him stay until morning when she could ask for answers. Slowly, Kate drifted off to sleep.

The next morning, the sun's soft white light snuck in through the blinds and shined onto the bed, waking Kate up. She turned over to find Yoga Dick lying beside her still asleep in a peaceful slumber. She stared intently at him. In her head, Kate replayed the scenes from last night piece by piece, trying to figure out what happened. He probably sensed her glare because it was not long before his eyes opened. He stretched out, breaking into a big smile and reaching up to give her a peck as if nothing happened.

"Morning," he murmured with a yawn.

"Good morning," she said curtly. Before she could part the words from her lips to ask him what had happened last night, he was rolling out of bed to get dressed and leave.

"I have to get to class." He sauntered around the room, picking up his clothes and gathering his things. "Have a great day."

"Yeah, you too …" Kate watched exasperated as he walked out the door.

He promptly vanished, leaving her in bed naked and longing for him but hurt and confused just the same. Technically, nothing happened between them, but it still felt like he had broken his six-month rule on being intimate … and in the process, he'd broken her heart as well.

Kate tried to rationalize his behavior to avoid feeling hurt and used. She could chalk up last night to not having sex and talk herself into being okay with it. Maybe it was part of his six-month rule. Maybe he did implicitly stick to six months before intercourse. She could handle it.

Little Katie stepped in. "Well, if his actions last night were not intended to seduce you into having sex with him, then why lay down on the couch to watch television with you and then arouse you and himself? What I don't understand is if he didn't want to have sex, he should have just said so, not jump off of you like he's changing poses without any explanation then fall asleep."

Kate couldn't argue with that, especially how she was feeling. She hoped he would call so she could straighten things out and rid herself of these mixed emotions that were making her sick.

Several days later, she did end up hearing from him, intermittently, via text messages:

"God baby your body is such a playground—"

"You are so f'n sexy—"

"I really want to see you, but I am short on time this week."

"Kate, you've heard all this before," Little Katie reminded her.

❈

A week went by before Kate decided she was ready to attend yoga class again. It was the only way to see Yoga Dick before he would willingly make time for her again. She convinced herself that as soon as he laid eyes on her, he would not be able to resist her.

Little Katie rebutted. "Even though you didn't have intercourse with him, he still got what he wanted from you, and now he knows he could have you anytime. Men are interested in the chase. You removed the challenge, and it took less than six months. Pay attention to the signs. He's not aligned with you, because if he were really into you, *he* would be making time for you."

Kate ignored her and instead framed the scenario she hoped for in her mind as she practiced her yoga. One look at her, and his desire for her would resurface. He would remember the outlines of her body and take her away where they could be together again, this time falling in love.

After class, Kate stole a few minutes of his time to have a word with him and find out when his schedule would open up for her. He was short on time he said, and there was no way he could spare her any of his time in the upcoming days. He didn't fall for her like she imagined he would, and Kate complacently chose to let it go and just wait for him. After all, they were getting closer to the six-month mark, and she'd be foolish to walk away now.

"It's sad to see you wait for this Dick, Kate," Little Katie said compassionately. "I wish you could see that he has the ability to make time for you if he truly wanted to, but he's selfish and living in his own little world with his selfish little rules."

"But I want to wait it out until the six-month rule is up to see where he stands." Kate was adamant.

"Why can't you see that it was up after three months, and there will be no fourth, no fifth, and no sixth? And besides, why do you want to wait around to see where he stands?"

Kate didn't know what to do. She was so confused, and even though she was tired of waiting, she didn't want to put this relationship to rest just yet. She wanted to give it a fair chance by reaching six months.

Then Kate got the text that was the clincher.

"Hi beautiful, I am going radio dark for ten days. I am taking ten days for me without any distractions aside from work. Don't read that wrong, you are not a distraction, you are a loving blessing."

"Huh? What exactly does he mean by 'radio dark,' and did he just passively call you a distraction?" Little Katie inquired.

"He means he's not going to contact me for ten days, and even if I do reach out to him, he won't respond." Kate replied, ignoring Little Katie's follow-up assumption.

"What is up with his rules and time lines—ten days, six months? Kate, you need to let this one go. Snap out of it and realize that *he* is letting you go."

Kate wasn't ready to accept Little Katie's advice. Instead, she complied with Yoga Dick's request and didn't contact him for the ten days. But those ten days were agonizing. She filled her head with crazy, self-doubting questions. The warrior goddess who had met Yoga Dick a few months before was beginning to fade.

Did he not find me attractive enough? Did I say something wrong? Is he seeing someone else? Is he sleeping with someone else? Kate had to know the answers.

So she searched on Facebook to check out his profile and see what he had been up to. There was the answer in a picture. Blonde, young, pretty … and at a baseball game with him and his kids. The blow was painful, but Kate dug deeper as if it wasn't enough. Clicking her way over to blondie's Facebook profile, she saw her in yoga positions that in Kate's mind made her yoga practice look amateur. Kate talked down to herself. *I can't keep up with that. She is way out of my league.*

"You know what, Kate? *She* is way out of *his* league." Little Katie came to Kate's defense. Blondie has nothing on you, and she also has nothing to do with you. Seriously, stay focused on who *you* are."

"Right now I feel like I don't know who I am." Kate felt powerless. *Why did I wait around for this toadd with his rules, time lines, and control? How could I ignore the signs?*

"I am glad you're finally opening your eyes to see the bigger picture, although I'm sorry you had to find out this way. Now you need to realize this choice of his is not about you; it's about him. He's on his own journey, and you are on yours."

It wasn't that easy for Kate to digest what Little Katie was saying. She was hurt. She was exhausted. She was confused. She didn't get this whole journey talk, because as far as Kate was concerned, she was on a journey with him, and her heart was in the right place the entire time. This was about her and her happiness. All she wanted was to give their relationship a chance and give him the benefit of the doubt.

Kate felt shunned and diminished. She felt like she took twenty steps back from where she had started this adventure. She was starting to think she was the one who had the problem. Then she heard from him ten days later:

"I miss, adore, and respect you so much. Are you busy tonight?"

And in that moment, Kate was ecstatic and relieved to hear from him. Everything she had told herself ten days before would prove to be wrong because *he* wanted to see her again. Kate sent him back a heartfelt "Yes!" in a text message.

Little Katie hung her head low and frowned.

❁

A few minutes after Yoga Dick showed up at Kate's house, all the excitement she felt to pick up where they left off took a sour turn terribly fast as soon as Kate asked him the question that she wanted to know all along.

"So the last time we were together, what exactly happened? Please shed some light on that for me."

"I love you so much, honey. What I mean by that is I really cherish so much about you. I think you are an incredible woman, and I hope we can maintain a level of ongoing friendship without romantic aspects." That was his self-serving bullshit response to her.

It had not been the answer Kate was hoping for. She was devastated and in disbelief at first, but then she got this incredible rush of anger, which made her realize something she wasn't prepared for. In the next instant, all sorts of questions and mixed thoughts raced through her mind. One of them being, *If he came back to me with a commitment, would I be willing to forget everything I've been through with him and how he's made me feel second to everything?* It was time to be honest with herself. And the real answer that came was *no*. It was over.

※

The decision brought a huge relief to Little Katie. Reinforcing the lesson learned here, she asked, "When is it appropriate to date a Yoga Dick?"

Kate's answer to the above question came out without any uncertainty. "Never! He loves having a classroom full of women he could prey upon who are dressed in scanty, tight-fitting workout gear with boobs falling out and sweat dripping from their tight little twenty-something-year-old bodies that he can ogle at from all angles as they bend over in a downward-facing dog pose."

Little Katie added to it. "When you find yourself in a scenario like this one, my advice to you is to walk that dog right out the door and take up long-distance running!"

Kate had experienced a huge revelation, which she shared with Little Katie. "Honestly, when all those questions and thoughts raced through my head after him telling me we could remain friends without being romantically involved, it knocked me back into my senses. He had all these women bending and contorting in all kinds of positions, and I too was one of them bending over backward for him—and not just in class.

"He never asked what would work for me. I never saw him bending over backward for me. A relationship this frustrating has no future. I am worthy of so much more than a self-serving Dick who will only make time for me when it's satisfying and convenient for him."

So to pick out a man who would treat Kate far better than this Dick did, Little Katie put together some questions for her to contemplate—self-reflective questions to help her make better choices and decisions whenever she met the next prospective toadd. Replying "no" to just one of these questions would be a clear sign he was not the toadd or relationship to take into her next adventure if she had learned anything at all.

☐ Is this serving me?

☐ Is this caring to me?
☐ Is this loving toward me?
☐ Is this kind to me?
☐ Am I uplifted by this?
☐ Is this extending freedom to me?
☐ Does this feel manipulative?
☐ Can I share this with others?

"And as far as Yoga Dick goes, all the answers to the above are 'no'! Time to let go and move on," Little Katie instructed.

In her pain, Kate struggled to see the point of seeking love. "Easier said than done, Little Katie. I am tired of heartache. I've just had it with these horny toadds!"

Update

One year later Kate heard from Yoga Dick. He texted her, asking if he could see her again.

"I have to see you after class if you'll let me. Can I come over to your house? I have something I want to share with you."

Of course, Kate hesitated. It took a lot of healing to get to a place where she could see him without wishing he would change his mind and want to be with her. She still periodically attended his yoga class, but as the months went by, she buried their romantic relationship in a closet along with all the other skeletons. Kate managed to move on, and now he occupied a place in her friend zone.

After seeing his text, she contemplated the idea for a few minutes whether she could see him outside the studio safe from having any other feelings besides friendship after all this time. She wondered what he wanted. One morning she opened her front door and was greeted by his sweet James Dean-looking face as he peered in hesitantly with his tail between his legs.

"Kate, I want you to know that I did some work on myself and found out that I have a block toward commitment."

Little Katie swiftly emerged. "No duh, yogidick!"

"Go on," Kate coaxed, trying not to laugh at Little Katie's remark. She was curious.

"I have been working through this blockage and anxieties that I have. I want you to know that I think you are the most amazing woman. I think about you all the time … a lot more than usual, actually. There is a fire growing inside of me. You remain one of the few women I find easy to love … and I still love you. I always have."

Yoga Dick's look was sincere, but Kate caught herself. It only appeared that way behind that cute face of his.

As she studied him, he took a few steps closer to her and cradled her face in his hands. "I want you. Would you consider taking me back?"

He must have seen the indifference in Kate's eyes as she looked at him without any shred of hope except for a kindhearted smile. There were no more sparks or romantic emotions left toward him. She surprised even herself with such an autonomous reaction. Her body language said it all as he released his hands from her and drew her in for a hug. Holding her tightly, he then said, "If you change your mind, I am here for you always."

If only he could read minds, he would have known what Kate was really thinking. *Oh, my love, but it is too late. You had your chance with me. In fact, all of you Dicks had your chance with me. What gives?*

Meanwhile, Little Katie was doing a happy dance over her decision to let Yoga Dick go. It came with a price, though, because Kate was flooded with resentful feelings and vexed emotions brought on by Yoga Dick's narcissistic attempt to reenter her heart, which he had contorted and bruised a year before.

"That's it! I am so spent over this dating thing. No one ever tells you that finding love is going to be such an exhaustive challenge. I'm not sure I can do this anymore. I feel like saying *fuck it*, and I'll just start treating men the way they've treated me!" Kate shouted fiercely.

Little Katie tried to divert Kate's thoughts. "What good would that do, Kate? That would only lead to one emotional disaster after another. Maybe at the time it will feel good, but ultimately, it will amount to emptiness inside you—a void that you will unsuccessfully attempt to fill with more dysfunctional, horny toadds, resulting in more heartache. It won't serve you in the end. I can assure you that hopping around from toadd to toadd for revenge is never going to make you whole. And that's not what you truly want."

"But I've had it! I'm not listening right now, Little Katie. Enough!"

Little Katie looked at Kate with a pool of tears gathering in her eyes as she attempted to utter words of hope. She too felt Kate's pain.

Kate put her hand up as a signal for Little Katie to stop speaking. The conversation was over. She turned away to head back to Dickland and the enchanted pond.

Little Katie knew it was her cue to step back and let Kate go and potentially reach rock bottom yet again. If Kate carried out the next adventure as she described, with revenge, it would be the most damaging. Although, there would only be one way to go after falling down that dark pit—up.

Maybe it's exactly what she needs, thought Little Katie. *I'll catch up with her eventually.*

Kate ran back to the enchanted pond, stripped of her goddess armor and choosing to wear an invisible cloak instead. She wasn't sure how she would navigate her next adventure, but she sure as hell knew she wasn't going to be prey to another toadd; instead, he'd be hers.

Spirals of grey smoke and a bitter smell from a cigarette led Kate back to the enchanted pond. *That's exactly what I need right now. All I want is to take a long, silky drag from it and to gaze at the other end into the eyes of the next Dick who I will carry off with me into my new adventure.*

Kate was going to do exactly what she set out to do.

12

The Elevator Dick

EMBRACE CHANGE ... AND NEVER SMOKE

Angry tears streamed down Kate's face, brought on by the frustration she was feeling as she furiously whipped along the path back to the pond through tangled woods, pushing the thorny vines and branches away from her. With every pounding step she took, the earth trembled underneath her feet, mud flinging from her heels. She was panting from all the running, forgetting to breathe as rage boiled up inside of her. She couldn't contain herself from shouting out loud up at the skies, to the wind, or to anything that could hear the echo of her shaky voice.

"I am so tired of these adventures! I had *enough* of trying to find the Dick who I'm meant to be with! ... The one?! My Prince Dick Charming?! ... I'm pretty sure there is no such thing. It's all *bullshit* ... What my mom told me and what Little Katie has been teaching me!"

Kate cried frantically as she reminisced about how she had stood by and watched lovers come and go, and the ones who go when you don't want them to are the ones who steal a piece of you. She was done. From now on, she swore to protect herself and not fall back into the clutches of another thieving lover.

"The next toadd is going to play by *my* terms, *my* time, and *my* rules! Fuck 'em!"

Picking up her speed so Little Katie wouldn't be able to keep up, Kate managed to leave her behind, and she was happy with that. Not that Little Katie was trying to keep up with her, though. Little Katie knew where this train was headed and could not, for the time being, bear to watch. Kate didn't care about anyone or anything at this point. She was emotionally numb from head to toe and didn't want to hear one more silly piece of advice.

"I just want to escape," Kate kept blurting out.

Little Katie managed to overhear the sharp words echoing through the woods. She was close by, peering through the trees as she kept Kate within her sights. "Uh-oh, not *that* word again. I'm going to have to keep an eye on her."

The whiff from a cigarette was summoning Kate. A smoke was exactly what she wanted. She finally arrived at the edge of the pond where she set her sights on the poor horny toadd who would suffer the wrath of her emotions as she reveled in the conquest. Kate sat down in front of him. A cigarette was hanging from his mouth. He searched her eyes for a hint of her intentions, but she returned a blank stare.

Feeling exhausted like she had just outrun a charging lion in a desolate desert, she pulled her knees up close to her chest, hugging them, and stared up at the night sky. She wished that the stars could talk. Maybe they could tell her what they saw in her future from way up there. *Do they know how disconnected I feel from my heart, my body, and my soul?* she wondered. She gave the horny toadd a side-glance. He still hadn't taken his eyes off of her. She knew he could see her face in the moonlight and glistening tears on her cheeks, but she didn't care and didn't offer any explanation.

Reaching over, she stole the smoky stick from his lips, put it between hers, and took a long, deep drag from its wet tip. She closed her eyes as she absorbed the satisfaction delivered in that single inhale. But the smoke was so strong she coughed and gasped for air. Once Kate pulled herself together, she began to laugh hysterically.

Kate looked over at the horny toadd with her chin jutted upward.

"What are you doing tonight?" she asked.

Without any qualms, he jumped into her lap.

"Wannanother smoke?" he offered.

So, what do you do when you need to kill the switch on your broken heart, forget your ex, and release steam? You plan a girls' night out. Kate and her girlfriends had long been waiting to get together and paint the town red. They managed to find a weekend they were all free and arranged to meet for happy hour at their favorite watering hole. But it wasn't just any watering hole. It was *the* watering hole you went to when flying solo and wanting to mingle and let go. Exhausted from her dating adventures, Kate was looking forward to spending some time with her squad and letting her hair down. And so it was no surprise that she happened to meet Elevator Dick at a bar.

The night was meant to be about Kate having fun. She wasn't interested in whether she'd be meeting anyone. She was going out to spend some time with her girlfriends and drink her sorrows away. *So what should I wear? I should dress for comfort.* Going through her closet, Kate decided on a backless maxi dress with a built-in bra and slip. No bra, no underwear needed. When she slipped it on, it fit just perfectly for a summer night.

Kate looked at her reflection in the mirror, ironing out the dress against her body—the fit and the slit showing leg made her look sexy. *Very sexy, if I do say so myself,* Kate thought. She wasn't trying to go for an attention-grabbing dress, but what the heck. She was comfortable, and she wasn't looking. If she didn't send out that vibe, no predators would take notice, she reasoned.

It was around eight o'clock in the evening when Kate decided to get the party started. She headed over to the wine bar a few minutes earlier than planned. She wanted to have a glass of wine on her own to take the edge off her bitter and vengeful mood toward men and decompress by the time her friends got there. The barroom was almost standing room only when she arrived. Fortunately, she zeroed in on one lonesome barstool calling her name from across the bar. She careened her way to it and coolly sat, crossing her legs just so to reveal her sculpted calf from the slit in her dress.

She felt slightly empowered and sexy that she had no undergarments on, and she must have unwittingly emitted the feeling because she could feel all eyes on her. She swore the only attention she was trying to get was from the bartender who was taking forever to ask for her drink order. All day she had been craving the taste of a chilled, oaky Chardonnay.

Then it hit her as she was waiting on the bartender. She glanced along the bar and realized that there were only men sitting where she was. Kate caught one guy looking at her, but she quickly dropped her gaze and withdrew her empowerment. Now she needed that Chardonnay. She just couldn't handle another adventure right now. All she could think of was, *Fuck men*. There was nothing pleasant about feeling that way, but it was what it was, and she wasn't going to be bothered with men. It was her night to escape with her girlfriends.

Finally, the bartender came toward her with a drink in hand. She hadn't ordered anything yet, so she looked puzzled at him. He said it was complimentary of the gentleman at the other end of the bar. Kate turned to bid a nod of gratitude his way, and her eyes were met by a good-looking charmer with dark hair, tan skin, and, from where she was sitting, a tight body. He flashed a gorgeous bright-white smile in acknowledgment.

This guy looked every bit close to her description of the kind of guy she had summed up on her Fairy Tale List, although she could tell he was much younger than her. Kate waited for him to turn away for a chance to take a closer look at him. Then she spotted it. He was wearing a wedding band. *Nope, hands off. Not going there*, she told herself.

"Good idea, Kate. You've been down this road before, and in your state of mind toward men right now, this sort of mix would be nothing short of flammable."

"Go away, Little Katie! You're not even supposed to be here. I know what I'm doing."

Kate's girlfriends soon came to the rescue. They arrived raring to go and ordered bottles of wine from the bar. They talked and laughed endlessly, drinking until they got to the point where they needed to eat soon before the wine made them sloppy. Browsing for a table, they noticed the bar was now sparse. They spotted a better seating arrangement that fit all of them at the other side of the bar. Elevator Dick was there too, sitting alone.

"He's married," Little Katie whispered.

Elevator Dick patted the seat next to him, motioning for them to come over as he looked Kate up and down.

I know he's married, Kate said to herself, as if that would interfere with her will to engage. She recognized the feeling that always got her into trouble—the tug of desire in between her legs was awakening.

"He's married," Little Katie said again, this time with force.

Reluctantly, Kate gave Little Katie the time of day. "He's so much younger than me. I'm just going over there to pull his chain. I'm not going to do anything more with him than just talking. Give it a rest."

"He's married!" Little Katie was even more assertive.

"That's right. I'm going to go over there and remind him what an asshole he is because he's hitting on me! All right … now go away, Little Katie."

Kate played along with him for a while, both of them flirting and bantering. But whenever she would bring up his wedding band, he was blasé about it, saying that his marriage was not working.

Clearly it's not, you asshole. You are here at a bar talking to me instead of home with your wife and kids, she thought. But come to think of it, Kate didn't actually care either. The liquor was clouding her judgment and disarming her from the anger she was feeling toward men. Teasing him while being seditious, she kept reminding him he was married. He would just laugh and shower her with flowery words meant to seduce her.

"You are so beautiful and sexy, baby."

And here she was again, reliving a past moment that had not served her well before. She was inebriated, and her longing for touch, love, and attention kicked into high gear with every eloquent, hearth-throbbing word that flowed from his mouth to her ears. It sent a high alert all the way down to her bare—*ahem*—energy.

In a moment of brief clarity, Kate searched for her girlfriends. *Damn it! Where are they?* They too were chatting with other men.

"Ladies, what just happened here?" Kate shouted out to her girlfriends over the blaring bar music. "Have we disbanded for men?"

They either didn't hear her or ignored her, so Kate kept chatting up Elevator Dick.

By this time, Elevator Dick had moved closer to her barstool. They were eye-level as she hung on his every word. Kate was trying to avoid the trance fueled partly by alcohol and partly by desire. That's when she felt him place his hand on her exposed thigh through the dress slit. She took his hand in hers to remove it, but instead, their fingers intertwined, and he started to move them up her leg toward her energy. Kate pulled herself together long enough to realize that they were on public display, and under her breath, she reminded him that he was married, hoping it would be a turnoff.

He then asked Kate if she wanted to step outside and have a smoke.

"You don't smoke, Kate," Little Katie managed to surface past the alcohol-infused fuzziness in Kate's head.

"I know, but I need a break from the bar scene and this charade."

"But don't you see where this is going?" Little Katie was every bit concerned for her.

Elevator Dick grabbed Kate's hand and led her out the door. She was more relieved that the petting at the bar was over. Perusing for a place where they could smoke and talk, he led her down a set of stairs. Kate stopped him.

"Where are we going?"

He turned back to look at her with those dark bedroom eyes. "There's a place down at the end of the stairs where we can smoke."

At the bottom of the stairs, she noticed an elevator. He walked over to it and pressed the button to open it. They crossed the doorsill into it.

"Why are we going into the elevator, because I'm pretty sure you can't smoke in here," she playfully remarked.

"Kate! You are so naive," Little Katie shrieked.

The door closed behind them, and he spun around to lock it. Kate started to get the gist of what was happening. Elevator Dick shot her an electrifying smile—the kind of look she'd seen in men many times before. It sent a tingling sensation up her spine. He gently grabbed her hips and pushed her against the wall. He then leaned into her and planted an erotic kiss on her smokeless lips, moving down to her neck with soft kisses while thrusting his power against her groin.

"Shit …" she said in a drunken haze. "Since when does let's get a smoke mean let's have sex?"

He shut her up with his sultry kisses and spellbinding eyes. Who was she kidding? By now, his lustful moves had her incredibly turned on. It was over for her at this point. She was all in, ready to take the dive. *Fuck the fact that he's married.*

They passionately kissed and groped like animals, devouring their last morsel. Before she knew it, he spun her around, bent her over, and lifted her dress. Surprise! No underwear. For a moment, Kate thought, *Shit, you asked for this.* Then she thought, *Yes, I did ask for this*!

He undid his belt, his pants fell to the ground, and off to the races they went! He entered her, and she moaned with pleasure. He felt so good inside that it negated the issue at hand. *So what if he's married.* But then, in a sobering three, two, and one … He was done.

Panting and agitated, Kate couldn't believe that she was once again left throbbing, dripping wet, and unsatisfied. "Is this how you're going to leave me? Par done?" she irreverently asked him.

He let out an awkward laugh in response to her question.

"Well, shit. What else is new?!" She let out a stifling laugh and shook her head.

Little Katie, of course, was not amused.

Kate's buzz started to wear off, and her head became clear in that moment. In a flash, she gathered herself together in case someone tried to use the elevator for its intended purpose. She and Elevator Dick headed back to the bar in silence.

As reality set in, Kate asked herself, *What did I just do?*

Little Katie stampeded back to answer her question. "You knew exactly what you were doing, but you kept on going. You're only punishing yourself even though you want to believe you were punishing him. Ultimately, you are the hurt one! You have spiraled right back to your old sex ways. But this time, what's even worse is that it backfired on you. You're the one who feels rotten about it, not him."

She was right. In that moment, Kate felt like she was walking back from a train wreck. She had hit rock bottom. Her girlfriends had stepped outside to look for her and saw them walk by. They and Kate alike looked confused. She was embarrassed. The shame started to creep in. The flood of memories from her previous affair encapsulated her.

They went back to the bar where Kate continued drinking to drown the shame, guilt, and remorse she was swimming in. It was mortifying on so many levels to think she had just become the other woman again, and she got nothing from it. She didn't even know who this guy was, and so much could have gone wrong. Her actions inflicted pain not only on her but on others, including his wife.

They awkwardly exchanged small talk after that, but for the most part, they kept their backs to one another. At the end of the evening, everyone had to go retrieve their cars from the valet.

His car arrived first, and before getting into it, he walked up to her and said, "I want to see you again."

Kate stated unequivocally, "No, we don't need to, and we will *never* do this *ever* again."

Elevator Dick jumped into his car and screeched off. And as Kate watched him drive away, she knew she had to make a change starting that very moment.

She never saw him again.

Little Katie waited until the right time to discuss this sordid incident with Kate.

"Kate, what were you thinking?"

"I wasn't thinking."

"Right … You mean you weren't thinking, or was it more along the lines of what you like to call escaping your pain?"

"I know it was a disgraceful reaction to the heartache I was suffering—a combination of being pissed and wanting revenge."

"So what are you going to do now?" Little Katie asked.

"Rise from the ashes. I realize I must change my ways."

"I'm beyond relieved that you recognize this and want to change. For starters, when is it appropriate to date an Elevator Dick?"

"I can answer that, Little Katie. Never! Elevator Dick was a one-night stand. If he got me into an elevator, it is only reasonable to assume that I haven't been the only horse in the stable. He more than likely has had other conquests in that very same elevator."

Little Katie helped Kate out of the wreckage with some humbling words of advice.

"This adventure, as bad as it seems, has helped you reach new heights in recognizing the signs in situations that will not serve you or your highest good. Don't resist this change you are feeling in yourself, because if you resist this, more Dicks like Elevator Dick will continue to show up in your life. You can't go back to the sexual patterns and behaviors you're used to. You don't like it anymore, because it's not who you are.

"The memory of all the past Dick adventures are just memories now, and you can file this one away with those too. They serve to teach you lessons so you can move forward, not to look back so you can keep reliving the same scenario over and over again. You're punishing yourself by doing so. Self-punishment does not promote emotional or spiritual healing; it simply adds to your emotional wounds. You must release all the guilt and shame and rancor and fury associated with every Dick you have encountered thus far in order to stop hurting. Learn from them and let go. When you look back at some of these adventures, embrace what happened and look at it as having done the homework to improve yourself for your next adventure."

Little Katie then listed several questions for Kate to start asking herself to help with the changes in her behavior:

- ☐ What is the change you are resisting?
- ☐ Why are you resisting that change?
- ☐ What are you afraid may happen if you change?
- ☐ What are the results if you keep repeating the same patterns and behaviors without changing?
- ☐ At what cost are you keeping these patterns and behaviors the same?
- ☐ What are the benefits of changing this pattern or behavior?
- ☐ What would you have to do to make the change?
- ☐ What is stopping you from changing right now rather than later?

Little Katie continued: "By answering these questions honestly and with an open, self-loving heart, you plant the seeds for personal, spiritual, and emotional growth, which you will reap and harvest for a more positive experience with the next Dick. Look at this as creating something new and better for yourself."

"I agree, Little Katie. I can see that I have been resisting change because I don't want to deal with facing the patterns I need to break. I tend to want to escape my torment and pain with sex, and I fear being alone or going without sex. But deep down in my heart, I do want a healthy relationship, free from my fears and the repercussions of a sex-based relationship. I want to find the right Dick, but if I keep repeating the same actions, I will keep attracting the same Dick and risk continuing to relive the past. The cost for keeping the same behaviors and patterns is pain, heartache, and no loving relationship. I believe that if I stop these patterns and/or recognize the signs sooner, I will eventually find what I am looking for—whatever that is. It will take time for me to process all this, but I want to start to work on changing me now."

Everything takes time, and this process was no different. But one day Kate would look back and barely remember the person she was in that moment, and it would still seem like it was just yesterday. People never stop learning and growing and moving forward. That is life. Good things would be coming her way by choosing to change and stepping into her power. Kate could feel it.

"You're getting close, Kate. Let's go back to the enchanted pond and find a good place to begin."

13

The International Dick

LEARN TO SAY NO IN EVERY LANGUAGE

Kate couldn't turn the page to close that last chapter fast enough. It had not been her *finest* moment, although what she took away was worth its weight in gold. If people pay attention to the signs, they give a clue into what's going on in life and even offer direction. There may also be some kind of metaphor for life that seems to fit. In Kate's case, the adventure with Elevator Dick had quite an impact on her. She literally had sex in an elevator with a perfect stranger. She saw that instead of taking the elevator to climb new heights, she had actually taken it to hit rock bottom. And when the doors reopened, she didn't exit the elevator with a sense of accomplishment or the exciting new discovery of having been on another floor. In fact, Kate never got off on another floor. She just took a ride that brought her right back to where she had started. There was no fun whatsoever in that. And now, there she was on the brink of another adventure and wanting so badly to change her ways.

"I don't like feeling like this anymore," she said to Little Katie.

"What do you feel?" Little Katie asked.

"I feel remorseful, shameful, empty, and disgusting. You name it, I feel it." Kate couldn't make eye contact with her. She couldn't even face her own image in the mirror at the moment.

"Okay, so we know you don't like how you feel right now," Little Katie said, trying to look at Kate through the windows of her wounded soul. Remember those feelings when you go on your next adventure, but don't dwell on what happened either. You don't want to keep feeling this way; what you want is to avoid ever feeling like this again. Associate the behavior with how you are feeling, and then it will come naturally to steer clear of this repeated pattern from now on."

Kate lost it in her last adventure to the point where she didn't want to hear any of Little Katie's advice, but she was back, fully in and practicing all the things she had taught her.

"But the issue that keeps showing up for me is my drive for sex. When I'm feeling empty or dry of love and a toadd shows up and showers me with flattery, I soak it all up. That's when I become weak, and not just in the knees. I tend to drop my goddess armor and lose my power, giving into that feeling I call love."

"It's time you recognize and realize that they are just sweet-talking you to get what they want." Little Katie asserted.

"It's difficult for me to discern their true intentions because I gauge love on how they make me feel. When they show me they're interested and attracted to me by giving me compliments and saying nice things, I immediately feel good about myself. The barometer in my mind says, 'If you feel good, then this toadd *is* good.' I believe they are saying these things to me because they are just as into me as they say they are, and not because they are just interested in sex with me. I know it sounds naive, but I believe in the language of love." Kate tried to explain herself to Little Katie, hoping she could shed some light on things.

"But most of the time they are not. Kate, you are an easy target, and they can see you coming a mile away from the enchanted pond. So to arrive at the destination of love, what are you going to do differently from this point forward?"

"I can't answer that with any clear certainty right now," Kate readily admitted, as her attention strayed and she glared toward the pond. "I see a toadd in the distance. Strange … He has a suitcase on his lily pad. I've got to go check him out. Later, Little Katie."

"I'm glad we brought all this up to the forefront," Little Katie called after Kate. "The answer to that question will be revealed in this next adventure. Stay focused on change and pay attention to what this toadd wants and what he says to you."

Kate heard Little Katie, but she had to move fast not to lose him. Before she could reach his lily pad, an object suddenly flew through the air toward her. His suitcase? She caught it as he simultaneously jumped into her arms. Walking toward her next adventure holding both toadd and suitcase, Kate thought, *Well, this should be interesting. I wonder what gives with the suitcase.*

✦

"Please be sure to have your passport ready prior to boarding your flight. At this time, we are boarding all first-class passengers," Kate heard the gate attendant as she made her way through the line of people waiting. She was excited to finally visit her best friend in London, England. She had lived there a little more than five years now, and for one reason or another, Kate had put off visiting her—but not anymore. She had never been out of the country, so she figured there was no time like the present. After the Elevator Dick fiasco, Kate was looking forward to exploring new sights and new people, *sans men*. She figured the long plane ride would be perfect for her to take advantage of some me time to read, catch up on some movies, and, of course, get some much needed sleep.

Kate was oblivious to anything around her as she checked her smartphone for last-minute messages while waiting to board. She had a message from her girlfriend saying she would be waiting for her at the airport, a message from her client agreeing to reschedule an appointment, and an affirmation from a Facebook page she followed—just what she needed. She closed her eyes as she recited the calming words in her head. A voice broke her concentration—it was her turn to board. She quickly gathered her carry-on and purse. With passport and boarding pass in hand, Kate was more than ready for this adventure.

She found her seat and carefully removed her headphones and tablet from her bag before placing it in the overhead bin, trying not to get in the way of the other passengers boarding behind her. As she turned to sit down, she noticed the empty seat beside her. *I hope I don't get a snorer*, she thought. Then she saw *him* walking up the aisle toward her seat.

Kate didn't know if it was her intuition kicking in or just the intense smell of cologne that made her turn to look in his direction, causing their eyes to meet. *Please don't let it be him*, she said to herself as she promptly looked away. *I can't bear ten hours of him and his fragrant Euro Paco Rabanne disturbing my hopes of a relaxing and enjoyable flight.* Before she could raise her head to see where he would be sitting, he was already standing right in front of her.

She looked up at him, and he looked down at her smiling. Then she heard in a strong, broad accent. "That is my seat."

"Oh, I'm sorry." She twisted around to get up. She thought he was talking about her seat. Then she realized he was going to sit next to her. Hopefully, he had not heard her, or maybe he didn't understand what she said, but she awkwardly pretended to get comfortable and not look embarrassed.

Kate looked over at him, and he smiled again as they exchanged a friendly nodding gesture. This time Kate took a good second look at him. *Good gosh, how could I overlook how gorgeous he is?!* He was scrumptiously delicious, like a Magnum Gold caramel ice cream bar. And to boot, he was dressed very sleek and stylish. The only thing she couldn't guesstimate was his height, because she was sitting down when he approached her, but she did sneak a peek to size up his legs, and they were bulging from his jeans throughout.

"Pull yourself together, Kate. Remember this trip is about you taking care of yourself. Stay focused!" her little travel companion reminded her.

"You're absolutely right." Kate put her headphones on to try to ignore her plane mate. But he started talking to her.

"So why are you heading to London?"

Politely, she responded, "To visit a friend."

He pressed on. "Is that *friend* your boyfriend?"

She blushed. "Oh no. Just my girlfriend." Kate didn't want to volunteer the fact she didn't have a boyfriend.

But then he blatantly asked, "Do you have a boyfriend?"

Bothered, not just by his fragrance but also by how brazen he came across with his prying questions, Kate could barely tolerate answering him. "I don't even know your name. And no, I don't."

Little Katie warned, "Ugh, Kate … You've just opened Pandora's Box."

He kept on talking. During the course of their conversation, Kate found out he was from the Mediterranean but lived in France. He traveled a lot for work and periodically went to the States just for that. And as her luck with men would have it, it came out that he was married.

"Though," he said, "unhappily."

Ah-ha! Kate thought. *I'm not playing this hand. Happy or not, he's a married man.* She cut him off straight away. "Okay, well, I'm sorry about your marriage. I'm a bit tired now, so I'm going to watch a film and take a nap."

It was a long flight, and Kate slept most of the way. She only got up a few times for bathroom breaks, which meant he had to get up and let her out, leading to a few short conversations. During one occasion when she returned to her seat, he took advantage of her not wearing the headphones, leaned over, and told her, "I waited to board the plane so I could watch you longer. I was very hopeful we would be seated together."

"Huh, I didn't notice you. Why were you watching me?"

"Because I think you are so beautiful and elegant."

"Thank you," Kate said uncomfortably and motioned to her headset as she put them on. She shrugged his compliment out of her mind along with his innuendos, not wanting to give any importance to it, but apparently, he was thinking about her more than she cared to consider.

After that, Kate purposely kept her headphones on for the remainder of the flight to avoid any further conversation, but as the plane was descending, he tapped her on the shoulder and motioned for her to take the headphones off so he could talk to her. She kindly obliged.

"I was wondering if we could exchange numbers. I am in the States quite a bit, and I think you are a really nice person. It is rare to find that in a person these days. I would love to meet with you and take you out for coffee when I am there."

Kate paused for a minute to consider his proposition. She chose to be nice and sincere. "I am fine with that, *but* just to be clear, you are married, and I am *not* interested in anything else but coffee."

International Dick agreed, and they exchanged phone numbers. Kate supposed she'd probably never hear from him anyway, and by the time she was back in the States, who knew when he'd be returning there, if ever.

Little Katie was shaking her head back and forth but didn't say a word to Kate.

After a few days in London and enjoying the sights with her friend, Kate's phone lit up. *Ring, ring.* She was receiving a FaceTime call from International Dick. Kate was confused because they had discussed him getting in touch with her when he was in the States, not in London.

It's probably a mistake, she thought. She declined the call, but within minutes, he called again.

Hmm, maybe it's important. Maybe I left something on the plane, and he has it. Kate answered the call.

"Hi, babe," he said as if they had known each other for years.

"Uh ... hi, *babe*?" she questioned.

He ignored her comment. "How are you? Sorry to bug you, but I cannot stop thinking about you."

"Oh boy, here we go," Little Katie chimed in.

"Oh, that's nice, but why are you thinking about me?" she asked him, confused.

"We had such a nice conversation on the plane, and I enjoyed every moment of your company."

It was becoming very clear to Kate where he was going with this.

"Likewise, but again, I just want to be clear. You're married, and I'm not interested in having anything to do with you other than possibly as a friend. Are you sure you understand this?"

"I understand, really. But you know how it is in a marriage."

"Yes, I do. And I want to be perfectly open with you. That's your problem, not mine. I don't feel comfortable talking to you. Where is your wife?"

"She is working."

"Oh okay, so would she be okay with you talking to me and telling me these things?" Kate asked.

"Our marriage is over," he assured her. "She is sleeping in another room."

"Well, why have you not filed for divorce?" He opened the door with his brazenness before, so she felt like she had a full pass to question him.

"It is a bit more complicated than that. We have two small kids."

Ugh! Kate's frustration with this conversation put her in a frenzy.

Trying to hold back from telling him off, she retorted, "I'm not buying it, my friend. I have to go now. When you get divorced, you can call me." With that, she hung up and dismissed him altogether.

Within minutes, he was texting her and telling her how beautiful and sexy she was. "You are so kind, and it is so rare to meet someone like you."

Oh no, there are those damn complimentary words again. Why can't I shake them off? Yes, I am skeptical about this guy, but what gives? Why is he that into me after such a short time?

Little Katie decided to try to jog Kate's memory. "Simple as this: he's good-looking for one, and also, you get intrigued when a man shows interest in you and showers you with affectionate and sweet words. We talked about this. Just remember how you felt after the last Dick encounter."

"You're right, but I just want to check him out on social media first. I am intrigued. I have to find out whether he's in a miserable marriage." *What if he is being truthful with me?* Kate pondered. As she perused his page, she saw he only posted and added pictures that had to do with himself.

"I don't see a wife," she pointed out to Little Katie. "Perhaps what he's telling me is true."

"Regardless, he's still married. Because he is notably aggressive in pursuing you, you need to be equally aggressive in saying no to him.

Just as Kate was about to abort Facebook, he caught her online and messaged her.

"Let me see you. I want to FaceTime you, babe. Let me see you. Send me a picture."

Instead of giving in, Kate listened to Little Katie and immediately shut down her social media. Something just didn't feel right. Kate left London without hearing from him again. She was glad that he had stopped trying to contact her while she was still there.

✽

Kate had a great time in London, but she was also glad to be home. No sooner had she touched down on US soil did she hear from International Dick again. "I want to see you. I will be in the USA very close to you—just a plane ride away. I will send for you."

What the hell does he mean that he will send for me? Kate curiously considered the invitation but swiftly declined. "Sorry, I'll be out of town when you are here."

"Then I will come see you. I would love to see you and feel your energy. Why are you not answering me? Take my American number. It would be great to chat. You look so amazing in your photos on social media. I want to see you. I want to feel you move and kiss those amazing lips. I'd love to be with you, hang out, and get crazy pleasing you. Send me a photo of you."

He was pushing all the right buttons.

"As much as I would love to reciprocate, you *are* married with kids," Kate replied.

"We have been down that road, babe. You know my situation. Yes, I have kids, but we all do. Send me a pic. I want to feel your touch and make you feel as amazing like you are. Relax. Let me please you and feel you move. What are you doing now?"

"I know we have been there before, but how fair is that to me?"

"I know, babe."

"Look, great to hear from you, but I'm tired and heading to bed." Kate was putting her phone down when it immediately lit up again.

"Look, I hate my situation." Spoken like a true Dick.

"Don't hate it because you have two beautiful kids. Plus you have sex with your wife!"

"Yeah, but it is not that great. No bonus. It is like let's-try-to-fix-things type of sex, but it does not fix anything. I want to feel you, and you know it. I want to see your smile, feel your touch, and taste your lips. You know how we make each other feel."

Funny enough, Kate could feel a certain sensation around her, like his aura was present.

She texted back: "Look, I get it. But you made that choice. You are stuck with it. I want and deserve more. I know what you want from me, and at the end of the day I would be the one left empty."

"Send me a picture of you. Look, I am not stuck, and I will get out. You never know what can be with us. Just feel me and allow it. Feel me, Kate, feel how I make you feel. Amazing, sexy, and beautiful. YOU are so elegant and amazing."

There was a brief pause before he texted again. "Babe, where did you go?"

"I'm figuring out how to respond."

"Stop overthinking, babe. Just allow. We both want it and feel it."

"Please stop calling me babe." It was weird that he talked to her like they already knew each other intimately.

"You don't know, babe, what can happen after just one day at a time enjoying each other. Feeling each other. Smiling together, pleasing each other. Just be and explore."

Little Katie surfaced and couldn't take any more of his shenanigans. "Are you not sensing how he's trying to manipulate you with his words? Because that's all this is—words. All talk and no action."

On one hand, Kate knew Little Katie was exactly right, and she should put her phone down. On the other hand, Kate was partial to continuing with this just to see where it led.

International Dick was not giving up. "Feel me, babe, taste my lips."

Her phone lit up this time with a cocky image of himself—not a suggestion to his face.

Oh my gosh! He just sent me a picture of his power! Does he realize that we're chatting over Messenger?

"Do you feel it, Kate? Feel my hands rubbing you, lifting you up on top of me."

Kate was now beginning to get excited. *But I can stop myself,* she said to herself.

"Yes, you *can*, Kate," Little Katie exclaimed.

"Feel how warm your body feels. Let me see you. Feel me behind you kissing your back, touching your hips as you move taking me in, all of me. Feel how hard I am. Don't fall asleep on me."

Kate didn't respond.

"You look amazing, babe. I know you feel all of me inside you. Feel how thick my cock is. I want to give you more of everything. I want to travel with you, drink wine with you, make dinner for you, take care of you …"

Now she thought he was talking straight from his dick, even though what he was suggesting was everything that she desired from her Fairy Tale List.

"Taste us. Babe, where did you go?"

"Again, I'm not sure how to respond to this," she was compelled to reply.

"I know you are touching my power, and it feels amazing. I want to travel with you and explore things. I know we will have amazing times, babe. Feel our energy. Let me fly you to me for one night while I am in the States. You are really beautiful. I really mean it."

It was tempting. *It does sound exciting—to have someone fly me to him because he wants to see me.* Kate found herself considering his proposal.

"Kate, he doesn't *just* want to see you," Little Katie snapped.

International Dick was internationally relentless. "My marriage is shit. I just want to send you love, babe. Thinking about how beautiful you are. I know we will cross paths. You are so amazing. Just be ready when we do see each other. Oh, by the way, you are so beautiful, hot, and sexy, and I go crazy but I like it. I hope you're having lots of amazing dreams of me pleasing you and making you feel amazing all over. Kisses everywhere. What are you doing?"

"Trying to go to sleep," Kate lied. She didn't want him to know he was succeeding in tempting her with his verbal *and* graphic sexual advances.

"Would love to help you sleep and make you relax, feeling me touching you. Let me see you."

"What part of sleep do you not get?" she replied while repeating in her head, *I can stop myself.*

"Are you alone?"

Shit. She was alone. She wanted to lie and tell him she was busy, but she didn't.

"Uh … I am … alone."

"Let me see you. Let me see you naked. I want to see you naked in your bed. FaceTime?"

He was calling her within seconds. Kate held the phone up in her hand and read the notification that it was him, but she paused before answering it. *This is not what I want*, she said in her head while persuading herself to believe that she if she answered they would only have a friendly conversation. She slid the green button to answer.

"You know, I don't feel comfortable talking to you. Where is your wife?" she said in an almost scolding tone.

"She is working."

"Oh, she sure does work a lot. Now please understand that the only reason I answered your call was to personally remind you that you're married, and I don't want to be the other woman. Plus, you probably do this with other women in every country you visit."

"Nice admonition," Little Katie bolstered. She knew Kate needed the confidence.

"You are the only one, babe. Let me see you. Take off your clothes, and let me see you."

"Boy, you're very pushy, and I don't want to do this, honestly. I appreciate all the kind words and …"

All of a sudden, he pulled out his very *large* power and showed it to Kate on FaceTime! She felt her face go flush as he started in on himself, repeating how beautiful and sexy she was.

Kate's throbbing desire began.

"Take off your clothes, and let me see you, babe. All of you."

Then it happened … She caved. Part of her still reluctant, she chose to engage him, angling her phone so he could watch as she slid her nightie off.

"Separate your legs, babe. I want to see your beauty. I know you feel all of me inside you. Feel how thick my cock is. I want to give you more of everything. Touch yourself."

Kate felt trapped. She could have easily hung up the phone and blocked him. *What is wrong with me?*

"Take your fingers and slide them down your belly and touch yourself. That's it, babe. I see you are so wet for me. Slide your fingers up and down your energy as I stroke mine. That's it, babe. Can you feel me? I know you feel our energy merging. I know you can feel me touching you."

And for a split moment, Kate thought she could feel his energy, as if he were in the room with her. She let her legs open wider to let him enter. Except for one *huge* problem, and it wasn't his cock. *He's not here!* Then the phone slipped out of her hand onto the floor, and she snapped out of her sexual trance.

What the fuck am I doing? What is this? Phone sex? Her voice of reason suddenly kicked in. She realizes she should've told him off from the moment Last Tango in Paris started in on her with his pickup lines. Kate grabbed the phone from the floor for one last admonishment.

"You are all the way across the world, married, and you manipulated me into having phone sex with you! Leave me alone!" *Click.* That was the end of that conversation, as well as her momentary lapse of judgment.

"Ah, Kate. So glad your phone dropped! You are getting better and better at recognizing your submissive patterns. Let's get to the bottom of what happened here. We'll begin with this: When is it appropriate to date a married International Dick? Never, ever. There is no passport to enter that region. When it comes to no, there is no language barrier. You have to learn how to say no with international policy and conviction.

"All International Dick wanted was phone sex from you. He didn't once stop to consider your needs and wants. He manipulated you from the get-go. He ignored your repeated logic that he was married and you were not interested in having a relationship with a married man. You were clear with him and told him that you wanted and deserved more. No matter how miserable his relationship is, he is still married—not your problem. However, he read you like a novel and knew exactly how to sweet-talk you to get you to relent.

"In this case, what you should have done was deleted his number or, better yet, blocked him. It's important that if you say no, you follow through with full responsibility—no guilt, no shame, no remorse. Although I congratulate you on pulling yourself together before you crossed the border of no return."

Little Katie was never one to sugarcoat things, and Kate heard her loud and clear.

"I agree. I should have stuck with no and followed through. But if saying no is so important, then why is it so hard?" Kate really needed to identify her weakness with saying no.

"Saying no is hard for you because you're nice. You don't like to make people feel like you don't care. It makes you feel guilty to think you are making them feel bad by saying no to them, but in reality, you're not making them feel bad. You need to change this behavior of yours. When someone asks you to do something that makes you feel uncomfortable, then that is a sign that it should stop. When you disregard that feeling, you get caught up emotionally with all the sweet talk.

"The way to look at it is that you are saying no for you, not to let that person down. You are saying no for your own benefit because it doesn't work for you or doesn't make you feel good. And if you were to concede to do something against your best interest, you'd be hurting you, not them. Let them know you come first and need to honor your own feelings. If that hurts someone else's feelings, then they are not thinking of you. Saying no is nothing against the other person. You could try to explain things to them if it makes you feel better, and that way, you are off the hook. But International Dick is not worth anything other than a simple N-O. No."

Little Katie's words filtered through Kate and helped wash away those old insecure feelings about what others thought of her that she kept buried and the need to be loved by everyone. Little Katie was right; Kate didn't want to hurt people's feelings, so she found herself going along with them even when she didn't want to, just to be able to save herself from an awkward moment or having to feel guilty—when, in reality, she would end up in an even more awkward situation or, worse, feeling horrible toward herself. That pattern took her away from experiencing self-loving possibilities.

"I know this adventure never would have worked out. He is married and lives across the world, and we are from very different cultures," Kate confirmed to Little Katie.

"Great lesson learned. Say no at an international level, and stick to it. As shallow as this adventure was, the enchanted pond is deep with more charming Dicks to sift through." Little Katie nudged Kate to get back in the saddle.

Kate was shocked that Little Katie was okay with her sifting through more Dicks. *What does she know that I don't?*

Excited to return to Dickland and have the possibility of having the right toadd leap into her arms was all Kate looked forward to.

"Let's go!" they both said at the same time. Finally, Little Katie and Kate were on the same wavelength.

14

The Football Dick

STOP THE PLAY AND SETTLING FOR LESS THAN YOU WANT

International Dick was a pretty hysterical moment—Kate would be the first to admit. While she felt a twinge embarrassed that she gravitated toward her old patterns, by the same token, she felt proud of herself for coming to her senses and putting the fire out before getting burned. It was a narrow escape. Then, all of a sudden, Kate had this epiphany.

When she was a little girl, she used to love lighting matches—watching the flame until she could feel the burn on her little fingers before blowing it out. It was a game to her. She would keep the match lit as long as she could stand it, each time trying to endure the flame a little bit longer. Her mother had caught her a few times and reprimanded her for it, trying to scare her with stories of disfigurement and loss of limb. But no harm, no foul. Kate kept on playing with matches until one day she couldn't put the flame out. Lo and behold, she suffered a second-degree burn and burnt the floor when she flung the match away. Thank God nothing more serious happened, but it did leave a scar on her finger to remind her and scorched the linoleum tile floor to remind her mother for years to come. Kate suddenly understood how she had played out some of her childhood antics into adulthood, albeit on a different level.

Mind-blowing, she thought.

Little Katie remembered doing that. She saw an opening in the fabric of Kate's memory box as Kate was beginning to grapple with memories from her childhood, comparing them to her past and present adult behaviors and patterns as she uncovered the similarities. Little Katie first explained that there was no need for embarrassment.

"You see, Kate, you have, and most likely will again, fallen for the wrong Dick, but in a way, it's only natural because what we do and how we make choices does stem from our childhood. Let me walk you through this and explain as we head back to the enchanted pond."

Intrigued by Little Katie's candor in admitting she had a hand in how Kate's love life had played out (because, ultimately, Little Katie was Kate's inner child), Kate followed along and carefully listened to the little one's every word.

"Have you ever heard people say that we are attracted to a mate or a partner based on our childhood upbringing? There is a theory that says we will end up with someone like our parents, meaning their traits. It is common to find yourself in a relationship that reminds you of certain aspects of your parents' personalities or feelings for someone associated with childhood memories of your parents. And in this case, it's true of your father."

Kate could see how Little Katie cut the pattern out from her childhood much like she had assembled that connection with lighting matches, but wait a minute … Kate wasn't ready to consider that she was attracted to men that reminded her of her father. That was crazy talk.

"Not so fast, Kate. Hear me out. I'm not done." Little Katie continued to contrive her own theory on why Kate always ended up with the wrong Dick.

"Everything we are discovering throughout these adventures has remarkably shaped your selection of a toadd, one Dick at a time. A father is a girl's first love—theoretically, he is the first male she receives nurturing from, thereby creating both her first feeling of giving love to a man and receiving love from a man. It seems natural that if you had a great relationship with your dad, then you're more likely to attract a great guy. However, if the opposite is true—as in our case because we didn't have a great relationship with our father—then guess what? Our first taste of love was not the fairy tale-type of love our mom led us to believe in. At the base of our experience, our father appeared not to show love and was intimidating, unemotional, distant, and a workaholic, so he had no time for us. We didn't feel loved by him."

So far, Little Katie was right on the money and continued to piece it together for Kate.

"This takes me back to the Disturbing Dick adventure long ago when you recalled the childhood trauma. Remember—we didn't feel safe and secure, because Dad did nothing to help or make us feel protected during that traumatic incident."

Going back in her mind to relive that memory, Kate remembered that her father appeared to dismiss and silence her and wouldn't listen when she tried to speak her truth. And whenever he would hear Kate trying to talk about stuff that she didn't quite understand to be disturbing, she could sense his doubtfulness by the off-putting look on his face. Kate never felt validated by her dad—not when she sought love, not when she sought support, not even when she sought safety and security. Instead, Kate felt like she was the one doing wrong.

"Yes." Little Katie agreed and understood because she was there. "And unbeknownst to you, as you grew older and tuned it out, it still set the standard for you in your search for love. These daddy issues have influenced you and the decisions that you've made in every Dick relationship you've been in so far."

"Let me get this straight, Little Katie. So allegedly—and I say *allegedly* because it's my own interpretation of my relationship with my father—what I needed from my father was to feel safe and secure. I needed to feel validated by him and have his approval of his little princess. Looking at it that way, I guess I was a needy little girl, but all I wanted was his attention. I can certainly see now that I depended on my dad to give me my identity." Kate sighed.

Kate continued to wrap her mind around the fact that all her deflated Dick experiences were a construct of a painful childhood. She uncovered more. She brought these deficits of love, approval, and protection into her relationships while trying to extract what she thought was love from them. Then it hit her like a brick.

"So in turn I developed a belief that in order to get love and attention and feel safe and secure, I have to have sex, because I established a connection between sex and fulfilling all those needs. I have kept repeating the same patterns with each Dick, blaming them and not taking responsibility for my perception of what happened, which is why these relationships always ended with so much pain and unanswered questions. In reality, I've never really been in love."

"That's right! You are getting it!" Little Katie felt like a mom on her child's graduation day.

"Whew! Unbelievable that it has taken me this long to understand, Little Katie. All right, so now that I've had this breakthrough, how many more Dicks do I need to size up before I find *the* Final Dick?"

Little Katie answered with utter assurance. "You *will* … When you stop settling for less than what you want and deserve. And only then will you finally uncover Final Dick."

"I get it, Little Katie." Then Kate saw a group of toadds in the distance tossing something around that caught her attention. "Thanks for opening up my eyes, Little Katie, but now I'm off to check out what these toadds are doing over at the enchanted pond."

I have to be close to Final Dick, she thought as she approached the pond. Kate could hear the sound of a whistle blow, and then she saw a ball hurtling through the air. Her inquiring mind had to know what this toadd was croaking about after the whistle blew. Standing next to the sidelines of the pond, she heard him yell, "Hut, hut, hike!" And the toadd, along with the ball, went flying through the air and into her arms.

"Good catch," he said.

Little Katie watched as Kate was underway to another adventure, knowing this would not quite be Final Dick. "But she is very, very close," she whispered dulcetly as she ran along to catch up with Kate.

It was a sunny and warm weekday morning as Kate sat on the patio of her favorite coffee shop, sipping her Cappuccino, eating a light breakfast, and going over her to-do list for the day when a gorgeous man walked by her table. It was impossible not to do a double take. His frame and stature made Kate break away from the task at hand to look at him. His handsome features came into clearer focus as her eyes watched where he was going. He headed toward another table close by. While Kate edged discreetly from her seat, wriggling around to try to get a better look, he caught her in motion. Nervously, she looked away and shoved her face with breakfast, pretending to be in lost in thought as she scrolled through her smartphone. All of a sudden, she heard a deep voice speak up. Kate's heart was pounding, hoping that he was talking to someone else and not to her.

"Excuse me. Excuse me." She kept hearing him call from his table. Kate could feel that energetic tug when someone is trying to get your attention. She was embarrassed enough that he caught her looking his way, but she became even more embarrassed when he said, "Excuse me, ma'am. You dropped something on the ground."

Ma'am?! Do I look like a grandma to be called ma'am? Kate thought. She bashfully looked his way with a grin, although a little peeved to be called ma'am. Then again, she was a little flattered she had drawn his attention for him notice she had dropped something.

"Oh, thank you," Kate said as she looked at the ground to look for whatever she had dropped. She couldn't see anything, so she looked around her chair on both sides and then under the table. She still didn't see anything. Finally, she turned to ask him what she had dropped. He was no longer sitting there.

Then she heard, "You have egg on your face." She turned to her other side, and there he was standing next to her in all his glorious presence. She imagined hearing angels sing as the morning sun framed his strapping silhouette. He was handing her a napkin.

Mortified, she grabbed the napkin from him and wiped her face.

He laughed and said, "I'm just kidding."

Kate timidly giggled with relief. "Oh, ha-ha. You are so funny … because I'm not even eating egg."

"Well, I guess the joke's on you," he said with a smile and walked away back into the coffee shop.

Kate was embarrassed pretty easily, especially when in the presence of an attractive man. Her guard slowly dropped, like a cube of sugar dissolving into a hot cup of java. And then she would find herself doing something like tripping over her own feet or, as in this case, forgetting what she was eating.

She decided to go inside for more coffee, thinking she would see him in there. His ego had sort of put her off, although not enough to forgo his attention and good looks. She made her way up to the counter discreetly looking for him as she tried to think of something clever to say when she came face-to-face with him. However, he was nowhere to be seen.

Bummer, she thought. *Oh well, no harm done. I'll just go back to my table and finish my coffee.* Except, there was no table. By the time she went back outside, it was occupied. Not only that, but every table was taken. Kate took a closer look at who had snatched the table she had left for only a moment. And, of course, *he* was occupying it. He looked over at her and smiled coyly.

Kate smiled back and said, "I guess the joke is still on me."

Irresistibly charming, he teased, "Yes, it is, and now you'll just have to sit with me."

He introduced himself as Kate pulled the chair back to sit across from him. She told him her name, and he asked how her morning was going so far and apologized for being facetious with her so early in the morning. Kate laughed and began a conversation just talking about everything and nothing as time trickled on. She found out he was a football coach in the local community, which gave them something in common to talk about, as Kate's son was playing tackle football. He gave some advice for her young son and told her what to expect as he got closer to possibly playing in college.

Kate made a point of steering the conversation away from anything too personal because she didn't think this chance meeting was going to lead to anything more than two people having a chat in a café. What she meant was, she knew where it *could* go, but at the time she wasn't ready for it to go there. On the other hand, she couldn't help basking in his gorgeous looks, losing herself in the movement of his lips with every word he spoke and wondering what they would feel like on hers. Her thoughts drifted away as her eyes unintentionally began sweeping his muscular arms and chest, trying to imagine how it would feel to have them wrapped around her body, and then looking down further to get a glimpse of …

"Hello? Are you listening to me?" He interrupted her trance with a chuckle, knowing full well that she was checking him out for the past God-only-knows how many seconds.

"Uh, yeah. You know, I better be going," Kate said flustered, as though it was the time she had been preoccupied with and not his physique. "It was certainly nice to meet you, and I am sure I'll see you here again soon."

As she started to get up from the chair, he stopped her and said, "I would love to take you out sometime. May I get your number?"

Oh shit. Here I go again, Kate thought. Feeling familiarly ill at ease with turning him down, she lightheartedly replied, "As long as there are no more jokes on me."

They then parted ways, him with her phone number saved in his phone and her with a flutter of anticipation to hear from him soon.

A few days later, they made a date to meet at a swanky restaurant in town. When Kate arrived, he was already there sitting at the bar—glowing like a Fourth of July sparkler. Or were those the sparks she was feeling?

Shake it off. Remember—just a drink, dinner, and nothing else, she told herself.

"You've got this, Kate. Since you've already detected his moderately sized ego, maybe you should investigate a little into what he does with his extra time, because he comes off as a bit of a player." Little Katie put it out there for Kate.

No sooner had she greeted him at the bar, he waved down the bartender and ordered her a drink.

"Little Katie, he just bought me a drink without hesitating, and you know men nowadays don't even offer, let alone actually buy a drink for a woman. I think perhaps he is a gentleman and not as egocentric as he appeared at the coffee shop."

"For some men, it's part of their game. Keep your defenses up, Kate. This player gives me the impression he has played the field, scoring his share of plays between his legs, and I am not talking about passing balls on the football field either."

Kate wasn't sure at this point whether Little Katie was being too overprotective or if she authentically did sense something foul in Football Dick. Kate decided to relax her guard and enjoy herself.

The conversation bubbled as they opened up more to one another, getting to know each other a little better. He kept the drinks flowing. Meanwhile, Kate felt herself becoming lightheaded and wandering in her own thoughts, unable to stop perusing his body with her eyes. She caught herself fantasizing about him again, aware she would be in trouble if she didn't get something to eat to absorb the alcohol. *I can't let the wine lower my inhibitions tonight*, Kate thought. She finally paused to look at the menu and order some food. They kept on talking over dinner and drinks.

Time took them by surprise again. She only realized it was late when she felt her eyes getting heavy. It was the same as when they were at the coffee shop. He was fun to talk to, and they seemed to hit it off. She noticed they never had that awkward silence that happens between two people who have just met and can't think of anything to say. She didn't want to spoil the evening, but she was tired, so Kate told him she was ready to go.

Throughout the entire night, he did not try to make a move on her. It seemed a little uncharacteristic of him because he was so flirtatious. However, when they walked out of the restaurant, a red flag went up for Little Katie.

"Can you give me a ride back to my car?" he asked Kate politely. "I'm parked across the street and could sure use the lift."

"Yep, there it is," Little Katie alluded.

"He just wants a ride. What's the big deal?" Kate brushed her off.

"Okay, if that's what you want to think. I see what he's doing. It's a classic blitz move."

"Sure, no problem. I'm over here." Kate signaled with her hand for him to follow her.

They got into her car, and he directed her to the spot where his car was parked. Kate drove right up to it and stopped, keeping her foot on the brake, assuming he was going to get out without lingering. Smiling, she turned to thank him for dinner and drinks, but it was clear he was thinking differently, because he leaned in for a kiss.

She let it happen. Kate had been daydreaming about feeling his lips on hers—no way was she going to shy away now. He delivered his kiss like a pro. She concentrated on his soft lips tenderly swiping hers as the bracing touch of his hands cradled her face. She could feel the throbbing between her legs. By this time, Kate had put the car in park. His juicy kisses quenched her longing for him. When she came up for air, reality hit her.

We have to get to know one another a little more before I let him whisk me away, she thought. Making that call was hard for her, especially because he made it very challenging to say no.

He continued kissing her as he whispered repeatedly in between breaths. "Let me come home with you, Kate. Don't resist me. Let me come home with you." He then began describing how he would take her into his arms and make love to her. It was Kate's fantasy too.

"It's a good time to take a time-out, Kate," Little Katie interrupted.

Kate gently pulled back and said to him, "I would like to keep doing this, but I am sorry. Not tonight. I'd like it if we could see each other again."

"Nice block, Kate," Little Katie said like a cheerleader.

Football Dick retreated like a gentleman and said, "I look forward to seeing you again."

※

Kate was going down lover's lane again, but taking a more cautionary approach. She used the magic of social media to gather intelligence on Football Dick before going out with him again. Was she just another move in his playbook, or could he really be setting his sights on her with the right intentions? She wanted to know. Kate went to his profile on one of the social media platforms and got her answer without having to do too much investigating.

He's engaged?! Kate felt drop-kicked like a football.

Normally, her flutter would have turned into sunken dismay, feeling like a fool, but instead, she was genuinely pissed off. Her gut was wrenching and spewing acid. *Not again!* Kate decided to confront him about the little secret he'd kept from her, so she got in touch with him and asked if he wanted to meet for lunch—on neutral territory during work hours so there would be no excuse for drinks, or anything else for that matter.

Days later, Football Dick greeted her with a grin from ear to ear, happy to see her. Meanwhile, she was fit to be tied thinking about how he could be stringing her along by keeping her in the dark on his engagement. Kate steadily kept her cool even though what she wanted to do was flip the glass of ice water over his head. She could barely hear anything he was saying, as her mind kept showing her images of a scoreboard in his favor with red flashing letters that spelled out: *He's engaged to be married!*

Unable to keep up the charade any longer, Kate said, "So, talk around town says that you're engaged."

Completely taken off guard, he looked at her as though she were speaking in a foreign language. "No, we are broken up," he said without hesitation.

"I see. Then why is it still on your profile?" Kate had her arms crossed in front of her chest.

He raised an eyebrow as if to imply she was a stalker. "I hardly ever go online, and I don't even care enough to sign on just to take it down."

"I see another flag in this play, Kate. It's red like the first one," warned Little Katie.

Kate wasn't letting him off the hook that easily. "Hmm … I would think that is something you would care to fix before you start to court someone, don't you think?"

"Yes, I suppose it would be good to do that. I clearly see this is upsetting to you," he said, trying to be sensitive.

"Yes, especially because I'm starting to like you, and then you act like your engagement or what you call a breakup is so trivial to you. If it is, then why didn't you mention it to me? Bottom line, I certainly don't want to be involved with anyone who is potentially getting married to someone else in the near future." Kate was ready to grab her purse and leave.

Football Dick took hold of her hand to stop her. "We are not getting married. She has some things to deal with, and for now, we're seeing other people," he assured Kate as he slid himself into the booth seat next to her.

Kate felt awkward that she was being so nosy. "Now what?" she asked him.

He looked at her with his heart-stopping eyes and grinned. "Now we continue where we left off in the car." He leaned into her, placing his full, rounded lips on her mouth. He quieted her with kisses until their food came out to the table. Football Dick managed to quell her suspicions by addressing his situation. Kate felt he had been honest with her. She figured that it wouldn't hurt to see where this would go.

After lunch, he walked her back to her car and wrapped his strong arms around her. His embrace made Kate feel safe and secure. She closed her eyes, taking in the moment of him holding her against his chest with the warmth of the sun on her face. He gave her a squeeze and then drew her away, coaxing her to look at him. As she opened her eyes, she gazed into his, and there was that all too familiar electrifying look she had become so accustomed to from a man when he wanted something from her.

"Let's go back to your place," he said seductively.

Little Katie interjected. "Think about what you're about to do. Don't you want and deserve more than a man who is getting over an engagement? Don't you want to know why they're not together anymore? This Dick is using you as a substitute. And how could you feel confident he's not playing other women besides you?"

"Well, right now, at this present moment, he is with me and not doing this with anyone but me." Kate was not going to let Little Katie intercept his pass.

◎

So much for just lunch, Kate thought as they both drove over to her house where they'd finally kick off their love affair. There was no mistake how much they turned each other on when their lips came together. Kate was ready to lose herself in ecstasy with him and sizzle in his burning passion. She believed they would inevitably fall in love, and it would begin with the exploration of each other's bodies.

It all happened so fast. He led her into the bedroom, kissing her and touching her in all the right places as though he had journeyed her body before. He knew her weak side, erotic points, and all the sexy subtleties that sent her into a euphoric state. The sensual pleasure he gave her was enthralling, not only with his power but also with his emotion. In a tender moment, he told Kate that a football accident had left him damaged and that he was not as powerful in bed as he once was. She was happy to be the captain of the team for him and slid on top of him so he could ease his way into her. And through the trenches of lovemaking, they both collapsed breathless with satisfaction before falling asleep in one another's arms.

Kate woke up to him putting on his clothes and getting ready to leave.

He assured her that they would meet again. As she watched him exit the room, she couldn't help thinking, *I hope I wasn't just played.*

"We shall find out soon enough," remarked Little Katie.

※

They kept their relationship going, but as time wore on, the relationship became increasingly more about sex and less about spending quality time like couples do. Also, their rendezvous were taking place later and later at night and always at Kate's house. She wondered what had happened for their relationship to take a turn. Although she was curious, she kept mum.

Then one night after an ardent trice in bed, he randomly and just casually mentioned to her, "I'm getting back together with my fiancée."

What kind of fuckery did I just hear?! Kate felt winded, like he had just sacked her on the playing field.

"Oh …" she said, regaining her breath. As calmly as she could, she added, "Really. Then why are you in bed with me?"

The echo of those words sounded comical to her. *He is in bed with me. We just finished having passionate sex, and this is how he demonstrates his commitment to his fiancée?* Kate busted out in hysterical laughter and asked, "Do you even know what you are doing, what you are thinking, or why you even want to get back with her? Seriously, think about what you're going to step back into, the operative phrase being 'step *back* into.' There is a reason why you guys broke up in the first place."

His response: "She has changed."

Kate cried out, "Oh. My. Gosh!" She fell back onto her pillow. "But *you* have not! You are laying here in bed with me!"

"Good catch." Little Katie applauded her for calling the penalty.

There is no doubt that Kate felt the chain saw rip through her heart when she heard those words coming out of his mouth, but in that moment, before she could feel the crippling effect of being duped once again, the obvious truth came crashing into her mind: *I fell for Football Dick via the same old pattern of all the other Dicks.* She reached out to Little Katie.

※

Trying to analyze where she had dropped the ball in this relationship,

Kate understood she just settled for Football Dick because she loved the feeling of the safety and security he supposedly brought to the field. She chose to allow this relationship to continue *not* because she thought he was the one, but because he was fulfilling her needs—to feel safe, secure, and loved in a man's arms. He was never going to commit to her, and every bone in her body knew it. His alleged ex-fiancée had always been waiting at the end of the goal line, while he was just throwing passes at Kate on the sidelines. All the signs pointed to this very outcome.

Little Katie spelled the lesson out for her in this adventure. "So I don't have to ask you when it is appropriate to date a Football Dick, because the answer is clear to you. You didn't have to let him come over to your house just because it felt familiar to you. You said yes not just to him but to your old self—the one who follows those old patterns. What you should remember, Kate, is that the only person responsible for whom you choose to allow to be in your life is *you*. You create your own story."

"Yes, you are completely right, Little Katie, but I've become more aware of identifying the choices that do not serve me. I am also getting better at being able to surmise where a relationship is headed by recognizing the signs and taking responsibility to make an altering decision to end it when it's not fitting with what I want or deserve."

Little Katie took Kate one step further. "If you're ever going to get what you profoundly want out of a relationship, you must stop settling for less than what you want. Don't simply recognize the signs, but take action in the present to heed the signs. Don't wait for the moment to pass, because it might be too late to avoid unnecessary heartache. Whenever you are confronted with a choice to either start, stay in, or break up a relationship, take a step back and weigh your options. Make a clear decision if the relationship is worth it by asking the following questions:

- ☐ Are you being honest about what you want and not making someone else's needs and desires more important than yours?
- ☐ Are you valuing your self-worth in this relationship and not lowering your standards by making compromises that you do not feel good about?

- ☐ Are you being mindful of what does and does not serve you in the relationship without holding on because you feel you are satisfying an old need?
- ☐ Are you choosing to practice self-love in this relationship in order to identify what you deserve and want, and not what you think you need to fulfill?

"Kate, you deserve to have everything in your life exactly the way you want it. Once you become clear about what you want and keep your mind constantly focused on that which you want for yourself, the who and the how will show up in the exact moment that is right and not a moment earlier. Football Dick wasn't the "who", and you knew it because you identified the signs and felt he wasn't for you. Now stay focused, and don't worry about "how" it will come to you. When you are ready in time, it will."

"Okay, Little Katie. I'm ready to create my own story. I think it's time we return to Dickland, so I can scour the pond again. I am feeling more worthy and deserving of Final Dick! I'm ready to chuck the old patterns because now I know what they are."

Little Katie was loving the maturity and conversion she saw in Kate. "It will all come to a head soon." She laughed impishly because she intended that naughty pun.

15

The Fitness Dick

SPOT THE PATTERN AND WORK IT OUT

Personal transformation is *never* easy. First, we are forced to reckon with the life we are unhappy with. And then we have to admit to ourselves that the reason we keep getting the same results is that we keep repeating the same actions. We've all heard this. Even Little Katie tried to get Kate to understand this simple concept—which, by the way, is a difficult one to swallow for someone convinced life sucks because of everyone else involved. *It's not me, it's them!* But what happens when a person gets to the point of feeling like she's tried everything to get a different result and those she's blamed are all the same? No matter how much of herself she gives, it's not enough, and she feels like she's back to square one. When that happens, it's time to rethink who's to blame.

Kate had either been strung along, cast aside, lied to, rejected, replaced, or heartbroken throughout every relationship. In order to survive another day, she had to swim through all the debris she had dumped into the pond to get to the other side. Otherwise, she'd become buried in a swamp of self-blame. Here she was, facing her transformation—a painful transformation. Yet, looking in the mirror was like looking at a new version of herself.

"Change," she heard, "because when you change the way you look at things, the things you look at *change*." The words sounded like they were coming from her own reflection in the mirror—not Little Katie, but a new Kate who was more than ready to emerge from this personal transformation.

The time has come for me to take a new stance in my quest for love, she thought as she headed back to the enchanted pond. Ever since Little Katie opened her eyes after Football Dick to the fact that she *did* deserve to have everything in life exactly the way she wanted it, Kate kept mulling over everything she had told her. *Once I become clear about what I want and keep my mind constantly focused on it, the how will show up at exactly the right time, and not a moment too soon.* It resonated so profoundly that it awoke in Kate the idea that it was time to write a new story. And in a way, she saw herself already living it—new Kate existed somewhere inside of her, and she was already getting a glimpse of her.

Timing was everything. Kate just had to keep her eyes open to notice the timely signs. As she practiced her awareness, in the distance she could hear a voice counting down. "In three, two, one, and rest."

Hmm, she thought. *Maybe this countdown has something to do with the timing that Little Katie is referring to? It must be a sign for me to follow.* Across the pond, Kate saw a toadd holding what looked like dumbbells as he struggled to lift them up over his head.

"What the heck is he trying to do?" Little Katie asked.

"Your guess is as good as mine, but I think I should go lend him a hand," Kate replied.

"Be careful not to hurt yourself." Little Katie had a strange feeling again about this one.

"Well, I'm not going to stand here and watch him get hurt if I can help it. I'll be careful."

Kate walked over to the toadd, who at that point could barely mutter a word, so she bent down toward him to help him out.

"Can you spot me?" he managed to ask as he placed the dumbbells into her hands and then jumped into her arms. Huffing and puffing, he asked, "What are you lifting today?"

"At the moment, apparently you," Kate said with a smile.

"Oh boy." Little Katie was wearing a smirk on her face. "This one looks like he's going to be quite the workout."

And off into the next adventure the three of them went.

Fitness Dick worked at a trendy fitness facility where Kate went to sign up for a strength training class. Her goal was to get her mind in alignment with feeling good about herself by becoming stronger physically. She figured a good workout routine would help her achieve that. The woman at the front desk suggested telling the instructor she was new. That way, he would make himself available to assist her if she had questions on any of the exercise machines.

Of course, it didn't help that Kate found him simply delicious. If she had learned anything about attraction, it was that even though she was not interested in pursuing anything romantic, Dicks smell out attraction just like a dog smells fear. She didn't need this toadd croaking for her attention, but what she did need was help using some gym equipment. So with no one else to turn to for help, she made it a point to turn off any radars that would signal she was trying to do anything other than that. Approaching him confidently to introduce herself, he turned around to face her and instantly put on a string of pearly whites from ear to ear that nearly blinded her.

"Uh-oh, Kate, don't read into this." Little Katie tried keeping her in line.

"It's okay," Kate assured her. "Even though he's clearly hot and has a rockin' buffed body, I'm not here for that. Besides, you should know that my observation is only indicative of a healthy sex drive."

"That's my concern. Your healthy sex drive, as you call it, tends to get you into trouble," she said with reprisal.

Trying to listen to and look at Fitness Dick as purely her instructor and not a potential Dick she'd like to get to know, Kate could feel her confidence wafting away and vulnerability taking over. She absorbed his voice as she listened to his instruction, and he gripped her attention with three-second glances he landed on her. She noticed he would tilt his head when he looked at her as though concerned with how she was doing. Even though he was professional on every level, she couldn't help swapping focus from her workout to checking out his incredible bicep when he swung his arm around to point her in the direction she should be facing. *Oops!* She had to shake it off in order to bring her mind away from where it was wandering.

"Good retreat, Kate, but maybe you should stick to the treadmill instead," Little Katie recommended.

"I don't want to come off like I can't handle the class and walk out. I'm staying here until we're done."

Meanwhile, Fitness Dick walked around the room to monitor everyone's movements and periodically check in with Kate. He took a short pause to demonstrate a few arrangements to add into their exercise routine—moves Kate wasn't familiar with: clean and jerk, snatch, and split jerk, to name a few. Kate was distracted by the names he called them.

"Those certainly don't sound like the kind of exercises a woman would do," she announced jokingly so he could hear.

"Don't worry, Kate," he said glancing her way with his striking smile and a laugh. "I'll help you out when we get to them."

His attention on her sent flutters through her body. She was flattered that among the entire group of gorgeous women in the room, he was noticing her. Turning on her sex appeal was automatic.

"Uh, Kate, what are you doing?" Little Katie asked.

"Just having a little fun flirting," she whined.

"You should probably focus more on your training intervals than on your flirting intervals. He's going to get the wrong idea. You are here to get an exercise workout, not to work out the instructor. That combination is not the kind of split training that's going to achieve the alignment you're looking for," Little Katie lectured.

Little Katie's constant sermon was irritating Kate. She was just trying to the make best of a difficult workout by lightening it up with some harmless flirtation. She was going to walk out of there sweaty and tired and nothing else.

But when Fitness Dick walked over to explain an exercise to her, the masculine scent of his cologne, powered by his pheromones, rebooted Kate's sexual attraction as he got close to speak into her ear over the loud music they were working out to. Instead of paying attention to what he was trying to explain, her mind went off track, envisioning what it would be like being with him.

"Kate. Kate … did you get that?" Fitness Dick was talking and looking at her with his head tilted to the side once more.

"Uh, yeah. I'm sorry. I got distracted," she answered playfully. "Could you demonstrate that again?"

"Ha! I see where this is going." He laughed and then walked away but turned around again, giving her the kind of sweet smile that would satisfy any sugar craving. The squint in his eyes told her he was definitely interested in satisfying it.

Ugh! What does he mean? Where does he think this is going? Kate caught herself again.

Little Katie was right. She was there to align her body, mind, and soul with exercise, not with fun and games. Kate worked out the remainder of the class without losing sight of her goal. When it was over, she made her mind up that he actually had a great teaching style. Not only was he funny, but he took the class to another level by motivating them with inspiring words. She loved his positivity.

After class, Kate went to thank him for all his help, but when she was walking over to him, he was already heading in her direction. Now in a nearly empty room, she felt a little embarrassed about how forward she had come off. But he was so approachable and easy to talk to that he put her at ease pretty quickly, which is what made Kate comfortable flirting with him in the first place. It came as no surprise that ultimately they ended up making a date.

The next day they met for lunch. He showed up looking just as hot and smoky in regular clothes as he did in gym clothes. Kate felt lucky to have the opportunity to get to know someone who seemed so refreshing compared to the kind of guys she had been meeting lately. She was interested in knowing his story; in particular, she wanted to find out if he was available. He was so easy to converse with that four hours later she had found out he loved to travel and workout (*obviously*), he loved to have sex but was not getting much of it (*shocker*), and he would like to do all those things with her (*is that so?*).

"That's nervy. He sure isn't wasting any time," Little Katie pestered.

"I'm giving him the benefit here because he's funny, smart, attractive, and super sexy," Kate said.

Kate was impressed by the way he effortlessly charmed her. Nothing he said put her off—that is, until he dropped the weight of his personal life issues on her.

When she asked if he was in a relationship with anyone, he admitted he did have a live-in girlfriend, which was a term he used loosely because they weren't sleeping together; they didn't even share the same bed. He was only living with her to help out with their kids, but there was no love lost between them. It was a joint venture of convenience until he could manage to find a way out. She had cheated on him several times, although they kept procreating—three children to be exact, all under age seven. And for the cherry on top, he had another child with his former wife.

Good Lord, that scenario is full of red flags! Then again, I suppose it's his problem, not mine, Kate thought, trying to see past the blazing bush.

Little Katie didn't want her sticking around for one more second. "How many more red flags do you need to identify? Do us both a favor and use your workout skills to exercise an exit plan."

"Not so fast." Kate still wanted to give him the benefit of the doubt, and so she dug deeper for a reasonable explanation.

"What's the story with the three kids? I mean, why are you still having children with someone you want to leave?" she asked him.

He assured her that he was in the process of leaving her.

That answer raised another red flag. *If he left her*, Kate wondered, *would he do the right thing by all those kids?* It seemed like he was trying to escape his situation, a strategy that Kate was utterly familiar with having attempted to escape a few times in her life.

By the end of their conversation, she felt somewhat disillusioned. Still, she was willing to see him again because she kept thinking about the signs that led her to him and how he possessed so many of the qualities she was looking for in a Dick. It felt easy to be with him.

"Why, Kate? He obviously has a lot of baggage—baggage that you don't need or want in your life. Reconsider what you're starting with this Dick. You see the red flags. Stop this while you can," Little Katie pleaded.

On the way back to the car, they exchanged phone numbers. Once they got to her car, he didn't try to kiss her. He just gave her a nice, warm hug goodbye. It felt good.

Kate's phone rang as she was driving out of the parking lot. Strangely, even though she had given him her phone number, he didn't call or text through a cell phone line. Instead, he was calling her through Facebook Messenger. *Why is he calling me through the Messenger app?* she wondered. *Is he hiding from his girlfriend?*

"Another red flag, Kate," Little Katie noted melodically. "That's a whole lot of red flags."

It seemed a bit shady, but Kate went with it and answered his Facebook call.

"Baby, do you know how badly I wanted to kiss you? I didn't want to let go of you. You are the most amazing, sexy, and beautiful woman I've ever met."

Kate heard all the sugar-and-spice words she loved to hear. He was showering her with the kind of dangerous compliments she inevitably fell for, but this time she was apprehensive.

"Thank you. That's sweet of you."

"I would love to see you again. When can we get together?" he asked, not wasting any time.

They agreed to meet the following week for lunch again. He offered to pick her up at her house. Kate felt like a safe choice because they were still in the initial stages of getting to know each other, he had been a gentleman on their first date, and it would only be a quick lunch because he had to get back to work for an afternoon class.

That day while she was waiting for him to show up, she pondered what he had said to her during their Messenger conversation. He had alluded to the fact that she was the type of woman he could see himself being with. Kate found herself venturing in the possibility he could get out of his situation, and they could start a relationship. Could they potentially make a go of this?

When she opened the door, to her surprise, he was holding not one, but two bottles of wine.

"Ha-ha … wine? Are we drinking?" she asked, sort of joking and a lot confused. *Another red flag*, she thought. "Don't you need to go back to work and teach a class? Shouldn't you be sober to do that?"

He pretended not to hear her.

Kate got a wineglass out for him and opened the bottle. She served herself a glass of water because she didn't want to partake of the wine, hoping he would feel uncomfortable drinking alone. As she poured the drinks, he poured his heart out—family problems, problems at home, relationship problems, and the usual pesky sort of problems that everyone has.

Kate listened as she empathized. She knew what it was like to feel inundated by problems without viable solutions. As he talked, he also drank. He downed the first bottle in under an hour. Not that she was timing him, but she was watching the clock because he had to get to work. He was drinking the wine like it was fruit punch. It triggered the familiar situation she'd had with Drunk Dick. Kate could see that Fitness Dick was trying to drown his sorrows by drinking them away.

As he shared more of his story, it became clear to Kate that this man was in a lot of pain. She almost felt sorry for him. Something inside of her knew she wasn't going to be starting a relationship with him, but she still cared and wanted to help him. At that point, the only thing she could do for him was to listen. He was now asking for another pour from the second bottle of wine. Kate deterred his request by asking more about his situation. He realized then that he might have said too much.

"Enough about me. Let's move on to you," he said, changing the subject.

Fitness Dick stood up from the table and maneuvered over to where Kate was sitting across from him. The look he gave her was magnetic and alluring. She knew what he wanted. Sensibly, she didn't want to go there, because she could see so much pain in him. All the signs were flashing; red flags were glaring.

He leaned into her and began the thrilling game of seduction, kissing her with teaser kisses on her face first. Then he moved down to neck kisses, sweeping his lips lightly across her jaw toward her mouth where he savored her lips with French kisses. The combination of his flattering words and the delicacy of his affection created a rush of intense overwhelming feelings of connection, attention, and validation inside her. It was a combination for disaster because it worked.

He took Kate's hand as he guided her out of the chair to face him, grabbing her by the waist.

"I really think you are gorgeous. Every time I see you at work I want to whisper in your ear how much I want you. I want to be inside you, I want to hold you, and I want to taste you." He certainly had the right pass to enter Kate's sexual realm.

At that moment, as they led each other to the bedroom, Kate instinctively knew that this was only going to be sex. Another sexual relationship with another Dick who had restrictions, rules, no time, and, in this case, too much pain—and with a drinking problem to match.

Why am I doing this? Yes, I love sex, but it is becoming clearer to me that this is not all that I want or desire. This is not good for me. I've had enough of settling for less than I deserve! But she didn't speak up, didn't stop the action, didn't break the pattern … She stayed quiet and kept responding to his affection instead.

He laid her down on the bed and ardently had his way with her while blurting out how much he needed this. Oh, yes, he used the word *need*. When he said it, she became aware that need represented to him what it represented to her: wanting attention, feeling deprived of love and desire, wanting a connection, and feeling wanted. It was apparent that because of the personal issues he was going through, he needed her to fulfill his needs in that moment.

When Fitness Dick finished with the needy one-way sex, they lay in bed without saying anything until the silence became unbearable. Then he exclaimed, "Wow, I so needed this! Well, gotta go back to work."

Kate would have liked to be able to say that she lay there in disbelief, totally misguided by her well-placed intentions, but she could tell where this affair was headed the moment he began to tell his story. There was no way she was going to be able to rewrite her story with his. She fell off track when she went from empathizing to sympathizing. As soon as Kate started feeling sorry for his situation, she lost her power to say no. She didn't want to be the one to fulfill his needs. She was fully aware this journey was his—and only his. The funny thing about this scenario was she could now see that, in effect, she had already traveled that same journey.

Kate decided then and there this would be the only and last time they had sex, or saw each other for that matter. She quit the fitness facility and called it quits with him via Messenger.

"I don't want or need to be a booty call, be hiding conversations, or be making calls through Messenger, and I'm not interested in a casual relationship. You are clearly still with your 'girlfriend,' and I don't want to be a part of that. I hope the best for you and wish you well."

Then she blocked him from her Facebook page—and energetically too.

So why didn't she speak up sooner and allow it to happen? Why did she settle for just sex again? To answer these questions, Kate had to take a hard look at who she was and what she had become. She was no longer Kate wanting attention or needing validation and approval, relying on someone to make her feel safe and secure, but for some reason, she had still associated that feeling of connection and taking care of her needs with sex. She had a moment of weakness. And she had to be okay with that because she wasn't shaming herself anymore or feeling distraught over another failed relationship. Confusion played a part as well. She was still in the process of finding out how this all worked.

But this time it wasn't like in her past adventures when she told herself she was sick and tired and she was going to change and then found herself going down the same path all over again. Kate was on a different wavelength now. Fitness Dick didn't play her; rather, she misinterpreted the signs and wanted to see him for the best person he was. You see, Kate swam that pond, and now she was taking responsibility for her actions. The time had come for Kate to change and transform. That she was sure of.

"So now where do I go from here?" That was the only question she had left to ask Little Katie.

"Okay, Kate. Here is the unanswered question: When is it appropriate to date your fitness instructor—in this case, Fitness Dick? And the answer to that lies in what you have learned so far. You answered it already by reflecting on the lesson you derived from this adventure. Now you know that in order for the right relationship to come along and thrive, you need to know who you are. So how do you know *who* you are?"

It sounded like a trick question, but Kate was able to discern what she meant. She categorically knew who she was *not* any longer, but she didn't necessarily know yet who she was now. To know who she was unwaveringly would be a process. So Kate started at the beginning, which was as far back as she could remember love.

She began to piece the puzzle together. "The first version of who I am was based on the dependency on my parents to love me and show me who I am. I cannot fault them for teaching me that I had to depend on them for everything, including love. Most parents raise children that way, but life eventually teaches us the lessons that perhaps our parents are not equipped to teach us. Thus, my adventures. Truth be told, I grew up not loving myself and expecting someone else to fill that void for me. When I didn't receive it, I became unemotional, distant, and disapproving of myself. I silenced my voice and dismissed the love I should have nourished in myself. I failed to provide the safety and security, the validation and approval for myself. I can see that was the old Kate—the Kate I have become is no longer needy or in need of attention."

Little Katie continued to forge the gateway to her illumination. "Yes, Kate, that *was* you based on, like you said, the experiences you have had. The way you describe how you felt about yourself started because of how you interpreted the messages from your parents, and subsequently, you kept on interpreting the messages from your love interests throughout your past in the same way. Consequently, this diluted your ability to maintain a successful relationship. How? Your beliefs canceled out your intentions."

"What do you mean by intentions?" Kate questioned.

"You have the intention to love, but you also have the need to feel loved, which is an expectation. Intention is pure, untainted by what your heart truly desires. On the other side of that is expectation formed by what the mind perceives to be true and the patterns it forms in your brain to create the scenarios that will fulfill your expectation. You haven't learned how to set an intention and not cloud it with an expectation, because your mind has still not unlearned the old patterns—those patterns that you identified after Football Dick going way back to what your mom told you and how you felt with your dad and your encounter with Disturbing Dick. All you remember is how good it feels to have sex, thereby placing the expectation on repeat, because not only do you like it, but it makes you feel loved. So you revisit it often because you want so much to feel loved. What you truly want is love that comes from the heart. That is your intention—love, not sex.

"However, the problem you encountered with Fitness Dick is that you remained silent and ignored those signs that led you down the same path of loveless relationships, leaving you feeling empty inside. Empty because you give of yourself not just physically but emotionally. You are on the right path to ending the pattern, and you started in the right direction by working on a new, stronger, healthier you. Now you can set the intention to be loved no matter the source. You can find love in any sincere relationship, not just an intimate one. Avoid falling into a sex trap by speaking up when you see the signs that are leading you to fulfill an expectation."

"*Not I get it!* A successful relationship begins by framing it in the mind. First, I have to break the habits that no longer serve the new beliefs I have and then set new ones that do. If I attach an expectation to an intention, then it is a false intention. But how do I do this?"

Little Katie was excited to see Kate's transformation taking place. "Align your thoughts with your intentions. You can start with these new practices:

- ☐ Stay focused on you by staying aware of the signs.
- ☐ Decide what you want and don't compromise.
- ☐ Believe you are worthy and that you deserve better.
- ☐ Lead with love and not the ego.
- ☐ Stop the relationship sooner to avoid the pain later.
- ☐ Speak up and know who you are.

"Kate, the way I see it, you have been a mouse trapped in a lion's cage all your life. You have kept silent about the love you are truly longing for, for too long. Some male figures in your life made you stay small, locked up in your cage without saying a word because of your neediness and lack of confidence. You never felt comfortable to speak up for what you want or don't want."

Kate made another connection. "I don't speak up, because I don't feel worthy of stepping out of my cage. Even when I recognized the signs, I stayed silent because I felt bad and guilty when I said no to a Dick. Either the response from him made me feel like he wasn't taking me seriously, or I felt bad to negate him, and so I continued to stay small and mousey."

"But that was when you believed in your story from the past. You don't anymore, Kate. You have grown from that. The real question now is can you be a lion, step out of your cage, and *roar*? Show everyone, including yourself, who you are. It's time for you to do just that! You said it. It's time to transform."

Little Katie was leading Kate out from the lion's den and into her kingdom. Maybe she was a cub learning how to walk, but she could feel a lioness growing into who she is.

Kate affirmed. "I am willing to roar. I am willing to speak my truth. It has taken me a long time of work and pain to get where I am today. I am still making mistakes, but I am working on myself. I am no longer trapped in a cage. I am no longer afraid to speak up and be transparent and authentic. I am no longer silenced by my guilt. From now on, I will live by a new mantra: set intentions, not expectations."

They headed back to Dickland's enchanted pond to find Prince Dick Charming for what Kate hoped would be the last time. She set the intention to simply love the next toadd she came upon and release any expectations of what her experience should be. Her intentions were strong, but her attachment to the outcome was low. The outcome would not disappoint her, because she had no expectation for one.

Intention comes from my heart, not my ego, she thought.

Little Katie was happy to hear that, but she knew even though Kate had learned to set the intention of love, she now needed to practice it. And with practice came a little more heartbreak and tears. But she had faith Kate would work it out with the next one.

I am now willing to be the lion, and I will roar! Kate said in her mind with conviction.

16

The Long-Distance Dick

BE CAREFUL WHO YOU GIVE YOUR KEY TO

What Kate learned over the years and through the course of her adventures was that a lover does not equal a commitment, and sex does not lead to love. Granted, it wasn't like she had discovered the New World. And while she was no pioneer on the subject of finding the one, having traveled the sea of love, she entered unchartered territory and came across occupied Dicks, abandoned Dicks, and even some war-torn Dicks who earned her the distinction of being an expert on misdirected love and sex—not that she was trying to win a medal for most Dicks explored either. The only reason Kate searched long and wide was to find love, and her quest was still not over. Surely, there was a toadd out there somewhere who was looking for her too. The saying goes, "There is someone for everyone." One thing was for sure: she was *not* going to give up on the love of her life. Kate didn't know yet who he was, but whoever he was, she knew their paths were destined to cross someday.

Kate began with setting an intention to find a toadd who matched her vibration and not an expectation of what she thought she needed. She went back to the enchanted pond with a different mind-set. Her new approach: no sex before being committed to the relationship, and it had to be a two-way street. So far, that particular act of intimacy had been the dagger of death in all her past relationships. Even though she didn't exactly cross that threshold with every Dick, in some way, shape, or form, they had crossed the line of sexual intimacy before becoming committed to one other. Kate came up with the idea that the next toadd she took seriously should be willing to hold out on sex until … *Until what?* she asked herself.

Little Katie interrupted her thoughts. "Yes, Kate, *what* exactly would that be?"

So many times Little Katie had vowed not to interfere and let Kate learn her own lessons, but she couldn't stay quiet for long. And even though Kate tried to shut her out too, she couldn't because only Little Katie knew her to the depth of her soul, and only she knew what Kate needed to hear for her own personal growth. She was Kate's voice of reason. She was her conscious awakening.

Kate wasn't sure how to answer Little Katie's question, but whatever it was that came after *until* was something she intended to figure out. She was at a point where she was letting go of everything that no longer served her. The patterns of past behavior and the so-called lessons she had cut out from them just didn't fit her anymore. Stepping out of her cage and removing her cape of ambivalence, Kate entered the banks of the enchanted pond with pure intentions and no expectations. She vowed only to give love—not sex, love.

"Somewhere out there in that big, wide-open pond there exists a toadd who wants me for who I am inside and not what he sees on the outside," Kate said with pounding determination.

Little Katie encouraged her. "Yes, that's the spirit. But don't bare it all either." She handed Kate a protective cloak for cover. "And remember you don't have to wear your heart on your sleeve in order to give love. Show only what is necessary while you get to know someone."

Staying clear of the horny toadds as she tuned out their loud croaks, Kate was led astray by unusual conversation doused in what sounded like a romantic dialect. Even though she couldn't understand a word of it, she nevertheless followed the echoes. They took her all the way across the pond. She walked for what seemed like ages until she got close enough to realize that this toadd was definitely speaking a foreign language, and a sensual one at that.

"God help me! He speaks the language of love."

"Amen to that, because you're going to need some celestial intervention for this one! He's dreamy, but keep in mind not all that glitters is gold. Even though he has the face of a handsome Zorro, Kate, underneath that mask, I see the face of a heartbreaker."

Kate, however, saw the face of her next adventure.

The handsome Zorro-looking toadd jumped up and down, vying for Kate's attention. She walked over to his lily pad and sat down next to him.

"Hello. I didn't quite catch what you were saying. Could you please repeat yourself?"

"Puedo sostener tu llave?" he said in Spanish.

"Oh, I'm sorry. I don't understand. Would you interpret that for me?"

"May I hold your key?" he said with a wide-brim, open smile.

The true interpretation of that question was not clear to Kate in that moment, although for now, it would be insignificant. She felt a strong, mysterious chemistry between them—a chemistry that ignited something in her beyond the throbbing between her legs. The connection felt far different from anything she had previously experienced. It was as though their frequencies had finally matched up. Everything about his presence made her feel like she could be her natural self. Kate's hope revived.

He leaped into her arms, and off they went into her next adventure.

꽃

Kate met Long-Distance Dick through a mutual friend named Debra. It all began spur of the moment. Debra, who lived in another town, called her up one day out of the blue and asked Kate to visit her. She had planned a fun weekend to include a group of friends and plenty of entertainment.

"Oh, and by the way," she said, "I want to introduce you to someone."

Normally, the old Kate would have jumped on that bandwagon for the sake of meeting a fresh Dick, but she was new-and-improved Kate now. She had adopted a new-fangled way of socializing, which was being okay with flying solo in a group of singles and couples, not depending on anyone to be able to have fun and enjoy herself.

Debra didn't know that Kate was going through a personal transformation, but Kate was up for some spontaneous fun and meeting new people, so she humored Debra to avoid dishing out her Dick version of the Ghost of Christmas Past and all the sordid details of it to her.

"Okay. I'm in." She'd find the right moment to tell Debra what was going on with her, but for now, *no expectations*, she reminded herself.

Even though Kate had visited her before, this time she felt a little out of her comfort zone because she was the outsider being introduced. Everyone else not only already knew one another but spoke a second language. They made their first stop at a restaurant bar where Kate ordered a curative cocktail to alleviate her linguistic insecurities and unwind. She soon got past the language barrier and engaged in the conversation when she could. She was open to making new friends, having a good time, and possibly even learning a new language.

Meanwhile, the person Debra wanted Kate to meet arrived later and conveniently sat in an open seat next to hers. A discomfited feeling came over Kate when Debra introduced her to him. Hot-looking men always made her feel the same way. They exchanged hellos, and she left it at that—no expectations.

After a while of imbibing and chatting, the group collectively decided to go to a place called the Basement. It was a place where a bunch of people were willingly locked in a room to look for clues and keys that would take them into the next room. The goal was to escape all the rooms under a certain amount of time. It wasn't Kate's thing, but she didn't want to be the party pooper, so she reluctantly agreed.

Before starting the maze, the director told them that no phones or purses were allowed inside with them, but they could use the lockers provided. Kate placed her belongings in one of the lockers, but she had no pockets on her where she could stash her key. She worried she would lose it if she held it in her hand, so she was trying to figure out where to put it. As everyone was waiting to enter the first room, Long-Distance Dick came over to her.

"Can I hold your key?" he asked.

Oh my gosh. What a considerate gesture, thought Kate.

"Yes, that'd be great. Thank you!" She was relieved that she didn't have to worry about breaking into the locker if she lost the key.

The doors opened, and Kate grudgingly went through the torture of the Basement. Long-Distance Dick was remarkably into it. Either it was a guy thing, or he was super competitive and wanted to win. Instead, Kate played along a little differently, walking around and pretending to look for clues when in reality she had been stealing glances at his ass—okay … the whole package. Some habits are hard to break.

They only had ninety minutes to find their way out, which felt like the *longest* ninety minutes ever. Everybody seemed to be engrossed and having fun, while Kate was bored and wishing she could go home. When they finally got out of there, everyone wanted to go for another drink except for Kate. She was done. Yes, a part of her did want to be in the company of Long-Distance Dick, but it was nearly midnight, and she was tired and ready to call it a night.

Of course, it didn't quite work out that way for her. Indeed, they all ended up at another restaurant bar, and either by force or by fate, Kate found herself once again sitting next to Long-Distance Dick. She got a case of the jitters—nothing a double shot of Patron Silver couldn't cure.

He lifted an eyebrow when he saw the server hand her the tequila shot. "Wow, I'll take one too," he said.

Kate shook her head and smiled. *Dude, I just want to relax and get through the night*, she thought. Again, no expectations. Bottoms up!

After a few more bottoms up, Kate was feeling revived and sociable. Long-Distance Dick and Kate began with small talk rapport—kids, jobs, hobbies, etc. The bar was nearly closing when they finished their drinks and decided to end the night. There was no telephone number swap, no flirtatious advances, no romantic hint at seeing each other again, and, above all, no expectations—just an inexplicable chemistry that was brewing.

When Kate got in the car with Debra, she wanted to know what Kate thought of him. Kate just told her she thought he was nice. Debra proceeded to give Kate the 411 on him. He'd had a sordid past with relationships.

Ditto, she thought.

The next day Debra invited Long-Distance Dick to a barbecue at her house with his kids. It soon became apparent he was a terrific father—very attentive. Why that would grab Kate's attention is no mystery. He came over to talk to her and shared a little more about his story—twice divorced, one kid from one wife, and one kid from an ex-girlfriend. Normally, this would have raised a red flag, but Kate wasn't expecting anything from him, so she didn't judge.

We all have our stories, and mine was just as harsh as his, she thought.

Again, they ended the night with polite goodbyes—no exchange of phone numbers, no expectations, just a brewing chemistry. Later that same night, Debra sent out a group text to both of them in order to share their contact information.

Kate texted back a breezy, "It was nice to meet you," and left it at that. His response was the same.

The next morning, Kate was on the road early to avoid traffic going home. Her thoughts gravitated toward her new gentleman friend. He'd left quite an impression on her. It was nice to finally meet a guy deserving of being called a gentleman. Kate mulled over the details of their meeting and embraced the newfound feeling of freedom from all the what-ifs and whatnots she usually experienced after meeting someone of the opposite sex.

Within a few days, Kate received an unexpected surprise. Long-Distance Dick texted her to ask if it would be all right for him to call her, because he didn't like texting. She was pleasantly shocked. *Wow, he wants to call and actually speak on the phone? How charming is he?!*

Long-Distance Dick had all the traits of a real Prince Charming, but Kate couldn't let her mind go running wild with her heart just yet. They had long conversations over the phone, and gradually they started to get to know each other a little more each time they spoke. He talked about business quite a bit, which made it sound like he had a lot going on in his life, whereas Kate didn't because she managed to design her life that way. She suspected he might be in the prime of building his career, but it didn't faze her at the time because they weren't jumping into a relationship. They were just talking and getting acquainted, although one thing was clear to Kate—he was adorable in her eyes.

About a month later, Debra invited Kate back out to her house, but this time she told Kate to bring her kids so they could hang out with hers. Kate arranged to bring her daughter along with her. In conversation with Long-Distance Dick, Kate casually mentioned that she would be in his neck of the woods with her daughter visiting her friend. He told Kate he'd meet up with her either at her house or for coffee, but that he definitely wanted to see her.

The first night she was there, he came over to Debra's house for dinner. It was a low-key gathering with adults hanging out and talking, while the kids swam in the pool, so they only had a brief moment to themselves. Even though Kate could feel a connection between them drawing her to him, it was best to keep a lid on the frothing emotions she was feeling. From what she could tell, there was definitely an attraction, but whether it could lead to more was something she had to wait and see.

When Long-Distance Dick left that night, they just nodded goodbyes to each other. As far as Kate was concerned, she would continue on the path of no expectations. Then, later that night, when she and her daughter were getting ready for bed, Kate heard a ping from her phone. It was Long-Distance Dick texting. The sentiment he expressed in his text both surprised her and made her heart skip a beat.

"You've probably heard this many times before, but I just wanted to say how beautiful you looked tonight."

It felt so sincere coming from him, especially because to Kate this Dick was very different from any Dick she'd ever met. Most Dicks tried to woo and seduce her straight off the bat, whereas he was being respectful and chivalrous while allowing the chemistry between them to simmer slowly. Kate decided they were just two people who liked each other. She thanked him and said good night and goodbye because she was set to leave in the morning.

He followed up with another text asking if she'd consider staying one more day. Curious about what he had in mind, her fancy-free self first checked with her daughter to see if she was okay with staying. She agreed happily because it meant she could miss a day of school. Kate confirmed with Long-Distance Dick that they would stay, and he promptly invited them to breakfast the next morning.

The plan was to meet him at his house. What Kate didn't plan on was him having such a stunning home. It was architecturally beautiful and set on enormous grounds surrounded by palm trees and colorful foliage. Inside the home was impeccable. The furnishings looked like a staged home tastefully decorated. Outside in the backyard was a saltwater pool that mirrored a tropical oasis with a built-in rock wall and waterfall. Kate couldn't help admiring how nice it was to meet a single dad capable of taking care of himself and his kids. The only thing she sensed off was that it had an empty feel to it—an absence of warmth she could not explain. The surrounding space echoed as they walked through the almost sterile home. Strangely, the home didn't feel lived in.

After a tour of the house, they went out for a nice breakfast. His kids and her daughter were interacting and laughing while they all enjoyed each other's company. When everyone finished eating, Long-Distance Dick asked them back to his house. Kate didn't hesitate to say yes, because her daughter was enjoying herself as much as she was. Once they got back to his house, he was very cordial, invited them to sit, and told Kate to help herself and her daughter to whatever he had.

"Make yourselves at home," he said.

Kate did, but he didn't. She noticed he was walking around the house doing things that made him look busy. When she concluded that he wasn't going to settle down, she finally asked if he needed help with anything. With that simple gesture, he looked at her as though she had just offered to lift a hundred-pound weight off his back.

"Yes, please," he said, exuding gratitude in his eyes.

Of course, Kate was happy to assist him with odds and ends throughout the day. The sooner he was done, the sooner he could settle so they could hang out and interact more with each other. But Kate was experiencing his normal busy behavior—something she could not have known at the time.

When it got closer to evening, he invited Debra and her family over for dinner. Kate was enjoying the moment, whether it was helping him, talking to the kids, or spending time with everyone around the dinner table. What she couldn't understand, or perhaps wasn't used to, was the space that he was keeping between them similar to the empty space in his home that echoed. Although she couldn't place her finger on what he was echoing through his actions.

Was there anything to his actions? she wondered. *Or am I reading into something that isn't there?* He had, after all, been the one to ask her to stay one more day and spend time with him and his kids. How could she get the wrong message? Then he surprised her again.

Kate walked over to the sauna end of the pool where the kids were playing, and Long-Distance Dick followed her, not noticing until she turned to sit on one of the rocks that he was there putting down a towel for her so she wouldn't get wet.

"Aw, thank you," she gushed. His unexpected attentiveness took her by surprise. *Gosh, he is such a gentleman*, she thought. *How sweet.*

The next few minutes he sat with her talking about their kids and how they seemed to get along. Then he changed the subject, thanking Kate profusely for helping him around the house. Again, it was as though she had hit a home run for his team. He was so happy she had offered and been helpful to him. Before Kate could even say, "You're welcome," his hands gently drew her face close to his, and then he puckered up and planted a quick, sweet kiss on her lips. With that, he got up and made his way back into the house. Kate sat there, head spinning and speechless while her heart fluttered a million beats per second.

What am I supposed to think of that? Again, *no expectations*, her thoughts reminded her. *But what if this guy could be the one?*

Over the next several weeks, Long-Distance Dick and Kate kept in touch nearly every day either by talking on the phone, texting, or emailing. It had been a month since they had last seen each other, and he had given her that unforgettable surprise kiss. He wanted to see her again, but this time they decided he would fly over to her. Kate arranged for a weekend stay at a resort-spa where they could both enjoy a mini vacation with each other and strengthen their relationship. What she didn't want was for him to get the wrong impression that they would be sleeping together. Their relationship was new and maturing, and so far, this long-distance arrangement was going well without complicating it with sex.

One day while they were talking on the phone, Kate asked him, "Are you okay with not sleeping in the same bed together?"

He said without hesitation, "Not a problem. I respect your wishes."

With him, Kate felt like she was opening a present on Christmas Day and finding exactly what she had asked Santa for. He always knew the perfect thing to say, and he always respected her wishes; this time was no different.

Kate could hardly wait to collect him from the airport, and when they saw each other, it was like picking up where they left off. It felt good to be with him again, and she was looking forward to finally spending some time alone together, getting to know what made him tick, and maybe paving the way for a deeper, more meaningful relationship.

Of course, he didn't know what Kate had in mind, because she didn't exactly share those thoughts with him. Men don't read women's minds, which she always tended to forget. He told Kate that he had reached out to a few of his friends and arranged to meet them for dinner. *Oh.* She was slightly disappointed that he had rearranged her picture-perfect weekend. But she had no expectations. She would just be open to receiving and being in the moment.

The moment took another turn when they went to register at the front desk, and she told the receptionist they had a reservation for a double room. After sixty seconds of keyboard ticking and looking at the reservation screen, they were told that the resort had booked all the double rooms, and the only rooms left were with king-size beds.

"What do you mean you're out of double rooms? I made the reservation a week ago!" Kate was about to start arguing. She could feel her stomach churning because she was being led into temptation through no fault of her own. She looked at Long-Distance Dick with a skeptical smile and shrugged.

"Don't worry about a thing," he said calmly. Then turning to the receptionist, he said, "We'll take it."

After checking in and freshening up, they took a cab to the restaurant where they were supposed to meet his friends. Everyone was nice and friendly, and Kate found herself in the moment and simply having a great time. The time drifted by while they enjoyed drinks, amazing food, and interesting conversation. She loved how things turned out so much better when she left worrying out of the picture. She had nothing to fret with him except for maybe a tad bit of ambiguity over what *his* intentions were. During dinner, he kept putting his hand on her leg and sort of rubbing it. It made Kate a little nervous because his touch ignited that throbbing sensation in her. She tried to dismiss it as just a gesture of affection and not an innuendo for sex.

She stopped drinking so that she could contain herself later. They finished dinner and took a cab back to the hotel. The return ride was nerve-racking. Kate felt a strong desire to kiss him in the cab. He kept talking about his friends while she sat as far away from him as she could and pretended to listen.

"Kate, you are in a good place." Little Katie urged, "Try to control yourself."

It was late, and both of them were tired and ready for sleep. Kate could feel some tension in the air once they got into the room. Neither one of them had mentioned anything more about their sleeping arrangements since he'd told her not to worry. She went into the bathroom to change into her pajamas, and all she kept thinking about was how she was going to say no to sex.

We are both adults, and for sure, it's not our first time around the block. There are only two choices here the way I see it. Either I give in to the sexual energy and set flame to the fireworks, or I take the high road and put a pillow in between to keep this long-distance relationship on course.

Kate consulted with her voice of reason. "Little Katie, I don't know how I'm going to shake him off if he comes on to me. I totally like this guy. He's everything in a man I've been looking for: smart, sexy, confident, and well put together. I don't want to mess this up. And if I say no, will he understand? I have a picture of us starting something special, and I don't want to blow it by having sex before being in a committed relationship. At this stage, we're still getting to know each other."

"You could tell him that, Kate. Stay strong and speak your truth," Little Katie encouraged. She too could sense Kate feeling backed into a corner when all she was trying to do was avoid another disaster. But Little Katie had to let her figure this one out and decide for herself just how ready she was to move on to the next level—sex.

Kate could hear the television turn on and felt relieved that he was watching because it would be the perfect distraction. They could talk about the news and then fall asleep. She awkwardly exited the bathroom and walked across the room, trying hard not to be sexy or turn him on, but she felt his eyes following her. The only light in the room was beaming from the television that framed his silhouette under the covers. When she went to climb into bed, he reached over and lifted up the sheets for her.

"Thank you," Kate said, still feeling self-conscious with every move she made.

She didn't want him to know she was nervously shaking, so she snuggled up to the edge of the bed, keeping as much distance between them as possible. As soon as Kate's head hit the pillow, Long-Distance Dick came over to her side and lay himself up next to her. The subtle scent of his cologne accompanied by his strong embrace and his skin against hers felt so good that it transcended Kate into that very moment, making her forget everything she had tried to tell herself to avoid this from happening. She knew she was doomed when he lifted himself over her and reached down to kiss her.

The firm weight of his body on top of hers felt like she had just connected with a lost piece of her. Kate could feel his power against her leg. She felt like a feather as it floated softly through the air slowly drifting with the breeze, undaunted by the thought of where she would land. Growing weaker and weaker wrapped in his arms, she responded to his caresses and kisses.

A thousand miles away, Kate could hear Little Katie. "Don't do this. It never ends well."

But Kate could no longer resist the soft touch of his lips, his tongue enfolding hers, and the tender way he felt her body. Kate heard herself moan in pleasure as he reached between her legs and stroked her energy. She knew there was no going back.

In an act of confirmation, catching her breath, Kate asked, "Are we really going to do this?"

"I want to surrender to you … I want to breathe you … I want to make love to you." He couldn't have said it more romantically with his sexy, longing voice. There was no escaping the moment and no reason for her to want to escape. She let go completely.

They carried on, exploring each other with their hands and fingers, lips kissing parts in ways they had not been kissed before, bodies molding into one another as they moved in sync with pleasure, each of them giving and satisfying the other for what felt like hours. Making love to him for the first time was so pure, so enigmatic, so natural, so beautiful, and poles apart from any past first-time lovemaking Kate could remember. In her soul, she knew that neither one of them had experienced this connection in such a long time. It was magical for her, and she could not get enough.

Once they came up for air, he continued to romance her with his words.

"Kate, you are such a great kisser and lover, so sexy and beautiful."

She began to panic a little bit. Kate had heard these same words from other Dicks, and part of her wanted to shield herself from them for fear they would morph into painful bee stings—words that sounded like honey but later left a burning wound.

She lay in his arms, recapping the evening. Sex was her Achilles' heel, and she was disappointed in herself for jumping into it. She could hear them coming—the berating thoughts to herself about what she had just done when all of a sudden, like a breath of fresh air, he said to her, "What happens if I fall in love with you?"

Love, she thought. Goose bumps crawled through her skin. She hadn't said the word *love* to anyone in years … well, except her children. And now he was saying it to her—well, sort of. Kate kept silent.

He said he was so happy. She kept silent.

He said making love to her was ecstasy. She kept silent.

Why can't I speak? There is nothing wrong with the things he's saying to me. Why am I afraid to say I too could be falling in love again? Again? Oh no, Kate thought. *Here I go again!*

"Kate, I don't think we've ever truly been in love." Little Katie came to her aid.

"What is love? What does love feel like then, Little Katie?"

"Ask Long-Distance Dick what he thinks it is, because maybe it means something different for a man than it does for a woman?"

So Kate asked him what love meant to him, and he said, "Love is respecting and being committed to one another. Once you have these two things on board, then the other things, such as honesty and trust, just fall into place."

She heard what he said, but compared to Kate's definition of love, it sounded nebulous. For Kate, love meant intimacy—a feeling of deep intimacy bound by unconditional love and no judgment. As for honesty and trust, they were the foundation of respect and commitment. She wasn't disproving or critiquing his definition of love. She simply defined it differently—just as Little Katie had hinted she would.

However, Little Katie proposed to observe it from another point of view before jumping into love.

"I think you should look at love from a place of loving yourself first. The reason we have not fallen in love is because you've been looking for it in someone else and giving your love to them with the expectation of receiving it in return. Your happiness does not lie in the hands of someone else, and neither does love. You have been searching for love outside of yourself, Kate, and that's why you've not found it.

"What if, instead, you look inward for that intimacy, acceptance, and unconditional love without judging yourself? Be completely happy with yourself and by yourself. Then when a man comes into your life, you will be capable of holding your own, satisfied whether you are with or without him. You started this adventure with the right intention of not introducing sex too soon. But because you didn't take the road less traveled, now you face the frightening possibility of walking down an old path unless you harness this lesson now. It's not too late to get back on course as long as you're willing to acknowledge that this relationship is not *the one* because you're still learning to define what true love is."

Everything Little Kate told her was fine and dandy, but there was one problem. Kate had drunk love's potion. She was in Wonderland with Long-Distance Dick, and she had this sensation of overwhelming euphoria. Even though she understood what Little Katie was explaining, she believed she was in the right place with herself. She did love herself, and she was excited that she could give love to him like she never had loved before.

"Yes, you are getting there, but there is just one more crucial lesson you need to learn before you understand real love," Little Katie declared.

The weekend ended, and Kate was riding unicorns with Long-Distance Dick at her side. They were on a high for each other—on top of the world. Kate embraced every moment.

※

Their relationship unequivocally blossomed that night they spent together, but it would soon hit a stunt in growth.

Since the day they parted, they spoke, wrote, or messaged each other as much as time allowed, always anticipating the next time they'd be together. The saying "distance makes the heart grow fonder" is a double-edged sword. Yes, they were longing for one another and holding onto the memories they had made, but on the other hand, time had a way of fading memories as well, and life carried on, filling the void with routines and responsibilities. They tried to sustain their relationship by connecting and communicating as much as possible, but the distance between them was taking its toll on both of them. The tank was running low on fuel, and it became apparent the day Long-Distance Dick sent Kate a distressed message.

"I miss you so much it hurts." His yearning sentiment was like a plunge to her heart. She missed him too. Although her schedule was to go to see him in a few weeks' time, instead of waiting she decided right then and there to allay his restless heart, as well as hers. She had the following day free without her kids, so she told him, "I could fly out for the day to be with you, if that's okay with you?"

She got an ecstatic welcoming reception from him when he said he would love it if she did and again when he saw her twenty-four hours later. They spent another memorable and, if possible, even more magical day together than the time before. He cleared his schedule to be with her and made her feel like his top priority. They couldn't get enough of one other being in each other's company, holding each other, making love countless times, and cherishing their time together.

But then something happened the next morning that Kate couldn't put her finger on. He woke up early with her for one more time of blissful intimacy before it was time to catch her flight. After making love, Kate showered and got ready to go. Meanwhile, Long-Distance Dick stayed in bed to get a few more z's in. She wanted to give him a long-lasting smooch goodbye so they could store it in their memory bank until the next time, but he just gave her a quick kiss, rolled over, and shut his eyes. He didn't even walk her down to the Uber. Something wasn't quite right in that moment, but it would remain a mystery.

Little Katie picked up on his lack of propriety and knew Kate was bothered by it. "Why didn't you ask him to walk you down to the car?"

"It is not my place to have to remind him what the proper etiquette is in this situation. Besides, it goes without saying. Here I am, leaving at the break of dawn to catch a flight after visiting him on a whim because he missed me—okay, I missed him too. But why should he need coaxing to walk me to the car and see me off? Especially since most of the time he doesn't need to take any cues from me."

"Is it possible you're making assumptions that he should know what the appropriate protocol is in this situation?"

"Maybe I am. Okay, I'm not going to make a big deal about it."

Kate decided to drop it and give him the benefit of the doubt because he only had a few hours of sleep left before having to get up again for work. Rather, she focused on feeling elated from having spent the past twenty-four hours with him. She felt so happy with the direction their relationship was headed. She decided that she was all in. She wanted to give him all of her. Kate would show him the kind of love she was capable of giving.

"He makes me feel like I have never felt before with a man."

Little Katie was quick to pick up on the third-party reference she made to how *he* makes her feel. "Kate, he does not *make* you feel any such way or any such thing. *You* are responsible for how you allow yourself to feel. And while it is a nice change to see you so loving and giving toward someone, by the same token, you should be so loving and giving to yourself first and foremost."

Little Katie didn't want Kate to have to check into the Heartbreak Hotel on her next visit to see Long-Distance Dick, and so she raised a couple of those red flags that usually warned Kate of the dead-end road she might be heading toward. Kate was already giving him the benefit of the doubt—something she was quick to do and that always led to her regrettable patterns.

"I don't want to have to point out the past to you again, Kate, but you are at a crossroad here," Little Katie warned.

"I know you're looking out for me, and I don't want to get hurt either, but in my heart, I know he undeniably is a different breed of toadd."

Little Katie could see some favorable differences between Long-Distance Dick and the past Dicks Kate had been involved with. She also knew there was something not jiving with him, but Kate was already madly in love, and in that state, she wouldn't even know where to begin to demystify *where*, *what*, *how*, and *why* she was like this for him.

"He lives several states away. How is it possible to totally know someone by only seeing them a few weekends out of the month? It's hard enough being able to figure out someone who you do see frequently," Little Katie pointed out.

"Because we're both occupied with work and kids, so the arrangement, for now, gives us the space we need to juggle home, work, and love life. He pursued me, and I know he has genuine feelings and good intentions. I'm willing to make it work at any cost for me to be able to feel this way about someone. He's worth it to me."

There it was. She said it—to Little Katie and herself. She was willing to go the extra mile for Long-Distance Dick. Funny enough, she already was.

"But are you worth it to him?" asked Little Katie.

Little Katie's rhetoric, though well-meaning, stung Kate to her core—to imply that he didn't think enough of her. Kate believed she was worth it to him; otherwise, he wouldn't be making the effort for her. Little Katie urged Kate to seek clarification from him. She could already see Kate start to lose a part of herself, as well as her power, which they had worked so hard to achieve.

The holiday season was approaching, and Kate was moved to do something extra special for him, something she had never considered doing before—not even for her ex-husband. Long-Distance Dick was bringing out a version of Kate that not even she recognized, but she loved it. She was daring and brave because of the love she felt. No other man had ever elicited these qualities in her.

Love letters starting pouring out of Kate. She wanted him to know how he would light up her life every single day. Her idea was to pen him one love letter a day up until the day they met again and wrap them up accompanied with pictures of her—professional boudoir photos. The love-inspired gift to him was *her*, in portrait and in words that spoke volumes of how she felt for him so that when he would be missing her, he could connect with Kate by way of this gift.

"Oh, Kate, that sounds nice, but what is he doing for you? He's doing nicely, receiving love at every level from you, but I don't see him taking action to reciprocate it. You said you wanted this adventure to be a two-way street. Instead, the direction you are headed in, again, is that single lane where the traffic is one-sided and with a tollbooth to boot. I'm afraid you're going to end up paying that hefty toll all on your own."

Choosing to ignore Little Katie, she just kept basking in love's glow, filling up on every moment she had with him. She imagined he would be swept away by her thoughtful gift and would inevitably fall in love with her.

"We'll see about that," said Little Katie in a doubtful tone.

Kate had already given Long-Distance Dick a love letter and had received an encouraging response from him that made her feel she was, in fact, on a two-way street:

Naughty and Nice:

I wonder what you are thinking when you see me. I don't know whether it is naughty or nice. But I do know I can feel your energy, your charge. When I catch you looking at me, or you kiss my hand, my lips, and hold me in your arms, I feel a part of you flow right through me. You and I are lovers. You want me. And it's no mistake. You are driven by your desires for me. Your passion burns, setting off my racing heart whenever you are ready for me. I crave you. I burn for you, looking forward to the day we are together again—to be touched by your strong presence that makes me feel like a beautiful, desired woman. I want you to know that I willingly reciprocate and wish to delight you like the deserving man that you are.

xoxo Kate

He responded with "60% nice, 40% naughty, 100% into you."

"See, Little Katie. He is into me," Kate relished.

She counted the days until she would see Long-Distance Dick again to surprise him with the gift of love letters and boudoir pictures. She personally wrapped the gift with lots of thought, tied with pretty black lace and arranged in an adorned wooden lockbox. The presentation was just as important as its contents. She couldn't wait to see the expression in his eyes when he opened it. She anticipated a magical weekend like the ones before.

Then, two days before Kate's scheduled flight, he told her they needed to talk. The telephone conversation knocked her sideways. She heard carefully what he had to say. As it became clear what he was saying, the words felt like bitter cough syrup going straight down into her empty gut.

"I am having a party at my house on Saturday night, and even though I want you here, I am not ready to tell anyone about us. And I'll probably have people stay over if they're drinking too much. Could you stay with Debra for the weekend?"

Kate's heart plummeted. Her magical illusion of spending the weekend with him, giving him *her* gift, and loving on him was shattered. The fact that he wasn't ready to tell people about their relationship was what caught her off guard more than the rest of what he said. It meant that she had to keep her distance from him in front of everyone. The distance between them now was more than she could bear at times, and she thought he felt the same way.

All she could think about was how she had spent so much time writing the love letters, booking the boudoir shooting at the last minute, begging them to take her even though they were booked to capacity, and then having the pictures developed express so she could get them in time for her trip. Kate was doing everything she could to demonstrate how much love she had for him, but now he was saying he had to hide her.

Her knee-jerk reaction was to reply, "I don't have to come out this weekend. We can do it another time."

"No, don't take it that way, Kate. I still want you to come. You planned it and have your flight scheduled." He reassured her he still wanted her to come that weekend.

There was no other way for Kate to feel except for hurt by his censorship of their relationship. Negative self-talk started to swirl around in her mind. *Is he not that into me? Is he embarrassed to be seen with me? What did I do to make him have this change of heart?* Me. Me. Me. She kept putting herself down as the one to blame for his actions.

That weekend would mark a big eye-opener for Kate. Her first night there she expected him to be distracted by all the party planning, but what she didn't expect was his blatant reaction to the present she gave him. When she handed it to him, he never remarked on the wrapping. When he opened it, he never remarked on the lacy details. When he saw it, he hesitated to remark what he thought of it.

"I love it," he finally said plain and dry.

Kate tried to believe his sincerity, but it was not the reaction she had built her hopes up for. Next, he carelessly threw the pictures back into the box with the collection of love letters that he had barely glanced over, locked the box, and stashed it in the hideaway drawer of his nightstand. Later, Kate would find it symbolic that he had found a secret compartment for her gift just like the invisible secret compartment he was keeping her in.

So far, it seems Kate had failed to make an impact with the gift of *her*, and the weekend was just getting started. They ended the night making love, but even the impact of their lovemaking felt more like a middle-of-the-night intimate encounter than the usual transcendent religious experience she had become accustomed to. She put his strange behavior down to his mind being occupied with all the party planning.

Then came the actual night of the party, which Kate was less than enthused about attending. She should have paid attention to her intuition and Little Katie and just stayed home. She got about as much attention from him as a dead plant. He asked her to keep their relationship on the down low, so as he wished, Kate hung around outdoors in the backyard most of the night. She kept her distance and acted as though she was fine with having to be hidden.

She checked in with Little Katie. "This is only temporary. We won't be like this forever. We are in a fairly new relationship, and contending with being in a long-distance one at that. After all, it's not like we've made a solid commitment to one other yet. Do you agree, Little Katie?"

"Kate, if he was really that into you, he would have introduced you at least as a friend."

The weekend continued with him being distracted and Kate longing for the same time and attention that he had given her before. She saw him retract a bit, but she was not going to give up just yet. She had gone into the relationship with no expectations, but the love she found with him was boundless, and all she wanted was to shout it from the top of a roof. He, on the contrary, and much to Kate's disappointment, had displayed some reservation and hesitation about exposing them as a couple. She reactively put her guard up, although she still left the holiday lights switched on to their relationship even though it felt like the festivities were over.

They managed to get through the holidays communicating yet missing each other, but when New Year's Eve came around, it became difficult for Kate again. They spent it apart because he said he wasn't feeling well. Trying to make the best of it, she went over to a friend's house to ring in the New Year. She was the only single person there. Even though she was used to being single and hanging out with her married friends, it didn't sit well with Kate, because she was in a relationship and felt like she was missing out on something special by not being with him.

When midnight hit, Kate was left sipping champagne alone and watching her coupled friends and their kids hug and kiss. She made up her mind in that moment that she wasn't going to spend next New Year's Eve alone. With that, came her decision to break it down to Long-Distance Dick and tell him exactly how she felt—no more hiding her and no more lonely holidays.

But in a sporadic turn of events and perhaps a rare alignment of the stars, they both decided that they wanted to fall madly in love with each other and would try to make this work. Instead of him backing away from Kate, he asked if she would consider moving in with him. This was all she could ever want—to be with him and share their world, possibly create their own perfect world. Kate started building a new illusion and figuring out how it would work out.

Little Katie could see the snags in the veil of Kate's illusions. "Kate, a minute ago you were considering breaking up for very valid reasons, and now, with one phone call and in one heartbeat, you're thinking of moving in with him. Where is he even coming from? Neither you nor he is making sense. Listen to your intuition; it's not fickle like he is. Your relationship is still not established, yet you're talking about sharing everything from the down comforter to the bathroom? Don't let yourself run away with this illusion, Kate."

Long-Distance Dick and Kate left it on the table to discuss another time.

The following month was virtually impossible for them to get together because his schedule was booked with business commitments. She also had work meetings out of town, but she wanted to stretch her efforts to keep in touch with him as much as possible, while he started to contact her less and less. The distance began to feel like the sun setting on their relationship. It became more apparent whenever she would text him and not get a response for a full day when not long ago he was quick to answer.

On one particularly tough day, Kate tried to reach him because the mere sound of his voice was all she needed to lift her spirits, but he didn't answer. She tried a couple more times throughout the day—still nothing. Before heading to bed that night, Kate thought to try him one more time. Finally, she got a response: "At concert." That was it. After that, he went radio dark, leaving her in the dark as well. No reason, no answer, no explanation. Nada.

There was a reason why people shouldn't have expectations—so they can't be let down. Kate wasn't expecting a whole lot. She only wanted a few minutes of his time to talk about their days and hear his comforting voice, which was like her medicine for a bad cold on days like these. But he didn't know what she was expecting and, essentially, set her aside so he could enjoy his concert.

I would've understood if he hadn't kept me in the dark and spared me more than two words, thought Kate. She felt bad to have been on the receiving end of a rude text message and couldn't help but think something was going on. *Last month he wanted me to move in with him, and now it's apparent he is pushing me away.*

She wanted answers from him, so the next day she sent him a text asking him to please call her. It took him a while to call, as she predicted. When he mustered enough courage, or perhaps decency, to finally return her call, it went down short and bitter:

"I don't have time for you. You are low priority in my life … I don't know what else to tell you."

Sudden death was the best way to describe what Kate felt in that moment. She couldn't believe what she was hearing. In an instant, her world came crashing down, leaving a hollow feeling in her chest where her heart was. She was devastated. All she could think about was how she had put her heart on her sleeve for this man, and he just kicked her to the curb undeservingly of any explanation.

Ending the call, Kate tried not to think about the bomb he'd dropped by distracting herself with work. Except when a million pieces of your heart are tearing you apart like shrapnel, it's hard to stop the stream of tears trying to wash away the pain.

Kate had to understand what prompted this, or she wouldn't be able to pull herself together. She chose to write him an email in a space of love because she wanted to remain committed not only to loving him but to love itself.

> Dearest Dick,
>
> Our last conversation was difficult for me. I just want to say that I know you are so busy, which has made it hard to connect with you over the past month so I thought this would be a better way to communicate and tell you what is on my mind.
>
> I see something has happened here, and it demands attention from me because, you see, I felt like I was in a relationship with you and you with me. While I am aware you are maxed out with your time in terms of work and the commitments you have are stressful enough without having to tend to our relationship, please understand that I don't want to add to your stress. I want to be the one who alleviates your stress and brings you peace when you need it.
>
> Being with you, I discovered an enormous capacity to love. I feel like I uncovered something very special in you—a gift to my existence. Awakening that inside of me was like finding the person who held the key to my heart. It's YOU. I believed you had similar feelings toward me.
>
> As time has gone on, we've been back and forth, trying to make it work, but now all I see is you having less and less time for me in your life. I, in contrast to you, am capable of defying the time against us by finding ways to bring us closer together. But I feel like the waves are drifting you away from me.

Perhaps we are not meeting the needs we both want as it stands, but I think we could find a way to bridge our relationship so we can find ourselves back to one another when the timing is better. Just because the tide has rolled out on our relationship doesn't mean we cannot wait for the tide to come back in. If we can accept that this is where we are and allow it without losing touch or closing the book to our story, we can keep it bookmarked to be continued.

For me, as I cannot speak for you, I look at our precious time together as a blessing that you opened up a beautiful space for me in your life to experience each other like we have. I have learned so much about myself being with you—most importantly, that I could fall in love again.

Feeling your presence and your energy is like Sunday worship for my soul. I have never had these feelings for anyone, mentally or physically, and now I know that this was meant to be reserved for you. Thank you for that.

I love everything about you … I think the world of you … I care so deeply for you. Know that I only want the best for you. With all that being said, do what you need to do, and if time permits in the future, we will be together again.

I quote you when I say, "We'll just leave it in God's hands."

xoxo Kate

As soon as Kate hit send, she felt a peaceful release. It wasn't closure or an ending; it was a mode of healing and a window to hope. Her words must have awakened Long-Distance Dick to realize they had something special between them because his response was to call her almost immediately.

"Kate, I am so sorry I hurt your feelings. I didn't mean to say that you are low priority in my life. I don't roll like that. I'm not that guy. The thing is whenever I've been in a relationship, the order of my life in terms of priority is God, relationship, kids, family, and then work. I don't want to bookmark our relationship just yet."

His words were the answer to her prayers. She resurrected in that moment. Her heart returned to its rightful place and started beating again.

They talked and worked through some of the kinks, and Kate came up with the brilliant suggestion that they try to make their relationship more of a casual one, casual in the sense that when she was in town or when he was in town they would see each other. No strings attached.

My boundless love for him can easily handle this, she thought. Kate was following the paraphrased saying of wisdom: "Let it go, and if it comes back to you, it was meant for you. If it doesn't, it was never was yours in the first place."

The point Kate missed was that instead of working toward a committed relationship like she had wanted in the first place, she was actually creating more distance between them emotionally. It didn't take long for her to realize she had bitten off more than she could chew. Kate was pretending to be okay with this arrangement while hurting inside.

Little Katie swooped in and gave it to her straight, while at the same time giving her strength. "This relationship is like watching two grown-ups on a teeter-totter—up and down. Neither of you enjoys the imbalance. You might be on a two-way street right now, but you've just lifted the brakes, and you're bound to lose control only to end up in a head-on collision. You deserve to be in a relationship of mutual appreciation and desire, not be fed morsels of love whenever he finds time to chuck some your way."

Kate knew Little Katie was right. She was settling for less than she deserved and, in turn, was suffering from the pain of holding it all together. She decided she had to end it and release herself from further pain and destruction, so Kate wrote him another email since the first one had gotten a far better response than any other form of communication.

> Dearest Dick,
>
> I want you to know that I am coming to you from a place of compassion and understanding of where you find yourself at this time. I didn't reach out to you sooner because it hurts me to address our failing relationship as

much as it must hurt you. And, of course, it's challenging to get you on the phone. So email it is …

First, I want to let you know that I spoke to someone recently in an effort to sort out how it is that two people like us, who really want to be together, are not able to make it work. What she told me was eye-opening.

Apparently, we've attracted each other because we share a similar trait that we fear and need to overcome—in our case, that trait is lack. We both lack something in a specific area of our lives that we are not fixing, thereby creating a hazardous zone. So analyzing this on my own, I came up with your lack is possibly time, and my lack is safety and security.

Looking at it from my point of view, what this means is I am sitting in fear of a relationship, just like ours, not working out, which, of course, stems from my absent-dad syndrome when I was growing up. So I may have either come off too strong or needy or both. (Ugh, and if that is the case, then I am so sorry because I know that must be repelling.)

What is wonderful about this discovery for me is now I know in my heart that I am safe and secure because I can take care of myself. My life has been a great discovery of the patterns I have forged in most all my relationships, and I've had to face that I was going through the motions of old patterns once again.

So I do not want you to feel guilty that you failed me, because you did not. You have always been upfront and honest about what you want. I have been afraid of being honest with myself and you about what I wanted for fear of what the answer from you would be—to not have time to give me what I want.

Now I can say without fear that all I wanted were two things from you: your love and your time to love me. Even though we shared some beautiful moments of love and passion, our relationship was being starved in the time between.

But I also understand that you don't have the capacity at this moment to have another draw on your heart. I hope you will understand that it is a big disservice to me when I want to share more with you, but you can't get past certain things, and I can't continue like this. I don't want to starve for you anymore—a relationship takes two to be nourished.

I'm happy that I got to know how you feel about me and especially that I was able to let you know how I feel about you with love notes and my actions toward you. I think you are an amazing man who deserves all the love and respect unimaginable, and I hope I was able to give that experience to you.

Know that even though you had a fear of depositing more time into your love life, that you were still able to attract someone like me. That's a good thing because I know a good man when I see one.

So with everything said and done, I have surrendered to *us* having been a wonderful moment in my life being fully present in love in a manner I have never shown before, and I am thankful that it was you who was the vehicle for my true love. Thank you for being open to me and all I had to offer.

I have weathered the worst of this storm, and I am a much better person because of you. I guess that leaves God and Father Time to decide what comes next. But for now, know that you can reach out to me anytime. After all, I am forever your friend. I am sure our paths will cross again. I only want the best for you.

xoxo Kate

Much like the first email, Kate's words must have made an impact on him. Long-Distance Dick called her later that day to discuss her letter.

She thought she had been pretty clear that they were done—case closed. But much to her surprise, he reopened their case by expressing the exact opposite of what she had written.

Kate's heart jumped back into the passenger seat—again.

"Do you love me?" Long-Distance Dick asked her.

"Yes, of course I do, silly. Didn't you read my letter?" Kate confirmed with excitement.

He had lowered the bridge to pave the way for them once again.

Kate paid him a visit, and they proclaimed their love for one another. The caveat was that they would still keep their relationship casual. *I have his love now, so what more did I want?* she thought. The truth: she wanted to change his mind. If she could hold on to his love for her if even by a string, she had one last-ditch effort to try to convince him to change his mind about them being causal.

Last-ditch effort … Yes, Kate was becoming desperate, resorting to what she knew best—*sex*. She just had to show him how good they could be as a couple. One more weekend spent with her, and he'd have no doubt how much their relationship was worth and want to shift gear from casual to commitment. She was worth it.

Kate was in a good place when Long-Distance Dick came into her life, and the way he proclaimed his love and desire for her was sincere and heartfelt. Then, whenever he pulled away, Kate allowed feelings of self-doubt to flood her thoughts; she'd lose her confidence and turn to sex as a crutch to support her. Here she was, hanging on for dear life to love, but at the same time wanting to give it freedom, hoping it would come back to her. He obviously failed to interpret what she meant because what happened next would transform everything Kate knew about love … and in a twist of fate become her saving grace.

This time Debra had a party at her house, and Kate was to see Long-Distance Dick there. It was getting late, and the anticipation was getting to be too much for her. He hadn't reached out to her, and she had no idea what was keeping him. He finally showed up much later. Their encounter was nothing short of awkward.

He said, "Hi there," and gave her a quick kiss on the cheek. That was the extent of contact between them, and they both ended up talking to other people for a good portion of the night.

After a few drinks, desperation started to well up inside of Kate. There was so much she wanted to say and do to him. She wanted to tell him exactly how she felt. She wanted to take him into the bedroom where they could be alone. She wanted to kiss him and make love to him like they did in the beginning of the relationship. Instead, she held back and played his game for as long as she could take it. Kate felt like a lion trapped in a cage. Finally, unable to restrain herself, she ripped through the party crowd to find him and spoke her truth. Her outcry took Long-Distance Dick aback.

"You aren't thinking of me when you act like this toward me. You tell me one thing, and then you do the opposite. Why are you ignoring me?" Kate asked him in desperation.

Then he asked, "What exactly do you want?"

Kate felt like a two-year-old in a candy store. She wanted every sweet in the shop but was being told she couldn't have any of it. She couldn't speak. She had no words to express herself in that moment, because if she opened her mouth, it would have come out like a tantrum. The fear of losing him paralyzed her.

Kate forced a brave smile, took hold of his hand, and squeezed it gently before walking away as tears clouded her eyes. He left the party not bothering to find her. He told Debra to say goodbye to her for him. The next morning, Kate was a bit more clear-headed in answer to his question, so she sent him another email.

> Dearest Dick,
>
> Hello, my love. Last night you asked me what I wanted. I was not expecting that question and didn't have the right words to express what I truly want. But I've had a chance to do some soul-searching, so here it is …
>
> The man I want:
>
> I have a man who has come into my life who is everything I am looking for. A man who sees me for who I am, what I love, and what I want to create in this Universe. He respects, supports, and encourages my calling in this world, which is a desire to help women globally, and he encourages me to keep growing so I can help others grow.

We both support each other in anything we do. We both have our respective careers, but we support one another's success. He adores me, and we have a strong friendship. He loves me unconditionally, is fully committed to me, and has eyes only for me. He's trustworthy, kind, funny, and makes me laugh when I get too serious. He is compassionate and passionate toward me. We also have a strong chemistry. He displays a very strong libido and craves me often. He is available for me whenever I need him. He communicates to me often with authenticity and honesty. We both can do magical things together even when we are not together. And when we are not together, it is okay, we have a strong bond between us of security and safety. We travel together to reconnect and bond. We have a lot of fun, and while we do work at maintaining our relationship, it is no effort at all. We also are active and keep healthy so we can enjoy each other for many years to come. We place each other first after God, and we are both in alignment with our spirituality. He is my partner in life, my source of loving energy, and the light that shines within me.

I am madly in love with you.

xoxo Kate

The message he wrote back in response simply said, "I'm flattered at how highly you think of me and us."

Someone had evidently gotten confused. Everything Kate wrote about was a fantasy she had of him and her. Yet, he did not make the distinction that she was describing the man she wanted even though she had written it clearly in the headline: "The Man I Want."

Kate thought about it, and all she had wanted was *that* exactly with him, and she tried desperately to create a happily ever after with him. Then suddenly, she wasn't sure he was capable of being *that* man for her.

Little Katie pointed out to her how her Fairy Tale List was evolving and changing with each adventure, and in doing so, she would begin to recognize that her love for Long-Distance Dick would too.

"I see," Kate said sadly, filled with the disappointment of what she was witnessing.

Long-Distance Dick decided that he didn't want a long-distance relationship. She understood what he was saying, but she didn't want to believe him. He said it hurt him too much. Kate held on to the notion that she could sex away his pain and continue to be there for him. It was what she wanted. But Long-Distance Dick also knew exactly what he wanted, and it was *not* a long-distance relationship with her.

Kate could see she was losing the battle, but she would make one more attempt. They had one last night together at his house after she sent him the letter to talk about their relationship. It was time to implement her last-ditch effort. She couldn't let him walk out of her life without fighting for the *us* she held on to. It was then that her loving intentions turned into desperate expectations. She stepped out of her lion's cage and spoke her truth, but it came at a cost.

She had a wee bit of liquid courage to anesthetize the hurt so she could face him over the pain she had been feeling the past several months. Climbing onto his lap and straddling him while fighting the urge and desire to kiss and make love to him, she gave voice to her pain instead and began to share the desires of her soul.

"I want you, and I want us to be together. We can be good if you would be willing to fight for us. Everything I wrote about in that email was the man I want, and I see in you that man. Don't shut me out, please. I know you care about me, and I know you love me. Why don't you open your eyes to see what I am offering you?"

He proceeded to silence her by repeating the same mantra he had many times before: "I *do not* have time for you in my life."

He said it to her with such conviction that Kate lost control and broke down in tears as she sat straddled on his lap facing him. His words cut through her like a knife. As Kate felt the sting of the deep wound he had just inflicted upon her, she cried, begging him to listen.

He silenced her again. "You're attacking me!" he accused. "All you're seeing is red, and I'm done talking about this. I'm tired and want to go to bed." He turned to walk away from her.

"Attacking? Is that what you call me wanting to love you?" she said with her voice cracking, choking from the tears.

She was devastated and could not see straight, not because she was seeing red in anger, but because she was bleeding red from having had her heart cut out. She couldn't bear to be in his presence one moment longer. She felt humiliated. She felt sick to her stomach. She couldn't breathe. She needed to flee from his spell that she was under.

Kate ran out of the house and called an Uber to pick her up and take her to her friend's house. She sat on the curbside waiting, crying. She searched for some tissue in her purse to clean herself up before the car arrived but couldn't find any. Kate quickly ran back to the house to grab some, but the door was stuck. She kept trying to turn the doorknob, but it wouldn't open. She finally realized the door had a lock on it. Yes, he locked her out of his house. It was the final blow.

There she stood in front of the door, lights out, door locked, sobbing, and kicked to the curb. *He is done*, she thought. She couldn't believe he left her outside late at night, crying and waiting for a stranger to pick her up. Again, her expectation was that he would come outside, carry her back into the house, and want to talk and fix things.

All I wanted was to love you and be with you, Kate thought as she walked away from the locked door, making her way back to the curb, head hanging low. She had failed to get him to see the picture she had visualized of them together as a couple.

This was a pivotal moment for Kate because instead of using sex to fight her battle for love, she had used her voice to stand up for what she wanted. The next morning she was still in a state of shock. Her heart was demolished beyond repair, but as the lioness that she was, she had to speak her truth again. So, she stepped out of her cage and wrote Long-Distance Dick a final email.

Dearest Dick,

Because I did not have a fighting chance last night …

It is not fair for you to be dismissive to me. I have always come to you from a space of love. My honesty toward you was never meant to be an attack, and I apologize if I hurt your feelings.

I'd like to say what I was not given a chance to say to you that night. I notice how you shut down immediately whenever I reveal something about your character. You don't give me a chance to explain what I see or why it matters. Part of any relationship, whether commitment or casual, is giving one another a platform to communicate and helping each other grow and learn from our faults; and when issues come to the surface, then we work through them to find a solution.

I always gave you the opportunity to speak up about what you wanted, but whenever I tried to do the same, you would tell me you didn't have time to deal with it and run from me. At the end of the day, what I am saying to you is that I want the opportunity to be seen and heard as well.

Do you know that all I ever wanted to do was to treat you like the well-deserving man you are? But you wouldn't let me. Maybe you didn't feel worthy of what I was willing to offer you. I'm here to say that you are worthy. My only downfall was that I wanted love from you in return even though you might not have the capacity to love on a level such as mine for whatever reasons you have, and that's okay. I was willing to patiently wait for you to open up to that possibility.

Your constant push/pull of my heart was not fair to me, and it wasn't fair for you to categorize us as a "casual relationship." If ours was a casual relationship, then why would you spend as much time with me as you did? I realize you had to move mountains to be with me this weekend, and I so appreciated every minute we had, which is why I cannot believe you thought this was casual. You even said yourself that "it is not about sex, Kate."

You know as well as I do that this was not causal. Yes, I said let's be lovers after you told me months ago that you had no time for me. But you also strung me along by telling me that you did not think "this chapter was over." So with that out on the table, it left me thinking that I had a modicum of opportunity with you. And it didn't help that you kept calling and texting me. You have a unique way of keeping it casual.

I held back a lot of my feelings for fear of how you would react and, more importantly, for fear of losing you. It was a way to protect myself from another broken heart. Although, how could you forget the conversations when we expressed our love for one another? I had to wonder if you had fallen and bumped your head along the way and got amnesia.

Whatever I said to trigger you last night, I apologize. I just want you to know that it was not meant to hurt you, only love you. My tears were from the frustration of you silencing me. I sat outside and waited for my ride because you made it clear you did not want me. Why would I want to be in your presence if you did not want to be with me?

But this morning, I believe in my heart that is not true. You were just hurting too. I know you love me, and it is a hard emotion for you to handle. Now we are both hurting when instead we could have been making love, knowing we have to steal moments in time to be together.

I don't enjoy always having to write out my feelings and send them to you. I would rather talk with you in person so you can't hide. But I hope with this letter you may have an understanding, a clearer picture of why we both hung on to the hope of making our relationship a committed reality, and it was not just an illusion of fantasy you escaped from.

Now that I have spoken my truth to you, please don't try to escape from the sincerity of my words. One day you will appreciate all I am as a woman. Above all, I truly hope you find what you are looking for. Mucho amor para ti.

xoxo Kate

His response came back to Kate via a text:
"I never misrepresented myself in this. You should have never offered

a 'casual relationship' if you were not serious. You don't live in reality. But I really wish you the best. I hope you believe that to be true."

Kate's eyes practically came out of her sockets when she read it.

"Wow, what a *Dick*!"

Little Katie put in her two cents. "Wow, spoken like a true *Oxymoron Dick*!"

※

Kate had given Long-Distance Dick the key to her heart since the moment she handed it over to him at the Basement. He had asked her for it, and she had happily conceded. What she had failed to see up until the moment of truth was that he kept her concealed like he did her gift box of photos until he finally locked her out of his life like he did his front door that fateful night. The symbolism was uncanny.

Kate mourned for a while, allowing her grief to take its course, especially in light of how suddenly the relationship had died without any closure. The only thing left to do was a postmortem dissection of the toadd in order to find out the cause of death.

Kate had never loved anyone the way she loved Long-Distance Dick. He had professed a love for her in a way that no other toadd had. She dove into the relationship headfirst. She ventured into uncharted territory that opened up her eyes and her heart to a completely new way of loving. She was inspired to write him love letters from the heart, journey at the drop of hat to be with him, and even thoughtfully gifted him boudoir pictures of her for whenever he missed her. She found herself sending him copious amounts of love energetically every chance she got. It was the first time that sex was not the focus of a relationship; it became more of the icing on the cake.

It all felt so real to Kate. As a result, she formed an illusion beyond a reality that he was comfortable with. Her expectations climbed higher than Long-Distance Dick could reach. At one point, he told her he could not handle what he described as a "failure to please you." He had become disappointed with his inability to cocreate Kate's fairy tale love. *My gosh*, Kate thought, feeling terrible she had placed her expectations on him.

Toward the end when she realized her intentions had turned into expectations, it was too late. The damage was done, and in Long-Distance Dick's eyes, it was too late for her to retract. He was not in a place like Kate where he could understand she had the ability to see her mistake and reset. And so, he ended it.

In accepting her loss, Kate started setting intentions of love sent in waves—not to him this time, but to *her*. She learned three valuable key lessons with this adventure:

- ☐ The key to falling madly in love with someone is *self-love*.
- ☐ The key to any relationship is *self-love*.
- ☐ The key to healing from the pain of love loss is *self-love*.

Little Katie knew Kate was finally coming full circle where they would soon be able to see eye to eye.

"Eureka! Now you're talking, Kate. You have discovered the key to love!"

Update

A few months later, Kate made a trip to see her girlfriend Debra, who had introduced the two of them. She reached out to Long-Distance Dick because she had left a few things at his house and wanted to retrieve them. Kate asked him if he would please give them to her friend, but he insisted on meeting her.

Why? I had such a hard time getting over you, she thought.

In an afterthought, she decided it might be beneficial to get some closure. Maybe he would give her some answers that could help her see the picture from his angle. Perhaps she would discover why she fell so hard for this Dick and why God/the Universe did not want them to be together. She agreed to meet him.

Inside a restaurant bar, Kate waited nervously for Long-Distance Dick to arrive. She decided against ordering a drink because there was too much adrenaline rushing through her body. Forget butterflies, she felt more like birds were ripping through her stomach. She hadn't seen him since he had locked her out of his house.

Why can't I forget that and let it go? she caught herself thinking.

She wasn't sure what this meeting was going to lead to, but she found herself thinking of what she wanted it to lead to. She wanted to hug him, hold him tight, smell him, feel his body against hers, and slowly kiss him in hopes that he would feel the same way. She had already learned this lesson. It was an unrealistic expectation of what she wanted. It had never served her in the past, and it was not going to serve her now.

Kate's nerves skyrocketed when she saw him through the window driving into the parking lot. She turned around to face the bar, her back to the window. She took a few slow, deep breaths and asked for divine guidance. Whatever the outcome of this reunion, she sensed it would take its course naturally and work out for the best.

The door opened, and Kate could feel his energy as he approached her. A soft breeze glided past the open door and awoke her senses to the familiar scent of his cologne, and she closed her eyes to brace herself. The tap on her shoulder didn't startle her, but it still gave her the chills.

"Hi there," said Long-Distance Dick.

Kate turned around as calm as she could and greeted him with a smile. He looked as hot as she remembered him being. "Hi." She instinctively moved to give him a hug and then realized she probably should not, turning it into an awkward hesitant advance.

He smiled back at her and opened his arms for a short pat. "Should we move to a table?" he asked.

"Yeah, of course," she replied, trying not to feel apprehensive.

They sat across the table from each another as Kate concentrated on not moving around nervously in her seat. *Keep your composure and relax. It's no big deal*, she reminded herself.

"I need a drink," she tensely exclaimed.

Long-Distance Dick ordered drinks, and then they began with small talk like two people who had never been intimate and were catching up like long-lost platonic friends. As Kate listened to him speak about what he'd been up to the last few months, she took notice that he had not been thinking of her nearly as much as she had been thinking of him. She had spent a lot of time struggling to find out what happened to them, tortured by her own demons, while he was living his life and had apparently moved on. Even though she too had been able to move on, she still ever so often wondered if time and space would ever again open up for them to be together in the future.

Then she brought it up … the last night they were at his house. She had to ask him what happened.

"I realize you told me not once, but many times, that you didn't have time for me in your life. I didn't listen, though. I wasn't honest with you because I thought I could change you. I wanted to have you fall in love with me so madly that you would change your mind and want to give in to a long-distance love affair. The last night we were together, I felt you treated me badly. I have to know. Why did you lock me out of your house?"

"Kate, I did not lock you out of the house!" he said in amazement. "I looked outside and didn't see you anymore, so I thought you had left. That's why I locked the door, but I didn't lock it to keep you out."

Kate listened, baffled at her own conclusions. She then opened up to him like she had wanted to so many times before face-to-face and not in writing. She explained to him exactly how she felt that night and wanted to know his side of the story too. They took each other through that dark, dreary night and shared in detail. As Kate listened, the pain and torture she had put herself through over the past few months melted away with every explanation he had.

She deduced that distance had been the culprit for the breakdown in communication between them, widening the gaps with disproportionate time spent together, which ultimately severed their connection. The night ended with closure for her.

As they got up to leave the restaurant, they gave each other a strong embrace in solidarity for the loss of a love they once knew. As Kate went to break away from his grip, he held on longer. She gave into him, closing her eyes and feeling his strong body against hers for the last time. When they pulled away from each other, Kate could feel the lioness' roar well up inside her. She looked up at Long-Distance Dick, and not withholding, she spoke her truth.

"It was great to see you again. You look smokin' hot, by the way."

Softening his eyes, he smiled back and said, "Great to see you too. And yes, you look amazingly beautiful."

Kate boarded a plane the next day not knowing if she would ever hear from or see Long-Distance Dick again. As the plane thundered for takeoff, she heard Little Katie say, "Your desire is to love, and it is your destiny to love. Just remember your destiny begins with *you*."

※

"Little Katie, I think the hardest thing to do in life is to let someone you love go when you realize that they are not the right match, vibration, timing, whatever it is. Now I know why this relationship had to happen, as painful as it was. He was the conduit through which I learned how to give love and receive love in a capacity I have never experienced before. That is the best lesson I have ever had in all my adventures.

Now I am aware that instead of placing unrealistic expectations on my romantic relationships, I will hold intentions instead. This mental reconfiguration releases me from the outcome, giving me permission to just be who *I am* and not be disappointed if, and when, it does not work out. Even though it is painful to lose the one you love, especially the deeper your love, self-love makes us capable of rising above the hurt and transmuting it into a positive lesson. We can either learn from it or run from it. I chose to learn from it. If I want to be loved, I have to be the love I am seeking to myself first."

Kate's breakthrough in this adventure left Little Katie with hardly anything further to say, except for her usual rhetorical question. "All right, so when is it okay to date a Long-Distance Dick?"

Kate laughed, knowing this would be the last Dating Dick question Little Katie would ever need to address. "Little Katie, it's time for me to start asking myself the question of when is it okay to date a certain kind of Dick. The answer will always be *never*. I could have read between the lines, heeded the red flags, and made better decisions when it became plain I was with the wrong Dick. I could have avoided heartache after heartache if I had ended the relationship at the first warning sign rather than choosing the benefit of the doubt. What happened was that I let my guard down with the excuse that I am too nice, when in reality I was too quiet. In order to please a man in return for love, I suppressed my voice. Speaking my truth is not a fault; it is a requirement for self-love." Kate was radiant as she spoke.

"Kate, you should keep in mind that you have an aura around you that certain men you attract have never experienced before, which draws them to you, and then they try to emulate your light. They hang with you for a while, but it is only a matter of time before their true colors come out, and they can no longer keep up the facade. That was a trigger point for you because you didn't know how else to interpret their flailing attention other than by measuring it against how *they* made you feel—responsible. When, in fact, the only responsibility you have is to *your* feelings of happiness and joy and love that do not come from how anybody makes you feel, only how you allow them to make you feel."

Kate considered, and even accepted, that perhaps her light did attract Dicks who wanted to brighten their dim space. From that moment forward, when a Dick approached her and before setting any intentions, she would focus first on what she was feeling—whether she was allowing herself to feel an emotion based on someone's attention or whether it was based on her own attention to self. To accomplish this, she came up with a list of question to ask herself in order to discern which all required a yes answer:

- ☐ Does this serve me?
- ☐ Am I being caring to myself?
- ☐ Is this loving toward me?
- ☐ Is this kind to me?
- ☐ Am I uplifted by this?
- ☐ Is this extending freedom to me?
- ☐ Does this feel honest to me?
- ☐ Am I able to share this feeling with others?

These were questions she could ask herself about every relationship situation, and not just when dating. After all, self-love is necessary to accomplish all good things in life. We all hold the Master Key of self-love, and as long as we maintain possession of the Master Key, we have the ability to fall in love, heal from the loss of love, and share vibrations of love wherever we go and wherever it is needed.

Little Katie had one last thing to say to Kate before heading over to the enchanted pond for the next adventure.

"Kate, your growth has taken leaps and bounds in this adventure. Now that you have released the blockage to love, you have opened the door to self-love and built channels through which you now give and receive love beginning with yourself. You are ready to take the final step—putting it all into practice. After all this time, Final Dick is really in the box, Kate. You do not belong buried in a secret compartment, in a nightstand, or locked away in a lion's cage. Step out of the cage and *roar*! And don't ever be led back into a cage again."

17

The Final Dick

LOVING YOURSELF IS THE KEY TO LOVE

When romantic relationships break up, they invariably end on a not-so-positive note—that is, one party is crushed, while the other comes out victorious but at the cost of some blood, sweat, and tears with no real prize to show for it. Or, both parties exit the battlefield exhausted and injured, loathing the mere mention of their enemy's name for years or even decades to come. Or, even worse, it could be so bad that neither party ever wants to retain a shred of memory of one another, pretending that it never actually happened and might even go so far as to have an identity change or maybe even a drastic sex change … It was that bad! Begging the question: Is there ever a happy ending? The answer is yes! Believe it or not, Kate found hers in a very surprising twist.

Even after all the misfit Dicks and unfortunate toadds Kate had kissed, sexed, and cried for, she rose from the ashes, faith unexhausted that she could experience her happily ever after, and not just through the lens of a fairy tale illusion. After Kate stepped out of her cage empowered by the lessons she absorbed and conclusions she drew throughout her many adventures and at last with Long-Distance Dick, she had never felt so free and so alive. She was no longer a naive, fearful, needy Dick lover. Kate had shed that skin and now embodied the priceless wisdom she had acquired:

"If I want to be loved, I have to be the love I am seeking toward myself first."

By setting loving intentions, Kate would have the ability to create a reality where her next relationship would play out like a symphony, and if fate would have it, it would end on a happy note, not with a bitter meltdown. When both parties of a relationship are in such a good place emotionally, spiritually, and mentally, and if, and when, they reach a point where a mutual split is inevitable, they have the ability to accept it as simply a time to move on. They have both learned as much from one another as they possibly could, and parting ways is the next natural step to take. No hard feelings.

When Kate was ready to head back to the enchanted pond, she asked her younger faithful companion if she could visit Dickland alone. Little Katie knew Kate was ready to face Final Dick. Receptively, she motioned with a nod and watched Kate fade away into the distance as she walked confidently on the path toward her Final Dick adventure. She would catch up with her later.

Upon arriving, Kate stood tall, casting a wide look around her and let out a big exhale. She took in the scenery, inhaling the fresh air around the pond and absorbing all its sights and sounds. The water was murky as usual, but somehow, it gave her comfort.

The enchanted pond has the feel of a wise old pond, she thought.

Closing her eyes, Kate listened to her surroundings and heard the sound of the toadds croaking. She let out a light giggle. She opened her eyes and squinted toward where the sound was coming from and saw a few of her past toadds. They were still jumping on their lily pads, trying to get attention from the next princesses who would walk in Kate's shoes.

As she watched the princesses and their Little Katie companions interact with the toadds, she wanted to warn them and rescue them from their impending adventures. However, it was not yet time to share her wisdom with them, because she had one last adventure herself to travel—Final Dick. She also knew that just like she was now in a good and happy place after having gone through the experience of the adventures that brought her to this juncture, those princesses also had their own journeys to travel before they too could feel worthy of love and see the pond in all its wisdom.

Kate sighed with happy relief. Placing her hand above her eyes to block them from the bright sunrays, she scoured the pond, hoping to come face-to-face with her Final Dick. A pair of eyes looking back at her raised her curiosity. This time, it was not a toadd vying for her attention or jumping up and down croaking for her. There were no shiny objects, clinking glasses, headstands, or any trickery involved. This presence that had caught her attention was quiet, peaceful, joyful, loving, and encircled by an aura of glowing light.

Kate noticed this presence stood on solid ground, not on a lily pad. Bewildered, she moved closer to it in a charily manner. She rubbed her eyes to clear her vision and could not believe what she saw. She had to do a double take as her jaw dropped in disbelief. For a moment, she thought it was the sunlight in her eyes distorting her view. But it was no mistake. The presence was a reflection of her!

Then she heard the shriek of a little voice. "Yes, Kate, it is you!"

Kate jumped out of her skin because she wasn't expecting Little Katie to be with her.

"Oh my gosh, Little Katie, you startled me! What are you saying?"

"You are Final Dick!"

Little Katie repeated herself, squealing with excitement. "I am telling you that you are Final Dick. You are true love's first Dick. You are the real Dick! Please stand up, stand tall, stand proud, and stand in your own power!"

Of course, I was the Dick all along—a Dick to myself for not loving me enough.

Kate turned back around to look at the pond again, and all she could see was herself. As the enchanted pond came back into focus, she noticed there were no more toadds. All the toadds were gone! Under the bright-blue sky, the pond's murky water was now clear and crystal-like, gleaming in the sun's beautiful white light. All that was in the pond were lily pads with colorful lilies that sparkled among the soft ripples of the shimmering water. Dragonflies, humming birds, and butterflies fluttered around. She had never seen it this way before. It was a breathtaking vision.

Her eyes fell on a sign posted on the bank of the pond. As she zoomed in on it, the words "Enchanted Pond" began to transform into "Miracle Pond." It was silent. For the first time, Kate could hear herself breathe and her heart beat. She closed her eyes one more time to make sure she was truly experiencing this miracle.

Suddenly, she understood. She had been coming to the enchanted pond for years with the same expectations and desires, creating a place that at times felt like a swampy marsh in her futile search for love. Now that she was no longer in search of something she thought she needed, the true miracle of the pond was revealed to her, and all she could see was the wisdom of it.

She closed her eyes, stretched out her arms, and lifted her face toward the blue sky. She spun herself around, breathing in the fresh air and letting the sunlight bathe her face as the breeze tickled her skin. This is what meditation feels like—a peaceful serenity and overwhelming love and joy.

In that moment, a message came to her from a place of stillness: "The path to a miracle is always through uncomfortable territory. And the source of a miracle is always unexpected."

Kate soaked in the sun along with the message she heard and embraced her Final Dick.

※

It was quite the revelation for Kate to have discovered who the real Dick in the pond turned out be. She had never seen it that way, but of course, it all made sense now.

Little Katie began the final lesson by asking Kate a different question this time. "When is it okay for you to fall in love?"

"When?" replied Kate.

"When you are aligned with who you are and you practice so much self-love that it fills you up and overflows into all areas of your life. Showing up for yourself, loving yourself, making yourself happy, and not being dependent on anyone else to make you happy is all I ever wanted you to achieve. You have arrived here, and that means, Kate, *you are ready*! Can you see, feel, and taste this now?"

"I can, Little Katie. I am overjoyed with happiness. The source of this miracle was truly unexpected!"

"Yes, I can see it in your eyes and the glow around your body. Tell me what else you see, Kate."

Kate shared her revelation with Little Katie. "I was looking for security and approval from a man, when the entire time I should have been asking myself the question, Why am I looking for security and approval from a man? Had you not emerged, Little Katie, I would still be lost not knowing where to find the answer, which was in me all along—my inner self, my inner soul, my inner being. I had to find myself and fall in love not with a man but with who I am. I was never in love with myself to begin with. I was never whole. Instead, I was dependent on everything outside of myself for security and support. I blamed everyone else around me for my love woes and stayed the victim for so long—throughout all my adventures. It's no wonder they did not work or did not last."

"So, Kate, the most important fact to remember is that in order to maintain this high vibration you are riding on, it will require never-ending work on yourself in order to keep positive, keep self-love nourished, and keep clear intentions for attracting the right match for you. One of the patterns you repeated was attracting a man who imposed unfair rules upon you and whose time for you was always restricted."

"True," Kate noted, "because even when I thought I was in a better place with myself and had found the right Dick who showed a surmountable amount of interest in me to the point that he wanted me to move in with him, I *still* wasn't ready to fall in love. It makes sense now that he couldn't give me more of his time, and I suppose it was a blessing in disguise in order to give me more time to learn this lesson in love."

Little Katie pointed out a final crucial fact for Kate. "And your definition of love has changed too. Sex is not the key to a man's heart. From Disturbing Dick to Long-Distance Dick, it took time for you to understand that your pattern of needing attention, safety, and security led you to sex much too soon in a relationship because of the feeling of emptiness and the longing to feel loved. The problem was you kept going back to the enchanted pond looking for a toadd to fulfill your needs, desires, and happiness in order to feel loved. All along, I wanted you to find *you* at the pond instead. You did that today, and you have finally come full circle. Now you know that you must love yourself, give attention to your needs, and provide your own safety and security first. Once you take those steps, the miracles begin to unfold. And here you are at the Miracle Pond."

Kate's adventures had come to a close. Together, she and Little Katie were moving into new territory—a territory that Kate should enjoy being in for the rest of her journey. She took one last deep breath, closing her eyes as she imagined a free fall from the skies. She daydreamed about every single Dick from her past and the valuable lessons she'd extracted from her adventures while reflecting upon each one:

- ☐ The Disturbing Dick: Introducing the inner child (Little Katie).
- ☐ The First-Time Dick: Be clear on what you want in a relationship.
- ☐ The Money Dick: Reject his rejection and money.
- ☐ The Gay Dick: Pay attention to the feedback.
- ☐ The Southern Dick: Face what is not working.
- ☐ The Controlling Dick: Time to commit to improving yourself.
- ☐ The Married Dick: Are you willing to pay the price and take responsibility?
- ☐ The Drunk Dick: Clean up your mess, not his.
- ☐ The Porn Dick: Ask for what you want or don't want.
- ☐ The Sexting Dick: Decide what pain you can tolerate from a relationship.
- ☐ The Yoga Dick: Be careful who you bend over backward for.
- ☐ The Elevator Dick: Embrace change … and never smoke.
- ☐ The International Dick: Learn to say no in every language.
- ☐ The Football Dick: Stop the play and settling for less than what you want.
- ☐ The Fitness Dick: Spot the pattern, and work it out.
- ☐ The Long-Distance Dick: Be careful who you give your key to.

And finally, the most revealing one of them all:

- ☐ The Final Dick: Loving yourself is the key to love.

Kate opened her eyes to see Little Katie with a big smile on her face. Except Little Katie now looked identical to Kate. She was no longer little. Kate had managed to transcend the pain Little Katie had been carrying for her, and her inner child was now in the likeness of present Kate herself. She had finally reconciled the childhood trauma, the distance she had with her father, and the unrealistic expectations placed on her by her mother. *Poof!* She had released it all.

"You can still call me Little Katie because I'll always be the little voice inside your head, Kate. Now let's celebrate that *we* have successfully redefined love one Dick at a time, and we should be so proud of our work and all our accomplishments!"

"I *am*. I feel vibrantly determined and good about loving myself, loving life, and, in a new twist, loving my Final Dick adventure … *me*."

The two locked hands, and as body and soul turned to walk away from Miracle Pond, Little Katie pledged, "You know I will always be with you, Kate. I will always love you. I will always be by your side to protect you and take care of you. You have been, and always will be, safe with me."

"I know, Little Katie. I can now say I feel the same way about you."

"Oh good, I'm so glad you're not going to hold it against me that you turned out to be the Dick in the room."

"No, Katie, I won't. But I still think you are a pain in my ass!"

And off into the sunset they went and lived happily ever after.

Epilogue

The Fairy Tale Dream Now

Once upon a time, there lived a little princess who, like many little girls her age, had a fascination with the magical fairy tales she read of the beautiful princesses who would be found and rescued by Prince Charming, fall in love, and live happily ever after. So it was no surprise this little princess wished for and fantasized about her own happily ever after—living the magical fairy tale of falling in love with a prince who would find and rescue her. Which she did. Well, sort of …

The question is, Did Kate really find *happily ever after*? Yes, she did. And she found it first in herself. Then, when she was not looking, a prince appeared like no other one had before. *He* is a man, not a toadd, not a dick—but a loving, genuine, real-life man. And his name is … Richard, not Dick. The fairy tale dream has turned into the fairy tale truth. How did she find him? She stopped searching for him. She lived only open to miracles. She has a *new* list that has to do not with what she wants but with what she is—happy and in love.

My Fairy Tale Truth and the Man I Am With:

- ☐ When I love and honor myself, my man is cheerful.
- ☐ When I am imperfect, my man is content.
- ☐ When I cherish the beauty in myself and in others, my man is captivated.

- ☐ When I love myself and love others unconditionally, my man is delighted.
- ☐ When I use my energy to heal and transform, my man is ecstatic.
- ☐ When I am present, my man is elated.
- ☐ When I see through the eyes of my soul, my man is joyful.
- ☐ When I release and surrender, my man is peaceful.
- ☐ When I speak my truth with love, my man is grateful.
- ☐ When I radiate love, my man is exultant.

The man who showed up for Kate did not come by way of her looking for what she wanted in a man; rather, she went looking for what she wanted for herself. This is how she will always show up for her man—living the miracle she really desires, treating him like the king he is, and enhancing his happiness because she is happy.

Your fairy tale dream is within you. The answer is within you. Grace is within you. The miracle of love is within you. Your fairy tale truth is waiting for you to embrace it with all its power and glory. Go after it, because as Little Katie said, "Your desire is to love, and it is your destiny to love. Just remember your destiny begins with *you*."

CPSIA information can be obtained
at www.ICGtesting.com
Printed in the USA
BVHW080325080319
542135BV00002B/95/P

9 781483 481654